Secrets of a Lady

Lords & Ladies of Mayfair

Laura Beers

Chapter One

England, 1813

The fog hung low to the ground as Miss Lizette Kent stood at her mother's grave, the skirt of her woolen black gown wafting in the wind. This is not how she envisioned her life to be. She was truly and utterly alone now.

She had been summoned home from her boarding school to the news that her mother had grown ill and was fading fast. By the time she returned home, her mother had already passed away, preventing her from saying her final goodbyes.

The smell of the dirt in the fresh grave churned her stomach and she wished that she would wake up from this terrible dream that she called her life. How was she going to move on without her mother by her side?

Her shoulders slumped as she fought the tears that were threatening to fall. She had already cried enough. Her mother would have told her to be brave and to embrace her future. Unfortunately, she didn't feel brave, and her future looked bleak.

Her eyes strayed towards the modest manor that was tucked away in the green countryside. She asked herself, what now? She had been trained to manage a household, but she didn't know what funds her mother had left her, if any at all. She still retained a small staff, but she believed they were there more out of loyalty to her mother than anything else.

If she was left penniless, she could always find employment as a governess to a wealthy family. She was fortunate that her mother had seen to her education. But that would take her far away from Bridgwater, which had been her home for most of her life.

Could she truly leave her home to step into the unknown?

Lizette leaned down and placed the bouquet of pink roses onto her mother's grave. Roses were her mother's favorite and she used to spend hours toiling after the rambling roses that occupied their garden. There was nothing more appealing than the fragrant smell of flowers drifting through the open windows of their manor. But now, who would tend to the roses?

A cloud of smoke rose from the chimney stack of the manor, and she knew that she had tarried long enough. It was time for her to return home. *Home.* Was it even a home without her mother there?

With a parting glance at the grave, Lizette turned towards the manor and started walking across the field. At times like this, she wished her father was still alive, but he had died- or at least that is what she had been told. She had no memories of her father.

Lizette arrived at the door that led to the kitchen and pushed it open. She stepped inside and saw Mrs. Everly stirring something over the hearth. The portly, silver-haired housekeeper had been with them for as long as she could remember and she also cooked for them.

"Good morning," she greeted.

Mrs. Everly gasped as she turned around. "Good heavens,

dear child, you gave me a fright," she said, placing a hand over her heart. "You can't go around scaring me like that."

Lizette's lips twitched. "You frighten entirely too easily."

"There is no shame in that." Mrs. Everly gave her a compassionate look. "Were you visiting your mother?"

"I was," Lizette replied.

Mrs. Everly wiped her hands on her white apron. "Come," she encouraged, "you should eat to keep your strength up."

She knew there was no sense in arguing with Mrs. Everly so she sat down at the round table. Mrs. Everly went about preparing a plate and set it down in front of her.

Lizette glanced down at the hearty breakfast and resisted the urge to push the plate away. She knew she needed to eat, but the thought of eating seemed overwhelming. She had so many things that vied for her time that she had little time for herself.

Mrs. Everly remained close and slid the plate closer to her. "Go on," she encouraged.

Lizette picked up the bread and took a bite. She chewed slowly, hoping to regain her appetite. But she found that she wasn't hungry.

As she placed the bread down, Mrs. Everly said, "If you don't eat more, you will wither away."

"I'm sorry," Lizette responded, "I am just not very hungry at the moment."

"That isn't like you."

Lizette gave her a weak smile. "Perhaps I will regain my appetite once I meet with my mother's solicitor."

"I doubt it." Mrs. Everly opened a cupboard and removed a bowl. Then she placed it down onto the table. "This may help. I know how much you love my marmalade recipe."

"When did you have time to make this?"

"I found the time since I correctly assumed that I would need to coax you into eating more."

Lizette eagerly reached for the spoon and dipped it into

the fruit preserve. After she spread it onto her bread, she took a bite, chewing slowly.

"It is just as delicious as I remember," Lizette said.

Mrs. Everly smiled. "I am glad that you approve."

"The cook at the boarding school would make marmalade with sweet oranges and it wasn't nearly as good as your recipe."

"That is because I have a special ingredient in mine."

"Is it love?" Lizette joked.

Mrs. Everly laughed. "No, it is cinnamon."

Lizette savored the marmalade as she ate, and she found herself immensely grateful that Mrs. Everly had not abandoned her when her mother died. She didn't know what she would do without her loyal housekeeper.

Mrs. Everly went over to the hearth and retrieved the ladle. As she stirred the contents of the pot, she asked, "When do you meet with your solicitor?"

Lizette wiped the crumbs off her hands before replying, "Mr. Billings' note indicated that he intends to call this afternoon."

"I do hope you receive good news."

"As do I," Lizette said. "Quite frankly, I could use some."

A knock came from the main door.

Mrs. Everly gave her a curious look. "Were you expecting anyone?"

"I was not," Lizette said as she pushed back her chair. "Most likely, it is someone from the village that wishes to offer their condolences."

Another knock came at the main door.

"That is odd," Lizette said. "Where do you suppose Stockton is?"

Mrs. Everly glanced over at the window. "Oh, dear, I forgot," she replied. "He is out with the chickens."

"Why is he there?" Lizette asked as she tried to imagine

the stoic butler amongst the chickens. It would be a sight to see.

"I asked him to select one for dinner since Thomas is no longer with us," Mrs. Everly explained.

"Where did Thomas go?"

Mrs. Everly frowned. "He left right after your mother died," she replied. "I'm afraid we haven't been paid for weeks, at least since your mother grew ill."

"I do hope to rectify that once Mr. Billings comes to call."

"I know, dear," Mrs. Everly said. "Besides, I just need a roof over my head and food in my belly for me to be happy."

As Lizette opened her mouth to respond, pounding came from the main door.

Mrs. Everly placed the ladle down and remarked, "It would appear that the matter is quite urgent."

Lizette started backing up to the door. "I shall answer it."

"You?" Mrs. Everly asked.

"I can answer doors," Lizette said.

Mrs. Everly looked unsure. "I don't know if that is such a good idea."

"It will be fine," Lizette responded as she turned to depart from the kitchen. She made her way towards the entry hall, where the pounding hadn't ceased.

Lizette reached for the door handle and opened the door.

Mrs. Bennett's hand stilled in the air and she exclaimed, "Good gracious! What has become of you?"

Lizette forced a smile to her lips as she addressed the village's most notorious gossip. She was the last person Lizette wanted to converse with.

"What can I do for you, Mrs. Bennett?" Lizette asked, hoping her voice sounded cordial enough.

Mrs. Bennett lowered her hand and displeasure was etched on her face. "I would have you know that I was waiting quite a long time for someone to answer the door."

"I do apologize but everyone is rather busy at the moment."

"Too busy to answer the door?" Mrs. Bennett pressed.

Ignoring the woman's question, she repeated her previous one. "What can I do for you?"

Mrs. Bennett extended a basket with a cloth covering the offering. "I had my cook prepare some biscuits for you."

"That was most thoughtful of you," Lizette said, touched by the act of kindness.

Leaning forward, Mrs. Bennett lowered her voice. "The whole village is worried that you are struggling to put food on the table."

Lizette tensed. She should have known that there was more to the gesture than just being kind. Mrs. Bennett was no doubt using this visit to obtain information about her.

"You need not worry about me," Lizette said.

"I just hired on your groom, Thomas, and he told me that your mother didn't have the funds to pay him," Mrs. Bennett pressed.

"I am speaking to my mother's solicitor today and I hope to get everything sorted out," Lizette responded.

"He would be your solicitor now, dear, since your mother is dead," Mrs. Bennett pointed out.

"That he would."

Mrs. Bennett strained her neck as she tried to look over Lizette's shoulder and into the manor. "Do you have any servants to tend to you?"

Lizette tightened her hold on the basket. "A few remain," she remarked vaguely.

"If you do need anything, please let me know at once," Mrs. Bennett said as she met Lizette's gaze.

"Thank you." Lizette held up the basket. "And I do appreciate the biscuits."

Mrs. Bennett's gaze left hers and perused the length of

her. "You are entirely too skinny, Child. No man wants to marry a twig."

Lizette had about enough of Mrs. Bennett and she placed her hand on the door. "I wish you a good day," she said in the most pleasant voice that she could muster up.

She didn't wait for Mrs. Bennett's reply before she closed the door. "What an infuriating woman," she muttered under her breath.

Stockton stepped into the entry hall and said, "I do apologize for not being here to answer the door."

"No harm done," Lizette responded.

"Would you care for me to take the basket to the kitchen?" Stockton asked as he held his hand out.

Lizette extended the basket to him. "Thank you. I think I might go for a ride."

Stockton nodded. "Give me a moment and I will saddle your horse."

With a slight wince, Lizette asked, "Did John leave, as well?"

"I'm afraid so, Miss," Stockton replied. "But I am proficient at saddling a horse."

"As am I," Lizette said. "My mother thought it was an important skill to have."

A sad smile came to the butler's lips. "Your mother had her own unique way of doing things, did she not?"

"She did," Lizette agreed. "She seemed to scoff at propriety."

"That she did, and she will be sorely missed."

Lizette fought the familiar urge to cry at the mention of her mother. "That is kind of you to say," she said. "If you will excuse me, I need to go change into my riding habit before my ride."

Stockton tipped his head. "Yes, Miss."

As Lizette headed towards the stairs, she realized that no

matter how far away she ran on her horse, she would never escape this unrelenting grief that she felt in her heart. Would she ever be able to think of her mother and not cry?

———————⁓———————

The sun was bright and shining but it did little to squash the growing irritation that Mr. Tristan Westcott felt as he rode through the small village of Bridgwater. He had far more important things to do than fetch Lord Ashington's grand-daughter, but here he was. It was a task that was wholly beneath him.

A black coach trailed behind him with liveried footmen and a surly companion for Lady Lizette. He intended to collect her and be on their way as quickly as possible. Lord Ashington hadn't given him many details on Lady Lizette, but he assumed that she would be like most women in high Society. Pompous. Patronizing. That had been his experience with these women, at least until he had been named as Lord Ashington's heir. Now the same women were batting their eyelashes and offering him coy smiles.

It was infuriating and he had no intention of ever falling for the parson's mousetrap. He was a smart enough man to know that a wife would bring nothing but misery into his life. He was much better off alone.

Tristan watched as a group of boys kicked an inflated pig's bladder around in a circle. They all had bright smiles on their faces, and he envied their naivety. They had no idea how exhausting life could be; how it grated on every nerve until you are forced to recognize that you are unable to have the life that you had always envisioned.

As he left the village behind, Tristan's eyes roamed over the countryside. Lord Ashington had informed him the manor was just outside of the village, set back into a field. In the distance, he saw a manor, but it was much smaller than he had been expecting. Surely that wasn't the home that Lady Crewe had lived in with her daughter.

Tristan turned down the road that ran in front of the manor. The closer he got, the more he realized that it was worse than he had previously thought. The stones around the corners of the home were crumbling, the bricks were showing signs of wear and the landscaping was unkempt. No servant exited the manor to collect his horse. If he didn't know any better, he would think this manor had been abandoned.

It was a far cry from the many grand estates that Lord Ashington owned. His townhouse in London was pristinely kept from the simplest flower in the gardens to the painted ceiling in the entry hall.

Tristan dismounted his horse and extended his reins to a footman. He removed his riding gloves and slipped them into the pocket of his great coat. He approached the coach and rapped on the door.

It was opened and Lady Anne met his gaze, albeit with an annoyed look on her face. "Yes, Mr. Westcott."

"Wait here," he ordered. "I'm not entirely convinced this is where Lady Lizette resides."

"Very well," Lady Anne said before closing the door.

Tristan walked up to the main door and knocked. It was a long moment before the door opened slightly and a young woman stared back at him. She had chestnut brown hair pulled back and pinned in a simple twist at the base of her neck. Her lips were pink, pursed at the moment, but full and nicely shaped. Her eyes shone with intelligence, and she was wearing a black gown, indicating she was in mourning.

"May I help you?" she asked in a soft, yet purposeful voice.

Tristan realized that he had been caught staring and fumbled for a calling card in his waistcoat pocket. He knew the rules in the countryside were rather lax, but he still intended to behave as a gentleman should.

He extended the card towards the young woman. "Will you inform Lady Lizette that I have come to collect her?"

She accepted the card and glanced down. "I'm sorry, Mr. Westcott, but there is no one here by that name."

"Do you, by chance, know where Lady Lizette lives?"

"I'm afraid you have been misinformed," the young woman said. "I am *Miss* Lizette Kent and I reside here."

Tristan had so many questions, but he decided to ask the most obvious one. "Are you not the granddaughter of Lord Ashington?"

"I am not."

Tristan lowered his voice as he asked, "Are you a servant here?"

He realized that was the wrong thing to say when her eyes grew fiery. "I bid you good day," she said before she slammed the door shut.

Raising his hand, he pounded on the door. He wasn't sure what was going on, but he had no intention of leaving until his questions were answered.

The door opened and a short man, presumably the butler, opened the door. "May I help you?" he asked.

"Where did Lady, er, Miss Lizette Kent go?" he demanded. He wasn't entirely sure why Lady Lizette wasn't making use of her title, but he would play her game... for now.

The butler's face remained stoic, despite the dirt that was crusted along the hem of his black trousers. "I'm afraid she is unavailable for callers."

"I just spoke to her," Tristan said in exasperation.

He held up his calling card. "I have your card and I will see that Miss Kent gets it."

Tristan stared at the butler in disbelief. "That was the card that I personally handed to Miss Kent, just a moment ago."

"Yes, but, you see, I found it on the floor. Perhaps she dropped it," the butler said. "Will there be anything else, sir?"

"I am not leaving until I speak to Miss Kent."

"Very good, sir," the butler said before he closed the door.

Tristan remained rooted in his spot, stunned, before he lifted his fist and pounded on the door again. He had never experienced such blatant rudeness before.

The door was promptly opened and the butler asked, "May I help you, Mr. Westcott?" His voice held no hint of irony.

"I demand to speak to Miss Kent."

"I am aware, but she is not interested in speaking with you," the butler said plainly.

"She doesn't even know why I am calling on her."

"Frankly, I don't think she cares."

Tristan stifled the groan on his lips. He didn't have time for this, and Lady Lizette was starting to grate on his nerves.

Through gritted teeth, Tristan asked, "Will you kindly inform Miss Kent that I have important business to discuss with her?"

"Excuse me for a moment," the butler said before he closed the door.

Tristan could hear hushed voices coming from the other side of the door, but he couldn't quite make out what was being said.

The door opened and the butler asked, "What do you wish to discuss with Miss Kent?"

"That is between me and Miss Kent," Tristan replied.

The butler turned his head and whispered to someone that was standing behind the door. He brought his gaze back to meet Tristan's. "She has a meeting with her solicitor soon. Would you mind coming back tomorrow?"

"I do mind," Tristan grumbled. "Is Miss Kent behind the door?"

The butler's face grew expressionless. "No."

Did Lady Lizette take him for a fool? "I think she is behind the door."

"You would be mistaken."

Tristan placed his hand on the door and shoved it open, causing the butler to step back into the modest entry foyer. "Miss Kent!" he exclaimed. "A word, if you don't mind."

Lady Lizette stepped out from behind the door, her hand on her hip. "You have some nerve barging into my home, uninvited."

"I need to speak to you."

"No, you need to speak to Lady Lizette and that person does not exist."

"I think she does."

"You would be wrong."

"Why would I be here if I was?"

Lady Lizette shrugged. "I don't rightly know."

Tristan reached into his great coat pocket and pulled out a piece of paper. He was glad that he had the foresight to write down some basic information about Lady Lizette before leaving Town to fetch her. He held it up as he asked, "Is Elizabeth Kent your mother?"

She dropped her arm to her side. "Yes, she is, or at least, she was," she said as some of the fight drained out of her.

"Was your father- William Kent?"

"Yes, but—"

He cut her off. "William Kent was the Earl of Crewe and his wife, Lady Crewe, was your mother."

"That is impossible," Lady Lizette said. "I would know if my mother was a countess."

"Apparently not," he muttered as he shoved the paper back into the pocket of his great coat.

Lady Lizette grew rigid. "I do not know what you are attempting to prove, but I will not stand here and have falsehoods spewed at me."

"I was sent by your grandfather, Lord Ashington. He is

requesting your presence in London," Tristan said. "I am here to escort you there."

Lady Lizette shook her head. "I think not."

"You have little choice in the matter."

"I beg your pardon?"

Tristan took a step closer to her. "I do not know what kind of game you are playing, but I am not interested in playing it with you. You will go upstairs at once and see to your trunks being packed."

Lady Lizette's lips drew into a flat line. "No."

"No?" he repeated back. No one dared to defy him. He was heir to Lord Ashington- one of the most powerful men in England.

"I am not going anywhere with you," Lady Lizette said. "I don't know you, and I most assuredly do not know this Lord Ashington."

"He is your grandfather."

"I have no grandfather."

Tristan's lips twitched. "Everyone has two grandfathers. Do I need to explain the reasonings behind that."

A faint blush came to Lady Lizette's cheeks, but her voice remained steady. "You most assuredly do not. I merely meant that my grandfather has never made himself known to me before. So why should I believe you now?"

"You will have to trust me."

"But I do not know you," she countered.

Tristan bowed. "Allow me to rectify that right now," he started. "My name is Mr. Tristan Westcott, and I am heir presumptive to your grandfather, the Marquess of Ashington."

"Do you expect me to believe that my mother hid the fact that I was a lady all these years and that I am the grand-daughter of a marquess?"

"I do, because it is the only logical explanation."

Lady Lizette clasped her hands in front of her. "I contend

you have been misinformed and I have no intention of traveling with you to London to sort this out."

"But you must!"

"Even if what you are saying is true…"

"It is."

"…then why didn't my grandfather come himself?"

Tristan opened his mouth but closed it. He wasn't entirely sure of how to answer that question. It was a fair question, but she couldn't possibly understand the demands that were placed on Lord Ashington's time.

He decided to just be honest and hope that this maddening young woman would be somewhat reasonable. "Your grandfather is a very important man, and he was unable to leave the House of Lords at this time." There. That was the truth, whether she appreciated it or not.

Lady Lizette held his gaze, her expression giving nothing away. "I'm sorry, but it just seems too inconceivable to me that my mother kept such a profound secret from me," she said. "I'm afraid it is time for you to go, Mr. Westcott."

As she went to walk past him, he reached out and gently grabbed her arm. "We are not finished here."

Lady Lizette squared her shoulders. "Do you intend to force me to go to London?" she asked, challenging him.

"No," he replied as he released her arm. "I would never do something so dishonorable."

"Then we have nothing more to say to one another."

"I should warn you that I am not one to give up so easily."

"That is something we have in common," Lady Lizette said.

Tristan watched as Lady Lizette hurried up the stairs and disappeared down a hall. He wanted to follow her and press his point, but he knew it would do no good. With any luck, she would mull over his words and realize that he was speaking the truth. He just needed to give her time, and time was something that he did not have a lot of.

"Vexing woman," he muttered under his breath.

The butler stepped forward and asked, "Will there be anything else, sir?"

Tristan let out a sigh as he realized he was going to be in Bridgwater longer than he had intended. "Is there a coaching inn in this godforsaken village?"

Chapter Two

Lizette sat by the window in the drawing room, and she could feel the warmth of the sun on her skin. The needlework in her hand was long forgotten as she replayed in her mind the conversation that she'd had with Mr. Westcott earlier.

It was inconceivable that her mother wouldn't have told her that she was the daughter of an earl. No. Her mother wouldn't have kept such a secret from her. They told each other everything, or at least she thought they had. Surely Mr. Westcott was wrong.

But what if he wasn't?

What if she was who he said she was? Was she truly the granddaughter of a marquess? She had heard of Lord Ashington- everyone had. He was well-respected amongst his peers and was a champion of the poor. He lobbied for clean water to be accessible to the people in the rookeries. She had read articles in the newssheets that highlighted his charitable nature and, by all accounts, he appeared to be an honorable man.

If what the newssheets said was accurate, why would her mother keep her from her grandfather? It didn't make any sense at all.

The manor was eerily quiet as the few remaining servants went about completing their tasks. She hoped her meeting with Mr. Billings would be beneficial and she would be able to secure the funds to pay her staff.

Stockton stepped into the room and announced, "Mr. Billings has arrived and is requesting a moment of your time."

"Please show him in." Lizette leaned forward and placed the needlework onto the table. She had met Mr. Billings only a few times, mostly in passing, but her mother seemed to have confidence in his abilities.

Mr. Billings stepped into the room with a satchel in his hand. He had a narrow face, long nose, and a cleft chin. His dark hair was swept to the side and had a distinct shine to it.

He bowed. "I wish to offer my condolences," he said in a sincere voice. "Your mother was a remarkable woman."

"That she was," Lizette agreed. "Would you care to have a seat?"

Mr. Billings walked over to an upholstered armchair next to her and sat down. "I would imagine that you have many questions for me."

"I do, but I am not quite sure where to begin."

Mr. Billings placed the satchel onto the ground and removed a piece of paper. "Your mother was a frugal woman that managed to live on very little."

"Did she have any source of income?"

"Yes, she did manage to procure funds from the properties she owned, but it wasn't much," he said. "She did little by the way of upkeep and some of the properties have fallen into disrepair."

"How much would it cost to fix up the properties?"

"Far too much for your means," Mr. Billings replied.

Lizette dreaded asking her next question. "How much is left in my mother's estate?"

Mr. Billings extended her the paper and pointed to the

total at the bottom. "Your mother left behind approximately one hundred pounds in her account."

"One hundred pounds?" Lizette asked.

"Yes, but I'm told that number will be much lower once you pay your staff," Mr. Billings responded.

"How am I going to survive on such a small sum?"

Mr. Billings gave her a look that could only be construed as pity. "I'm afraid you will have to let your household staff go and seek out employment."

Lizette had already considered that possibility, but she was hoping for another outcome. She didn't want to go to work as a governess for a wealthy family. If she did, her future would be determined. She would never have the opportunity to find love and get married. Her focus would just be on her charges.

"What if I sold the manor?" she asked.

Mr. Billings' eyes roamed over the drawing room. "I could send out some inquiries to see if anyone is interested in purchasing this manor, but it would require extensive work to bring it up to snuff," he said. "I daresay that the lands surrounding the manor would be much more enticing for a buyer."

"What do you think the estate would be worth?"

"I can't answer that, but I do believe you would receive considerably less than what it is worth, considering the state of the manor," Mr. Billings replied.

Lizette did find one thing odd, considering her mother's financial state. "If what you are saying is true, how did my mother manage to pay for my boarding school?"

Mr. Billings reached into his satchel, pulled out another paper and extended it towards her. "Your mother had been receiving quarterly deposits into her account from an anonymous donor, and with those funds, she paid for your school."

Lizette reviewed the paper and saw the dates that the payments were recorded. "You don't know who the donor was?"

Mr. Billings shook his head. "Mrs. Kent never told me, and I never pressed the issue," he said. "But the payments stopped after your mother passed away."

"Perhaps the payment is just late," she asked hopefully.

"I do not think that is the case," Mr. Billings responded. "The donor was most likely acquainted with your family since they knew you withdrew from your boarding school."

Lizette extended the papers in her hand to her solicitor. "I do not know of anyone that has sufficient enough funds to pay for my boarding school. I had just assumed my mother had been paying for it all of these years."

Mr. Billings returned the papers to his satchel and removed a small envelope. "Your mother asked for me to give this to you in case of her untimely death."

Lizette accepted the envelope. "Thank you," she replied.

"I do hope that her words will provide you with some comfort at this difficult time," Mr. Billings said, rising. "If I can be of any further assistance, please let me know."

"I will require the funds to pay the staff," Lizette requested. "They haven't been paid since my mother grew ill."

Mr. Billings nodded. "I will secure the funds at once."

Lizette leaned back in her chair as her solicitor departed from the room and let out a sigh. What was she going to do now? To some, a hundred pounds was a windfall, but she couldn't live on that forever.

With any luck, her mother's letter would shine some light on her current circumstances.

As she started to unfold the letter, Mrs. Everly stepped into the room and said, "I hope you received some good news from Mr. Billings."

"I'm afraid not," she replied. "The coffers are not full, and my mother's estate is not worth very much."

Mrs. Everly smiled but it appeared strained. "You must think of the silver lining."

"Which is?"

"You still have a roof over your head, a horse in the stable and food in your belly," Mrs. Everly said.

"Not for long since I most likely will have to sell the estate to make ends meet."

"Don't you fret," Mrs. Everly said. "When one door closes, another one opens. Just be patient and don't take the wrong door."

Lizette found her housekeeper to be entirely too optimistic at the moment. She held up the letter and revealed, "My mother wrote me a letter."

"Have you read it yet?"

She shook her head. "I haven't."

Mrs. Everly gave her a compassionate look. "I think this calls for a cup of tea."

"That would be wonderful," Lizette responded. "But I thought my mother used the rest of the tea leaves."

"I may have saved a few for an occasion such as this," Mrs. Everly said. "I will be back with a tray."

Once Mrs. Everly stepped out of the drawing room, Lizette unfolded the note and smiled at her mother's handwriting. It had always appeared so regal to her.

My dearest Lizette,

If you have been given this letter, it means that I died before I could tell you the truth of who you are. You were born Lady Lizette, the daughter of the Earl of Crewe, and the granddaughter of the Marquess of Ashington.

I have wrestled with what I should reveal to you about your father, considering he was a troubled man. I do not want you to think less of him, because he loved you more than anything. He tried to fight his demons, but he eventually succumbed to them.

Your father and I thought it was best to keep you tucked away in the countryside to keep you protected from the harshness of the truth. We may have been wrong for doing so, but we wanted to keep you safe.

Everything we have done has been to protect you. You must believe me.

Lizette lowered the paper to her lap. What harsh truths were her parents trying to protect her from? Nothing about this letter made any sense.

Mrs. Everly stepped into the room with a tray in her hands, and her steps faltered. "You know," she said matter-of-factly.

Lizette held her gaze and asked, "Did you know?"

"Yes, but I was sworn to secrecy by your mother," Mrs. Everly said. "She told me that she gave a letter to Mr. Billings that explains everything."

"But it explains very little."

Mrs. Everly came to place the tray down onto the table. "Just know this- your mother loved you very much and she wanted what was best for you."

"By hiding the truth from me?"

"She thought she was doing right by you."

Lizette folded the paper and slipped it into her pocket. "She mentioned that she was trying to protect me from the 'harshness of the truth'. Do you know what that was?"

Mrs. Everly shook her head. "I knew very little."

"Why didn't you tell me?"

"I assumed it would be best to hear it from your mother," Mrs. Everly said as she reached for the teapot. "Was I wrong?"

"No, you weren't wrong," she reluctantly admitted.

Mrs. Everly poured a cup of tea and extended it towards her. "Now that you know the truth, what are you going to do about it?"

"I think it would be best if I took Mr. Westcott up on his offer to go to London and meet with my grandfather," Lizette said. "It would save me the expense of securing a seat on the mail coach."

"What of the manor?" Mrs. Everly asked.

"I don't rightly know," Lizette replied before she took a sip of her tea, "but I think it might be best if we let the staff go so they can seek out other employment."

Mrs. Everly nodded with approval. "I will let them know at once."

"Will you ensure that the staff is given an extra month's salary?" Lizette asked.

"That is very generous, but do you not require those funds?"

Lizette lowered the teacup and saucer to her lap. "I feel that it is the right thing to do, given the circumstances."

"I will see to it."

"Now I am in the uncomfortable position of seeking out that vexing man."

Mrs. Everly smiled over the rim of her teacup. "I caught a glimpse of him. A very handsome, vexing man."

An image of Mr. Westcott came to her mind. She thought of his dark hair and his long sideburns. He had straight, white teeth, tanned skin and brown alert eyes that studied his surroundings. His gaze seemed very astute. She'd wondered what he'd seen when he looked at her. Had he known she'd admired his appearance, albeit briefly? She most assuredly hoped not.

"Some *might* consider him handsome," she reluctantly admitted.

Mrs. Everly seemed amused with her response. "Anyone with eyes would."

Lizette pressed her lips together as she considered her next words. "He is not unfortunate to look at."

Mrs. Everly leaned forward and placed her cup down onto the tray. "Shall I send for him?" she asked. "Stockton informed me that he is staying at the coaching inn on the edge of the village."

"That might be for the best."

Tristan took a sip of his watered-down ale as he sat in the main hall of the coaching inn. A group of men sat around a long rectangular table, their loud, slurring voices filling the hall. A barmaid didn't seem to notice, or care, that they were deeply into their cups and kept bringing them new drinks.

He glanced down at the amber-colored liquid and wondered how long he would have to be in this blasted village. His job was simple- retrieve Lady Lizette and take her to Lord Ashington. Yet the maddening young woman refused to see reason.

He chided himself on losing his temper with Lady Lizette, but she was being entirely unreasonable. It wasn't his fault that her parents had hid her lineage from her. Regardless, it did not change the fact that she was a lady. Most women would be elated to discover an elevation in status, but not her.

Tristan pushed the nearly full tankard of ale away from him. Lord Ashington had not told him how stubborn his granddaughter was or how incredibly beautiful she was. Did he even know? If not, then Lord Ashington would no doubt have his hands full with his granddaughter.

Botheration. He didn't have time for this. Lord Ashington had placed him in charge of running his estates while he immersed himself in politics. For every moment he spent here in Bridgwater, he was losing precious time. Estates simply did not run themselves. They took time to fully understand the complexities of the properties and realize their potential worth.

A blonde-haired barmaid sashayed up to him and asked, "Can I get you anything?"

"No, thank you," he replied, barely sparing her a glance. The last thing he wanted was another drink. He could barely tolerate what he had now.

Her eyes perused the length of him. "You don't look like you belong here, Mister."

"I have some business I need to see to in Bridgwater." His response was intentionally vague because he had no intention of striking up a conversation with the barmaid.

"It sounds serious," the barmaid remarked with a teasing lilt in her voice.

A man shouted from across the hall and the barmaid turned her head to acknowledge him. "Excuse me," she said before she walked off.

Tristan was relieved to be alone with his thoughts again. But it was short-lived.

A dark-haired man with small, rounded earlobes came to sit down next to him. He was dressed in a green jacket and a paisley waistcoat. His hair was slightly longer on the sides than what would be considered fashionable, most likely in an attempt to disguise his earlobes.

"Can I buy you a drink, Friend?" the man asked.

"I'm not your friend," Tristan grumbled, reaching for his tankard. "And I already have one."

"What about the next round?"

"I do not intend to stay that long."

The man looked amused by his response. "Rumor has it that you have come to whisk our Miss Kent away to London," he said. "Is there any truth to that?"

"My business is my own," Tristan replied in a firm voice.

Shifting on the bench, the man said, "I have heard that she has fallen on hard times now that her mother died."

Tristan brought the glass up to his lips, not bothering to

respond to the man. He had no intention of speaking to him about Lady Lizette.

The man continued. "I had considered offering for her. In fact, my father was encouraging me to do so. A union between us would make sense because her land borders ours," he shared. "She is handsome enough to tempt me, but her lowly status kept me from doing so."

Tristan wondered how this man would respond once he discovered that Miss Kent was, in fact, Lady Lizette, grand-daughter of one of the most powerful men in England. But he had no intention of revealing the truth to him. He just wished he could be there when the smug smile was wiped off his face when he discovered Lady Lizette's true lineage.

"Now, I shall just wait until she is forced to sell her lands, and I will get them at a fraction of the price," the man said, rubbing his hands together.

"How chivalrous of you," Tristan muttered.

"It is not as if I do not sympathize with Miss Kent's plight, but I must put my personal feelings aside when it comes to business."

Tristan brought the drink down to the table and glanced over his shoulder. "Do you have no one else you can talk to? Surely, there is someone else."

The man chuckled. "You are not a man that minces words. I can respect that." He leaned closer and said, "I just find myself curious if you intend to take Miss Kent for your mistress."

Tristan tightened his hold on his tankard and growled, "Do you take me for a blackguard?"

The man gave him a pointed look. "Your garments are made from the finest material, leaving me to believe you are a man of means. How else would you catch the eye of the most beautiful woman in the village?"

"You know not what you speak of."

"Then enlighten me."

"Why should I do that?" Tristan asked.

"It is not as if I blame you," the man said. "Miss Kent would make a fine mistress to any man. Perhaps I will make a go of it with her."

The blonde-haired barmaid set a tankard in front of the man, the ale spilling over the top and onto her hand.

Reaching into his pocket, the man pulled out a white handkerchief and handed it to the barmaid.

The barmaid used it to dry her hand before she extended it back to him. "Thank you," she said.

The man put his hand up. "Keep it," he encouraged. "You never know when you might need it again."

The barmaid smiled as she slipped it into the pocket of her dress. "You are most kind, Mr. Slade."

Mr. Slade winked at her. "You are easy to be kind to," he said in a flirtatious tone.

Tristan resisted the urge to look heavenward. He was all too familiar with these types of men. His brother had been one of them. They seemed to crave attention from the ladies, not caring a whit who they hurt along the way.

He may not know Lady Lizette well, but he knew that she deserved better than what Mr. Slade would be offering. As far as he was concerned, she was under his protection, and he had no intention of letting her settle for a man such as Mr. Slade.

Tristan turned to face the man. "You will leave Miss Kent be." He didn't want to refer to her correct address for fear that would entice the man even further to press his suit.

Mr. Slade appeared unconcerned at his warning. "Or what?" he asked. "You will make me, dandy?"

"I am no dandy, and, yes, I will."

With a smirk, Mr. Slade said, "I think not. It would be in your best interest to leave Bridgwater without Miss Kent."

"I am not leaving without her."

"Then we have a problem, because I don't intend to let her leave," Mr. Slade said. "I also have designs on her."

Tristan shoved back his chair and rose. He had little doubt that he would beat Mr. Slade in a round of fisticuffs, but it would hardly be a fair fight. He towered over the weaselly man. "We shall leave it up to Miss Kent to decide her future."

Mr. Slade scoffed. "She is merely a woman," he said. "I think we would both agree that a woman must not be left to her own devices."

"I daresay that you are associating with the wrong women."

"Or you are overestimating them."

Tristan pushed his chair back into the table. "I tire of this conversation and, frankly, your presence."

Mr. Slade held his tankard up. "May the best man win."

"There is no contest," Tristan said. "Once Miss Kent sees what you are offering, she will want nothing to do with you."

"I wouldn't be so sure," Mr. Slade responded with a cocky grin.

Not bothering to dignify his words with a response, Tristan started to walk away, wishing that he could wipe that arrogant look off Mr. Slade's face. But he was a smart enough man to know when to leave well enough alone. Mr. Slade wasn't worth his time or notice.

Tristan stepped out into the cool night air and glanced up at the moon that hung in the sky. How was he going to convince Lady Lizette to return to London with him? He didn't dare leave Bridgwater without her and risk Lord Ashington's wrath. He was a kind man, but he expected that his orders were followed precisely as instructed.

A young, lanky boy ran up to him and said, "I'm looking for a Mr. Westcott. Do you know him?"

"I am Mr. Westcott."

The boy let out a relieved sigh. "I was told to tell you that Miss Kent would like you to call upon her tomorrow."

A thrill coursed through him at that unexpected news. "Please inform her that I will be there first thing in the morning," he said as he reached into his waistcoat pocket for a coin. He pulled it out and extended it to the boy.

The boy's eyes lit up. "Thank you, Mister," he gushed as he clasped the coin in his hand.

As the boy ran off in the direction that he had come from, Tristan felt a smile tugging at his lips. Perhaps he wouldn't be stuck in this village for too long. And it was a good thing because the entire village smelled of manure.

Chapter Three

With the morning sun streaming through the windows, Lizette paced back and forth in the drawing room as she tried to prepare herself for Mr. Westcott's visit. She knew she shouldn't be overly worried about their meeting, but she found herself rather anxious about it. What if Mr. Westcott changed his mind and refused to accompany her to London? No. He wouldn't do that. He was a gentleman, and he would do the honorable thing.

She stopped pacing. Was he truly a gentleman? He may look and act the part but there was a sadness to him that she found at odds with his boorish behavior. She might not have even noticed his conflicting emotions if she wasn't grieving the loss of her mother. Regardless, she would need to be mindful to keep him at arm's length on their journey to London. No good would come from associating with him since he was the most vexing of gentlemen.

Turning towards the window, she stared out at the garden. It had been her mother's place of solitude for so long, a place that she would retreat to when she needed to feel close to her husband. What would become of it? If she sold the manor, would the next owner care for the roses as diligently as her mother had? She doubted that and grew sad all over again.

Lizette leaned her shoulder against the window. How she wished her mother were here, leading her, and assuring her that everything would be all right. She needed to hear those comforting words.

Stockton stepped into the room and announced, "Mr. Slade has come to call and is requesting a moment of your time."

Lizette felt herself smile at the mention of Colin's name. "Please send him in," she ordered as she smoothed down her black gown.

"Very good, Miss," Stockton said before he departed from the room.

It was but a moment before Mr. Slade stepped into the room. He bowed and greeted her politely. "Miss Kent."

Her smile grew more broadly. "Since when did you stand on formalities, Colin?"

Colin returned her smile. "I suppose since I haven't seen you very often since you started at your boarding school."

"I am still the same girl that could best you at... well, at everything," Lizette teased.

As he walked further into the room, he said, "It is good to see you looking so well, Lizette."

She gestured towards the settees. "Would you care to sit?" she asked as she went to sit down on the blue camelback settee.

"I would." He waited until she sat down before he did the same. "I came to see how you are faring."

Her smile dimmed. "I am taking every day one day at a time."

"That is to be expected."

Lowering her gaze to her lap, she said, "My mother would say that grief is the price we must pay for loving someone so completely."

"Your mother was very wise."

"I thought so." She brought her gaze back up. "How long did it take before you stopped grieving your mother?"

Colin gave her a blank look. "I… uh… am still grieving her," he said, his words sounding forced.

"I notice that you are not wearing a black armband over your sleeve."

"Yes, but it has been nearly two months since her death," Colin responded. "One cannot live in the past if one wants to embrace the future."

"Oh, I see," she murmured, even though she didn't see. How could he so quickly move on from grieving his mother?

Colin's eyes left hers and roamed over the drawing room. "This room is exactly how I remembered it."

"My mother was not one for change," Lizette acknowledged as her eyes filled with tears at the mere mention of her mother. "I do apologize for my display of emotions."

Colin's eyes held compassion. "You have no reason to apologize."

Lizette offered him a weak smile. "I keep telling myself that it will be okay. Maybe not today, or tomorrow, but eventually."

"I wish I had your positive outlook on life."

"You misunderstood me. This is my new way of life, and I must accept it."

Colin moved to sit on the edge of his seat and reached for her hands. "You are not alone in this," he said. "There are many people in the village that care for you."

Lizette shook her head. "I have never felt like I truly belong here."

"That isn't true," Colin defended.

With a glance down at their hands, Lizette felt comfort in his touch and words. There was a time when she had fancied herself in love with Colin, but that was in the past. They had both grown up and moved on with their lives.

"I am glad for a friend such as you at a time like this," Lizette said.

Colin took his finger and started caressing her gloved hand. "I was hoping to be more than just a friend to you."

Lizette grew rigid. "Pardon?" Surely he didn't mean what she thought he meant.

"I know this is not the ideal time to speak of such things, but I can't abide the thought of you leaving Bridgwater with that blackguard- Mr. Westcott."

"Mr. Westcott is not a blackguard." Or at least she hoped that he wasn't. She knew very little about the man.

"I regret to inform you that I saw him at the coaching inn last night and he was blatantly flirting with the barmaid."

"That is disconcerting, but of little concern to me."

Colin leaned closer and said, "You don't have to be his mistress. You have other options afforded to you."

Her lips parted in disbelief and Colin must have taken that as an invitation to kiss her. He pressed his lips against hers and she felt absolutely, positively nothing. No stirring of emotion. No visions of the future. Rather, it was just a dull, awkward kiss.

She reared back and demanded, "What are you doing?"

His lips curled into a flirtatious smile. "I thought it was fairly obvious."

Rising, Lizette said, "I think you should go."

"I daresay that you are overreacting," Colin remarked as he rose. "I thought you wanted this."

She placed a hand on her hip. "What would give you that indication?"

"Truly?" Colin huffed. "You are the one that is leaving our village to be with Mr. Westcott."

"Mr. Westcott and I have no understanding, and I resent the implication," Lizette said. "He is just escorting me to London."

Colin took a step closer to her. "Stay here in Bridgwater... with me."

"You are asking me to marry you?"

He scoffed. "Of course not," he replied. "I want you to be my mistress."

Lizette found herself speechless. How dare he insult her in such a fashion?

Colin must have taken her silence for acceptance because a lazy smile came to his lips. "I see that you are considering it."

Lizette was fuming and she clenched her hands into tight balls. "No," she said firmly.

"No?"

"I will not be your mistress," she asserted. "I am no man's mistress."

Colin frowned. "You must understand that I cannot marry you since your circumstances have been reduced."

It was on the tip of Lizette's tongue to tell him that she was the daughter of an earl, but she decided to keep that to herself. She didn't want to encourage Colin. Quite the opposite, in fact. She had no interest in what he was offering.

"What if I bought your manor and allowed you to remain living in it?" Colin asked.

"But that would come at a cost," Lizette said dryly.

Colin put his hands out wide. "Nothing in this world is free. Everything has a price associated with it."

Lizette stared at him in disbelief. When had Colin turned into such a cad? He had always been kind to her when they were younger. Did he think asking her to be his mistress was an act of kindness? She certainly hoped not.

"I am not interested in what you are offering," she said.

Colin stared at her, his face growing hard. "You will regret this."

"I don't think I will."

Taking a step back, Colin asked, "What do you think will

happen to you once you lose your lands? Do you think anyone will want you then?"

Lizette pursed her lips. "I understand that you are hurt—"

He cut her off. "Hurt?" he asked. "Don't flatter yourself. You are just a stubborn woman, and your pride will be the death of you."

Clasping her hands in front of her, she said, "You should go."

"You will not dismiss me so easily—"

Mr. Westcott's commanding voice came from the doorway. "The lady asked you to leave."

Colin turned towards Mr. Westcott and growled, "This does not concern you."

"It does now," Mr. Westcott said, stepping further into the room. He appeared calm, but his jaw was clenched, and his hands were balled into tight fists.

With narrowed eyes, Colin seethed, "You can have her, but I won't be taking your castoffs. I am done here." He walked past Mr. Westcott without bothering to spare her a glance.

Neither of them spoke as Colin stormed off, slamming the main door behind him.

Lizette released the breath that she hadn't realized that she had been holding. "Thank you for what you did."

"I did nothing but simply encourage him to leave."

"It was something."

Mr. Westcott shifted his stance, appearing uncomfortable. "I do apologize but I overheard some of your conversation."

"Then you know of my shame."

His expression turned perplexed. "What shame?"

Lizette sat down on the settee. "I was asked to be the mistress of my childhood friend; someone that I had once dreamed of marrying."

"And now?"

"Didn't you hear him?" Lizette asked. "I am unmarriageable."

"As Miss Kent, perhaps, but not as Lady Lizette." Mr. Westcott walked further into the room. "You could have your pick of suitors. They will be lining the streets just to get a glimpse of you."

"You are prone to exaggeration, I see."

Mr. Westcott moved to sit across from her. "You didn't chastise me when I referred to you as Lady Lizette. Dare I hope that you have come to terms with the truth?"

Lizette nodded. "I have and I would like to go to London to meet my grandfather."

Tristan resisted the urge to smile since this was precisely the outcome he had hoped for. He didn't want Lady Lizette to know how pleased he was that she was agreeing to allow him to escort her to London.

He would fulfill his duty to Lord Ashington and then he would wash his hands of Lady Lizette. He could go back to managing the estates, a job that took nearly every waking moment, and focus on what was truly important- his legacy. He couldn't fail when so many people before him had succeeded. He had to prove to others- and himself- that he was worthy of such an honor.

Leaning back in his seat, Tristan asked, "May I ask what changed your mind?"

Lady Lizette started fidgeting with her hands in her lap. "My solicitor gave me a note that my mother had written and she explained that I was the daughter of the Earl of Crewe."

"Did she explain why she kept that from you?"

Lady Lizette hesitated. "She said it was to protect me."

"From what?"

"The harshness of the truth," Lady Lizette said as she blew out a puff of air. "But I have no idea what that means."

"Perhaps Lord Ashington will have some insight on that," Tristan suggested.

Lady Lizette seemed to perk up at his words. "I do hope that is the case."

"I must admit that I am relieved that your mother was in the right mind to write that letter to you," he said.

"As am I."

Tristan glanced over at the window and saw the sun reflecting off the panes of glass. "If we depart at once, we can arrive in London by tomorrow afternoon."

"So soon?"

"Is there anything keeping you here in Bridgwater?"

Lady Lizette's eyes roamed over the drawing room. "I suppose not anymore."

Tristan thought it would be best if he informed Lady Lizette of the dangers that they might encounter on the journey home. "The road we will travel on is frequented by highwaymen so I will expect you to follow my orders as precisely as possible."

"I understand."

"Good, because you are under my protection, for the time being, and I take that role very seriously," Tristan said. "I don't have time to coddle you."

Lady Lizette gave him a wary look. "Coddle me?"

"Just do as I say and we will get along swimmingly."

"You want me to follow you blindly?"

"In so many words, yes."

Lady Lizette visibly tensed and the lines around her mouth grew tight. "I think it might be best if I secure another mode of transportation to London."

Fearing he'd misheard her, he asked, "I beg your pardon?" What in the blazes was she about?

"The mail coach goes through Bridgwater and I could purchase a ticket," Lady Lizette said. "It would save us both the trouble of dealing with one another."

Tristan stared at this maddening young woman and couldn't believe she had the audacity to even suggest taking the mail coach. Did she not care a whit about her reputation? A mail coach was not an acceptable mode of transportation for the daughter of an earl.

Rising, Tristan said, "That is ridiculous. You will travel with me and that is the end of the discussion."

Lady Lizette rose and tilted her chin. "You seem to believe you have the right to tell me what to do, Mr. Westcott."

"I was sent by your grandfather to escort you back to London."

"Escort me, yes, but not dictate my every move."

"That is not what I am trying to do," Tristan countered. "I am merely telling you that I know the dangers that lie ahead of us and I don't have time for a simpering miss."

"And you believe I am a simpering miss?"

Tristan could hear the slightest warning in her voice, but he wasn't smart enough to leave well enough alone. "I don't know you well enough to make that determination, but it has been my experience that women of high Society tend to be all the same."

Lady Lizette crossed her arms over her chest. "You are rather quick to lump me in with those women, considering I only have just learned that I am a lady."

"I take no man's word for anything, but I trust my own experiences," Tristan said.

"Then I do hope to prove you wrong."

Tristan grinned. "I am hardly wrong."

"You are a cocky man."

"I have been called far worse."

"That doesn't surprise me," Lady Lizette said as her mouth drew back into a smirk.

Tristan looked heavenward. "Do you always make it a habit of speaking your mind?"

"I do."

"It is rather annoying."

Lady Lizette dropped her hands to her sides. "I disagree," she said. "It is much more liberating to speak the truth than pretend to be someone I am not."

Tristan had to admit that Lady Lizette did have a point, but he didn't dare tell her that. He would much rather have a woman speak plainly to him than hide behind coy smiles.

A knock came at the door, interrupting their conversation.

Lady Lizette turned her head towards the direction of the main door. "I wonder who has come to call since I wasn't expecting anyone."

Tristan knew precisely who had come to call. He had been so engrossed in his conversation to Lady Lizette that he forgot Lady Anne was in the coach. How could he have been so easily distracted? That wasn't like him.

A moment later, the butler stepped into the room and announced, "Lady Anne Astley would like a moment of your time, Miss."

A line between Lady Lizette's brow appeared as she turned her attention towards him. "Do you know a Lady Anne Astley?"

"She is your aunt," Tristan replied.

"My aunt?" Lady Lizette asked.

He nodded. "Yes, and she is not one that is accustomed to being kept waiting."

Lady Lizette went to address her butler. "Please send her in."

The butler had just turned on his heel when Lady Anne stepped into the room. She was a tall, slender woman with fading black hair. She was dressed in a rich green traveling habit and a straw hat sat slightly askew on her head.

Lady Anne's face was tight as she cast a disapproving look at Tristan. "I grew tired of waiting in the coach."

Tristan bowed. "My apologies, my lady, but Lady Lizette

and I had a few things we needed to sort out before I retrieved you."

"Have they been sorted out?" Lady Anne asked.

With a glance at Lady Lizette, he replied, "Not quite."

"Well, I am not one to wait for an introduction." Lady Anne turned towards Lady Lizette, her critical eyes sweeping over her. Finally, she spoke. "I was sorry to hear about the passing of your mother."

"Thank you," Lady Lizette murmured.

Lady Anne stepped closer. "You look terrible in that woolen gown," she said. "Black does not complement your skin tone, my dear."

"I am in full mourning of my mother."

"Yes, but it might be best if we forego the mourning period for you, considering the circumstances."

Lady Lizette blinked. "You don't think I should mourn my mother?"

"The French rules are not as strict as the English customs, and your mother was French, was she not?" she asked.

"She was, hence why I am adhering to their tradition by wearing the woolen gown."

With a wave of her hand, Lady Anne said, "We can discuss this on our journey back to London."

Lady Lizette's eyes turned towards him, and he could see the questions in her eyes. He rushed to explain, "Your grandfather thought it would be best if Lady Anne came and acted as your chaperone on the journey home."

"I am home, Mr. Westcott," Lady Lizette argued.

Lady Anne pressed her lips together. "This is hardly a home fit for a woman of your status."

"It suited my mother and me just fine," Lady Lizette argued.

"Yes, well your mother was just a vicomte's daughter that had fallen upon hard times," Lady Anne said. "It is of little wonder she would feel comfortable in a place such as this."

Tristan saw that Lady Lizette's back grew rigid and she looked as if she were about to give Lady Anne a tongue lashing, which would not help the situation. Lady Anne was a proud woman that held strong opinions and she was not one that he assumed took criticism well.

Interjecting, Tristan asked, "Are your trunks packed?"

Lady Lizette shifted her gaze towards him. "They are," she replied.

"Shall we depart then?" he asked.

"I wish to bring my horse," Lady Lizette said.

"I have no objections."

Lady Lizette looked relieved by his response. "Thank you," she murmured. "If you will excuse me, I shall go collect my horse."

"You mean your servants will collect your horse," Lady Anne corrected.

"No, I spoke correctly," Lady Lizette said.

Lady Anne put a hand to her chest, feigning outrage. "A lady does not retrieve her own horse," she explained. "It is simply not done."

"If not me, then who?"

"Any servant would do," Lady Anne pressed.

Tristan found it odd that Lady Lizette's eyes sparkled with mirth, as if she were enjoying her conversation with Lady Anne.

"I'm afraid we do not have an abundance of servants at this time," Lizette said.

"It only takes one to retrieve your horse," Lady Anne argued.

Lizette shrugged. "Yet I find it is a task that I enjoy."

"Surely you jest."

"I take saddling my horse very seriously, my lady," Lizette said. "If I do not saddle my horse correctly, then I could fall and die."

"More the reason for a groom to do the task," Lady Anne declared.

"And deny me the privilege of doing it myself?" Lizette asked. "I think not."

Tristan brought his hand up to cover the smile on his lips. It was evident that Lady Lizette was goading Lady Anne, and it was rather amusing to him. But he wouldn't dare admit that to Lady Anne, who was growing more exasperated by the moment.

Lady Anne lifted her chin haughtily. "What would people think if they knew you saddled your own horse?"

"I would imagine they would be impressed."

"You would be wrong, Child," Lady Anne said. "A lady must never get her hands soiled with work."

"Fortunately for me, I only just discovered I am a lady." Lady Lizette dropped into a curtsy. "I shall see to refreshments being brought up while I step out to the stable," she said before she hurried out of the room.

Lady Anne turned towards him with a panicked look on her face. "Don't just stand there, young man, do something."

"What would you have me do?" he asked.

"Go with Lady Lizette and help her retrieve her horse," Lady Anne ordered. "For heaven's sake, be a gentleman."

Tristan bowed. "As you wish, my lady." He didn't bother to wait for her reply before he went to find Lady Lizette and force his assistance upon her.

Chapter Four

Lizette found great pleasure in shocking Lady Anne. She knew she shouldn't find such enjoyment in that, but she did. Normally, she would request a groom to prepare her horse, but they had left to seek out other employment. Not that she blamed them.

She proceeded down to the kitchen and was pleased to see Mrs. Everly placing biscuits onto a silver tray.

Mrs. Everly glanced up as Lizette stepped up to the counter. "Are your guests still in the drawing room?"

"They are," Lizette confirmed. "I was just coming to see about refreshments for them."

Mrs. Everly gave her a knowing look. "You could have asked Stockton."

"I know, but I found I needed a reprieve from Lady Anne."

"Who is Lady Anne?"

Lizette pulled out a chair at the counter and sat down. "Supposedly, she is my aunt."

"That is exciting."

"Is it?" Lizette asked. "She seems like a prude."

"That is rather critical of you since you just met the

woman," Mrs. Everly said. "Just promise me that you will withhold judgment until you get to know her."

Lizette reluctantly nodded. "I suppose I can do that."

Mrs. Everly slid the tray towards her. "Biscuit?"

She eagerly reached for one and asked, "What am I going to do without your biscuits?"

"I have no doubt that your fancy new cook in Town will prepare something that you enjoy," Mrs. Everly teased.

Lizette took a bite of the biscuit before saying, "I am sorry that I can't take you with me."

"I understand why you can't."

"What are you going to do now?"

Mrs. Everly reached for a rag and started to wipe down the counter. "I intend to remain here and care for the manor, just as Mr. Westcott directed."

Lizette gave her a baffled look. "When did Mr. Westcott direct this?" And why did Mr. Westcott think he had the right to order her staff around? The audacity of that man!

"Mr. Billings informed me this morning that Mr. Westcott had given him the funds to maintain a small staff for the manor for a whole year," Mrs. Everly shared. "Did Mr. Westcott not tell you this?"

She felt the anger leave her. "No, he did not."

"I wonder why," Mrs. Everly mused.

Lizette had to admit that her respect had just grown for Mr. Westcott, but she wouldn't dare admit that to him. He was already much too cocky for his own good.

Mrs. Everly placed the rag down. "Furthermore, Mr. Westcott has requested repairs on the manor."

"That is most generous of him," Lizette admitted.

Reaching for the tray, Mrs. Everly said, "I should get these refreshments to your guests before they starve."

Lizette smiled. "I doubt they will starve."

"It is a chance I don't want to risk."

She felt her smile slipping as she asked, "What am I going to do without you?"

Mrs. Everly's face softened. "You will be just fine without me."

"How can you be so sure?"

"Because you are destined for great things, my dear," Mrs. Everly said. "You just have to believe it to be true."

Lizette felt her shoulders droop. "What if I fail?" she asked.

Mrs. Everly placed the tray onto the counter and met her gaze. "Failure is most definitely an option, but so is success. You just have to decide which path you want."

"You make it sound so simple."

"The first step in any journey is the hardest," Mrs. Everly said.

Tears pricked at the back of her eyes and she blinked them away. "I wish my mother was here," she murmured.

Mrs. Everly placed a comforting hand on her shoulder. "Your mother will always be a part of you."

"You must think me incredibly foolish."

"Never," Mrs. Everly responded. "There is nothing wrong with being fearful of the unknown, assuming you do not let that fear consume you."

Lizette sighed. "I wish I knew what the future holds for me."

"That would take the joy out of all the little moments along the way," Mrs. Everly said. "It is better to work towards the future you hope for, knowing that it could change at any moment."

"That is what concerns me."

Mrs. Everly removed her hand and reached for the tray. "What could go wrong?"

"So many things," Lizette rushed to reply.

"Do not overthink this, my dear," Mrs. Everly urged. "You have been given a great opportunity. Do not waste this."

Lizette knew that she had to make a choice. She could go forward in fear, or she could hope for the best.

Rising, Lizette said, "You are right."

Mrs. Everly gave her an encouraging smile. "The greatest thing you can do is trust and believe in yourself." She held the tray up. "Do you need any more encouragement, or can I take these biscuits up to your guests?"

Lizette laughed. "I think I have been properly encouraged."

"Very good," Mrs. Everly said.

After Mrs. Everly departed from the kitchen, Lizette walked out the back door and headed down the well-worn path towards the stable.

Lizette arrived at the stable and noticed that the door was ajar. She stepped inside and saw Mr. Westcott standing next to the stall that housed her horse. He was petting her nose and was speaking in hushed tones.

Lizette couldn't resist the opportunity to tease the boorish man. "I do hope you aren't waiting for Moonshine to respond."

Mr. Westcott dropped his hand and took a step back. "I came to see if you needed assistance with your horse."

"That won't be necessary," Lizette said, walking further in the stable. "My mother was adamant that I knew how to saddle my own horse."

"It would be my privilege," he pressed.

Lizette walked over to the stall and opened the door. "Thank you, kindly, but I do not require assistance."

Mr. Westcott glanced down at her gown and remarked, "But you are in a gown."

Lizette closed the door and reached for a brush that was on a hook on the wall. "I am, but it is of little consequence."

"I would feel more comfortable if I could assist you."

Lizette suspected that Mr. Westcott wasn't about to leave

her alone so she might as well make the most out of the situation.

Extending him the brush, she said, "You can brush down Moonshine."

Mr. Westcott accepted the brush and stepped into the stall. As he started brushing the horse, he asked, "Why did you name your horse 'Moonshine'?"

Lizette placed her hand on the horse's side. "She was born late at night, and I remember how the moon shone down upon her as she took her first wobbly steps." She smiled at that memory. "I knew that we would always be together after that."

Mr. Westcott continued to brush down the side of Moonshine as he met her gaze. "You are an anomaly, my lady."

"Why do you say that?"

"I do not know any woman that would saddle her own horse."

"Then you might not be associating with the right women," Lizette teased as she retrieved another brush.

"Apparently, I am not."

Lizette brushed Moonshine in downward strokes. "Have you never saddled your own horse?"

"I never said that I didn't."

"Oh, I just assumed."

Mr. Westcott paused. "I was not raised with a large household staff," he shared. "I learned from a young age to make do with what we had."

Lizette furrowed her brow. "How is that possible?" she asked. "Are you not my grandfather's heir?"

"I am now, but my brother held that title for many years," Mr. Westcott shared. "Frankly, we grew up as the poor relations."

She could hear the pain in his words, and it caused her heart to ache. "My condolences on the loss of your brother."

Mr. Westcott gave her a weak smile. "Thank you," he said. "It has been three years since he has passed away."

"Does it make it any easier?" she asked.

"I'm afraid not."

"That is what I was afraid you would say."

Mr. Westcott went and placed the brush on the hook. "May I saddle Moonshine?" he asked as he reached for the saddle that was secured on the wall.

"You may." Lizette stepped back as he placed the saddle onto Moonshine. "I wanted to thank you for providing the funds to pay my staff and to fix up the manor. That was most kind of you."

"It is what your grandfather would have wanted," Mr. Westcott said as he went about securing the saddle to the horse.

"Regardless, I would be remiss if I did not properly thank you."

Mr. Westcott glanced up from tightening the strap. "You are welcome," he said. "I know this is your home and I did not want to have it fall into disrepair."

Lizette's eyes roamed over the stable that was in desperate need of repair. "It might not seem like much to you…"

"A home isn't so much about the size, but the people that live inside of it," Mr. Westcott remarked, speaking over her.

Lizette looked at Mr. Westcott with newfound respect, knowing she felt as he did. "I concur with that," she said.

Mr. Westcott looked at her curiously. "Did we just agree on something?"

"I think we did."

"Let's not make that a habit, shall we?"

"I wouldn't dream of it."

Mr. Westcott grinned. "We did it again," he said as he yanked down on the strap. "We will need to be more careful in the future."

Lizette had to admit that she found this side of Mr. Westcott to be much more tolerable. Perhaps the trip to London wouldn't be as terrible as she thought.

———————————⟨~⟩———————————

Lizette had been entirely wrong about the trip to London being tolerable. It might have been had Mr. Westcott ridden in the coach with them, but shortly before they departed, he had informed them that he would be trailing behind them on his horse.

She fingered the strings of her bonnet as she stared out the window. She knew she was a coward, but she was attempting to avoid a conversation with her aunt. What did one say to an aunt that you only just discovered existed?

Her aunt's voice broke through the silence. "Are you well, dear?"

"I am."

"I only ask because you seem wildly interested in the countryside," her aunt said with amusement in her voice.

Lizette met her gaze. "I'm sorry."

"You have no reason to be sorry," her aunt said. "I was only just teasing you."

"I'm afraid I am not terribly comfortable with polite conversation."

Her aunt considered her for a moment before saying, "You will have to get over that since you will be thrust into high Society, and people will expect you to converse with them."

Lizette smoothed down her gown. "But I am in mourning."

"I do not mean to be insensitive, but your grandfather wishes to introduce you into Society once you arrive in Town."

"Can it not wait until next Season?"

Lady Anne shook her head. "I'm afraid not," she said. "If

memory serves me correctly, you just turned eighteen."

"I did."

"If I had my way, you would have been introduced into Society last year, but your mother would have none of that," her aunt said. "A young woman with your beauty must not hide behind a bushel."

"You knew about me?"

Her aunt smiled kindly. "We have known about you for your whole life, but we kept our distance, per your mother's request."

"Do you know why that was?"

"Let's not dwell on such unpleasant topics," her aunt replied. "We have an appointment with the dressmaker tomorrow afternoon. We will need to obtain a whole new wardrobe for you."

Lizette removed the bonnet off her head and placed it down onto the bench next to her. "What will the *ton* think if I forego the mourning period?"

Her aunt waved a hand dismissively in front of her. "The *ton* will be abuzz with the fact that Lord Ashington's long-lost granddaughter has returned."

"How can you be so sure?"

"Your grandfather wields a lot of power with Society," her aunt said. "Anyone that dares to cross him would be ostracized."

Lizette grew silent. "Was my mother ostracized?"

"No, your parents chose to keep you hidden away. They thought it was for the best."

"In the letter my mother wrote, she said she was protecting me."

Her aunt bobbed her head. "I do believe that is what they thought they were doing."

"Do you know what 'harshness of truth' that they were protecting me from?" Lizette pressed.

Shifting in her seat, her aunt replied, "It would be best if your grandfather explained that to you."

"I'm afraid I don't understand why that is."

"It is not a conversation that is to be taken lightly."

The coach hit a bump in the road and Lizette reached out to steady herself. "I forgot how much I hated riding in coaches," she muttered.

"Mr. Westcott informed me that you threatened to travel to London by the way of a mail coach."

"I did."

"May I ask why that was?"

Lizette brought her hand back to her lap. "Mr. Westcott kept coming up with ridiculous commands and wanted me to trust him."

"And you thought your only solution was to ride on a mail coach?"

Lizette gave her a sheepish smile. "I thought it was rather amusing at the time and I did get a rise out of Mr. Westcott."

"What if Mr. Westcott had called your bluff?"

With a shrug, Lizette replied, "Then I would have ridden in a mail coach."

"I would have loved to see my father's reaction if you had, in fact, ridden in a mail coach, considering he sent his finest coach for you."

Finding herself curious, Lizette asked, "What is my grandfather like?"

"He is a good man, but he is very busy in politics," her aunt shared. "He is trying to give the people in the rookeries access to fresh water."

"Do they not have the River Thames?"

Her aunt shuddered. "The smell that wafts off the River Thames is horrendous," she said. "It is more of a deadly sewer now rather than a fresh flowing river."

"I have read some articles in the newssheets about the conditions at the River Thames, but I had hoped it was just exaggerated in an attempt to sell more papers."

"If anything, it wasn't reported on enough," her aunt said. "People are dying in the rookeries at an alarming rate."

"Surely it can't all be blamed on the River Thames?"

"No, but it is a big contributor, and my father can only do so much. He is lacking the support of Parliament."

Lizette reached into the reticule that was around her right wrist and pulled out a fan. It was entirely too stuffy in the coach, or maybe it was because of the thick, black traveling gown she was wearing.

As she started fanning herself, Lizette decided to remark, "Mr. Westcott failed to mention my grandmother."

Her aunt's eyes grew downcast. "My mother passed away many years ago and we do not speak of her often."

Lizette felt awful for bringing up her grandmother and went to apologize, but her aunt spoke first. "My mother was troubled."

"My mother said the same thing about my father in her letter," Lizette said. "What does that mean?"

Her aunt shifted her gaze towards the window. "My mother and brother had real struggles in this life that they couldn't overcome," she shared. "Not everyone can handle the rigors of life and come out unscathed."

"What kind of struggles does an earl have?"

Lady Anne brought her gaze back to meet Lizette's. "A gilded life does not mean it is not without problems," she chided.

"I did not mean to imply such, but I am just trying to understand."

"Sometimes we must accept we don't understand everything and move on," her aunt said.

Lizette sat back in her seat. Now they were just going in circles and it was evident her aunt had no intention of sharing anything more about her father.

Her aunt cast her a disapproving look. "A lady does not slouch."

"But no one can see me in here," she argued.

"A woman must behave in private as well as in public," her aunt advised. "You never know who could be watching."

Lizette sat straight in her seat, all while grumbling about it in her head. They had been traveling for hours and her whole body seemed to be protesting with every rotation of the wheels. She didn't know how much longer she could take being cooped up in this coach, especially with Lady Anne as a companion.

Mr. Westcott rode by the window on his horse and appeared to be giving directions to the driver.

"I do hope this means we will be stopping soon," her aunt said. "I could use the opportunity to stretch my legs."

"I feel the same way."

Lizette let out a sigh of a relief as the coach began to slow down. She placed the fan back into her reticule and reached for her bonnet. After she placed it on her head, tying the strings loosely under her chin, the coach came to a stop.

The door opened and a footman extended his hand to assist them out of the coach. Lizette waited until her aunt had exited the coach before she accepted the footman's proffered hand. Once she stepped onto the dirt road, she withdrew her hand and breathed in the fresh country air.

A footman approached them with a basket and a blanket over his shoulder. "Would either of you care for some refreshment?"

As if on cue, Lizette could feel her stomach growl and she placed a hand over her stomach. "I must admit that I am famished."

"Where did this food come from?" Lady Anne asked.

"Mrs. Everly insisted that we take along a basket of bread, meats and biscuits," the footman shared.

"How thoughtful of her," Lady Anne said.

The footman pointed towards a cluster of trees on a small

hill a short distance away. "If you ladies have no objections, I will place the blanket down under those trees."

"That is a fine idea," Lizette responded.

As they followed the footman over to the trees, Mr. Westcott came up from behind and asked, "What is the meaning of this?"

"We are going to have a picnic," Lizette replied, speaking over her shoulder.

"Absolutely not!" Mr. Westcott exclaimed. "We have a schedule that we must adhere to if we want to arrive in London by tomorrow afternoon."

"Do not be such a bore," Lady Anne declared, making no effort to slow down.

Mr. Westcott met Lizette's stride. "Fine. We will eat quickly and I'll have you back in the coach before we waste too much time."

"You should know that I am a slow eater, young man," Lady Anne said as she winked at her.

Lizette resisted the urge to smile at Mr. Westcott's expense. It was clear that her aunt was baiting him and found amusement in it.

Mr. Westcott frowned. "If that is the case, it might be preferable if you ate in the coach."

"Then when would you eat?" Lady Anne asked.

"I am not hungry," Mr. Westcott replied.

Lady Anne arrived at the blanket and gracefully sat down. "Sit, Mr. Westcott," she ordered. "We will eat the food that was prepared for us, and we will take a moment to enjoy one another's company."

Mr. Westcott glanced back at the coach before he reluctantly sat down. "Yes, my lady," he muttered.

Lizette lowered herself onto the blanket and reached for a biscuit in the basket. As she enjoyed the delectable treat, she listened to the birds chirping merrily in the trees above them and she felt herself relaxing.

Chapter Five

Tristan was miserable. This outing was taking entirely too long for his liking. They had a schedule that they needed to adhere to, and they had no time to lollygag about.

The chirping birds grated on his nerves, and he could feel the sweat rolling down his back. It was too warm to be enjoying a picnic, even though the shade of the trees did provide some relief. But not enough.

Lady Lizette and Lady Anne were politely conversing with one another, and he felt no need to contribute to the conversation. Why couldn't they just eat in the coach so they could be on their way? It would be much simpler.

Tristan shifted uncomfortably on the blanket that did little by the way of cushioning the hard ground beneath him. He would much rather be in his saddle.

Lady Lizette cast him a curious look. "Are you not hungry?"

"I am not," he replied.

"There is more than enough," Lady Lizette encouraged, bringing the basket closer to her. "Mrs. Everly packed enough food to feed a small army."

"I thank you for your concern, but I will eat once we arrive at the coaching inn for the evening," Tristan said.

"That will be in hours." Lady Lizette removed another biscuit from the basket and shared, "Mrs. Everly makes the most delicious biscuits."

"I shall have to take your word for it."

"I thought you were the type of man that doesn't take anyone's word for it, and you rely off your own experiences," Lady Lizette remarked, using his own words against him.

"Usually, yes, but it depends on the situation," Tristan said.

Lady Lizette extended him the biscuit. "Go on, try it for yourself."

Tristan didn't want to argue with Lady Lizette, so he accepted the biscuit. "Thank you," he muttered before he took a bite. He chewed slowly, and he was forced to admit to himself that it was surprisingly a very good biscuit.

"What do you think?" Lady Lizette pressed.

Not wanting to give Lady Lizette the satisfaction of being right, he replied, "It is edible."

Lady Lizette gave him a look that implied she didn't believe him, but thankfully she didn't press him. "Would it be permissible if I rode alongside you for the next stretch of the trip?"

Tristan resisted the urge to groan. He rode his horse to be alone and the last thing he wanted to do was engage in conversation with Lady Lizette. He took no issue with her, at least not anymore, but that didn't mean he wanted to spend time with her. If he had his way, once they arrived in London, he would see very little of Lady Lizette.

Lady Anne spoke up. "I think it is a fine idea, especially since I intend to close my eyes for a spell."

Lady Lizette turned to him with a hopeful look on her face, and he didn't dare disappoint her. "As you wish," he muttered.

"Thank you," Lady Lizette gushed as she jumped up. "I shall meet you at the horses."

As Lady Lizette walked away with a newfound skip in her step, Tristan couldn't seem to stop himself from watching her retreating figure. He found it odd that she found joy in the simplest things.

"I do believe you made Lady Lizette very happy," Lady Anne said.

"I hope she doesn't tire easily since I don't plan on us stopping until we reach the coaching inn this evening."

"If that is the case, we should depart at once."

Tristan rose and went to assist Lady Anne in rising. A footman stepped forward to collect the blanket and the basket.

They started to walk back to the coach in silence, which Tristan preferred. He didn't have much in common with Lady Anne and, truth be told, she frightened him a little bit.

As he approached his horse, he saw Lady Lizette was being assisted onto Moonshine by a footman. She was the epitome of grace as she positioned herself on the saddle. After she smoothed down her gown, she adjusted the reins in her hands and gave him an expectant look.

Tristan accepted the reins from the footman and mounted his horse. Turning towards her, he said, "I hope you are proficient in the saddle."

"I am."

"Have you ever followed behind a coach for hours on end?"

"I have not, but I go riding every chance I get."

"That is hardly the same."

"But it is something," she contended.

The coach started rolling down the road and Tristan urged his horse forward. He was pleased to see Lady Lizette do the same. With any luck, they would ride in silence, and he would be alone with his thoughts.

But he was not so fortunate.

Lady Lizette glanced over at him. "Where do you hail from?"

"Oxfordshire."

"Did you attend Oxford?"

He shook his head. "No, Cambridge." He hoped by keeping his answers short that Lady Lizette would get the hint that he didn't wish to engage in conversation.

"That is a shame since you lived so close to Oxford."

"I suppose it was, but Lord Ashington preferred that I attend Cambridge," he said. "His father went to Cambridge, and his father, and his father... and so on."

Lady Lizette smiled. "I get the point. You must maintain a close relationship with my grandfather then."

"I have always had great respect for Lord Ashington but we are not particularly close."

"Whyever not?"

Tristan kept his gaze straight ahead as he replied, "Your grandfather is a very busy man, and he does not have time to coddle me. He focuses on politics, and I manage his estates. It is a tried-and-true formula for us."

"Do you think he will have time for me?" Lady Lizette asked.

"I hope so," he replied. He had no desire to lie to her, but it would be best if she kept her expectations realistic when she met her grandfather.

Lady Lizette's eyes grew sad. "I just hope my grandfather will tell me more about my father. I know so little about him."

"You and I have something in common," Tristan said. "My father served in the Royal Navy, and he died when I was just a young lad."

"Do you have any fond memories of your father?"

Tristan felt his lips curve into a smile. "Just one," he replied. "When he did come home, he would blow his whistle a short distance away. My brother and I would get so excited to hear the whistle that we would drop whatever we were doing and would run to him."

"What of your mother?"

Tristan tensed. "She is dead."

"I'm sorry," Lady Lizette murmured.

"It was sudden, for which I was grateful," Tristan said. "I do not think I could have watched my mother suffer."

Lady Lizette's eyes grew downcast. "My mother died so quickly I didn't even have a chance to say goodbye."

"What would you have said, if you had the chance?"

Bringing her gaze back up, Lady Lizette replied, "I would have thanked her for being the best mother I could have asked for."

"It sounds like you had a good mother."

"I did," Lady Lizette said. "Although I find myself frustrated that she never told me that my father was an earl."

"I can only imagine."

Lady Lizette's horse whinnied, drawing her attention. "Moonshine is expressing her discontent at this slow pace."

"My horse has had no issues with the pace that I have set."

With a glance at him, Lady Lizette asked, "What is your horse's name?"

"I saw no reason to give my horse a name," he replied.

"But everyone names their horses."

"Not me. It is a horse; not a person."

A line between her brow appeared. "You are a perplexing man, Mr. Westcott."

"I have been called far worse."

"No, you misunderstood me," Lady Lizette rushed out. "I did not mean to insult you, but rather I'm trying to understand your way of thinking."

"You are wasting your time, then."

Lady Lizette cocked her head. "Why is that?"

Tristan frowned. "Do you always pry into other people's business?"

"I am just trying to make conversation."

"There is no need," Tristan said, "as I am perfectly content riding in silence."

It was Lady Lizette's turn to frown. "I just thought it was a good opportunity to learn more about one another."

Tristan resisted the urge to look heavenward. Why did women prefer endless chatter to the silence? He had discovered that the quieter he became, the more he could learn about himself, and others.

Knowing she was still waiting for a response, Tristan said, "Once we arrive in London, we will both go our separate ways so there is no need to become more acquainted with one another."

"Oh," Lady Lizette murmured. "I hadn't considered that possibility."

"It is better that way," Tristan assured her. "You do not need me underfoot as you spend time with your family."

"I suppose not," Lady Lizette said, her voice lacking conviction.

Tristan felt like a jackanapes. Lady Lizette's entire life had been turned upside down and he was dismissing her out of hand. But didn't she see that it would be better this way? They weren't friends, but merely acquaintances. There was a reason why he didn't have too many friends. He preferred to be alone.

Lady Lizette met his gaze. "Will you be there when I meet my grandfather?" she asked in a hesitant voice.

"Aye," he replied.

"Thank you," Lady Lizette said, turning her attention back towards the road. "I shall strive to be quiet now."

Tristan knew that he should feel elated that Lady Lizette had stopped speaking to him, but he felt a twinge of guilt at that. Why couldn't he just leave well enough alone, especially since Lady Lizette was doing no harm by conversing with him?

But he enjoyed the solitude more.

The sun was low in the sky as they came up over the hill and saw a village in the distance. Lizette let out a sigh of relief since she was exhausted from being in the saddle. Her whole body seemed to protest every step her horse took, but she didn't dare admit that to Mr. Westcott. She had told him that she could handle the rigors of riding her horse behind the coach and she meant it. She refused to give up and give him the satisfaction of being right.

Mr. Westcott pointed towards the village. "We will stop there for the night."

Lizette tipped her head demurely. "Wonderful," she said as she could barely hold back her excitement. She wanted nothing more than to be out of this saddle and have her feet on solid ground.

"I must admit that you surprised me," Mr. Westcott said. "I expected you to give up on riding your horse and return to the comforts of the coach."

"I did tell you that I was a proficient rider."

"That you did, and I am pleased to know that you didn't exaggerate your abilities."

They continued down the road in silence until the coach came to a stop in front of a brick building with a thatched roof. A tilted sign above the door read- *The Crafty Squirrel*. The smell of freshly baked bread wafted out of the open windows, but the dried and ground up manure on the cobblestones quickly overpowered it.

Lizette reined in her horse and waited for Mr. Westcott to dismount. After he handed off his reins to the footman, he came around her horse and assisted her in dismounting.

Mr. Westcott withdrew his hands and stepped back. "Shall we proceed inside?" he asked, indicating she should go first.

Lady Anne's voice came from the door of the coach. "Mr. Westcott," she started, "you cannot possibly be in earnest? This dilapidated place looks like it will fall down any minute."

"This is the only coaching inn for miles," Mr. Westcott replied in an apologetic tone. "I'm afraid it is sleep here or on the road."

Her aunt frowned. "I will strive not to touch anything."

"That is the spirit, my lady," Mr. Westcott joked.

As Lizette took a step, she felt Mr. Westcott's hand on her elbow. "Stay close to me, my lady," he advised. "There could be dangerous men afoot here."

"I understand."

"Good," Mr. Westcott responded, removing his hand.

Lizette approached her aunt and said in an encouraging voice, "Surely it can't be as bad as it looks."

Her aunt didn't look convinced but didn't say anything as they walked towards the main door. As Mr. Westcott opened the door, a man barged out with a pale face and ran a short distance away before he started retching up the contents of his stomach.

"Lovely," her aunt muttered.

Eager to be inside, Lizette stepped through the door and stopped in the main hall. Round tables filled the room with men sitting around them. A woman, wearing a revealing gown, was serving drinks as men stared at her lewdly.

Her aunt leaned closer to her and whispered, "It is worse than I thought."

A burly man approached them with his hands out wide. "Welcome to my inn," he greeted. "My name is Mr. Condie and it is a pleasure to be serving you."

Mr. Westcott stepped forward. "I understand that you have rooms available."

"I do," Mr. Condie responded. "I have set aside rooms for you and your servants on the second level."

"Very good," Mr. Westcott said. "Do you have a private room where we could eat some supper?"

"That will cost you extra," Mr. Condie replied.

Mr. Westcott removed coins from his waistcoat pocket and extended them towards the innkeeper. "Will that be sufficient?"

Mr. Condie clutched the coins in his hand. "Follow me, sir."

As they walked through the main hall, Lizette felt uneasy by the attention she was garnering from the men in the room. They all seemed to gawk at her with a peculiar interest that frightened her. One dark-haired man even raised his glass towards her as she passed by his table, a sneer on his lips. She could feel his beady eyes on her even with her back to him.

Lizette felt like her heart was pounding out of her chest as she tried to appear unaffected, but she had never been so uncomfortable before.

Mr. Westcott must have sensed her discomfort because he offered his arm to her. "It will be all right," he said, leaning closer to be heard over the noise in the hall. "I won't let anything happen to you."

She remained close to Mr. Westcott, closer than what would be deemed proper, but she didn't care. He made her feel safe and protected.

Mr. Condie opened a door in the back and stood to the side to let them enter. "I will see to that supper now."

Lizette dropped her arm and went to sit at a small table in the center of the room. As she sat down, the chair wobbled beneath her, and she put her hands onto the table to steady herself. So much for being graceful, she thought to herself.

Lady Anne pulled out a chair as her eyes roamed the non-papered walls. "Where have you brought us, young man?" she asked in an accusatory tone.

Mr. Westcott leaned his shoulder against the wall. "This is a respectable coaching inn."

Her aunt pressed her lips together. "Maybe for ruffians."

"We only need to stay the night," Mr. Westcott stated calmly. "We can leave at first light, if you would prefer."

"If we don't get murdered in our sleep first," her aunt muttered.

"That is a pleasant thought, my lady," Mr. Westcott said.

The door opened and a young girl stepped into the room with a tray in her hand. She placed it down onto the table. "Will there be anything else?" she asked as she stepped back.

"Not at this time," Mr. Westcott replied.

The girl spun on her heel and hurried out of the room.

Lizette glanced down at the simple meal on the tray. It consisted of bread, meat, fruit, nuts and a generous helping of butter.

Her aunt reached for a piece of bread as she said, "Let's hope the bread tastes as good as it looks."

Lizette had no such qualms about the bread, or the other options on the tray. She was hungry and would gladly eat just about anything right now.

Mr. Westcott straightened from the wall and came to sit across from them. He reached for a piece of the thinly sliced meat. He chewed it for a moment before a disgusted look came to his face. "I would encourage you to avoid the meat."

It wasn't long before all the food, except for the meat, disappeared from the tray.

A yawn slipped past Lizette, and she brought her hand up to cover her mouth. "Pardon me, I must be more tired than I realized."

Mr. Westcott rose. "I will see to our rooms." He walked over to the door and stopped. "I do not think it is wise to leave you at the moment since the footmen are tending the horses. There is no one to stand guard while I am away."

"We will be all right, considering you won't be too far away," Lizette encouraged.

Mr. Westcott looked unsure. "I think it will be best if I remain."

Lady Anne spoke up, her voice stern. "We are tired, young man, and I want to adjourn to my room at once. Go about your business and I will watch over Lady Lizette."

Indecision crossed his features until he finally conceded. "Lock this door behind me and do not leave this room, for any reason."

Lizette and her aunt nodded their understanding and Mr. Westcott slipped out of the room. She rose and went to turn the key in the lock. Then she returned to her seat.

Her aunt turned towards her and said, "You must not tell Mr. Westcott this, but I have been in far worse coaching inns than this one."

"If that is the case, why are you giving Mr. Westcott a hard time about this one?"

A mischievous smile came to her aunt's lips. "It is fun to see Mr. Westcott squirm."

"That is terrible of you," she chided lightly.

Her aunt's eyes strayed towards the door. "Mr. Westcott is a good man, but I do not want him to become complacent."

"Do you think he will?"

"I don't rightly know, but I do not want to take the chance."

A knock came at the door.

Lizette rose and went to unlock the door. She opened it, expecting Mr. Westcott, but instead she saw the dark-haired man with beady eyes that she had seen in the main hall.

"What is the meaning of this?" Lizette asked.

In a swift motion, the man stepped inside, ushering her backwards and closing the door behind him. After he locked the door, he turned back to face them with a dagger in his hand.

Her aunt gasped.

The man's eyes landed on Lizette and he gestured with his dagger towards the window. "I want you to climb through that window and no one will get hurt."

Lizette knew that Mr. Westcott would return shortly. She just needed to buy herself some time.

Tilting her chin stubbornly, Lizette sat down and said, "No."

The man looked amused. "You don't have a say in the matter." He walked over to the window and unlatched it. "Now, go."

Lizette shook her head.

The man's eyes narrowed. "You do not want me to get angry," he said. "I can just as easily kill you as abduct you."

Her eyes darted towards the dagger in his hand, and she could feel herself shaking with fear. "I am not going to leave with you," she forced out.

The man closed the distance between them in a few strides and yanked her out of her seat. "I don't have time for your games," he said as he started pulling her towards the window.

Lizette dug the heels of her boots into the ground in an attempt to slow them down, but it didn't seem to work. He shoved her towards the window.

"If you don't go now, I will take you in pieces," he growled.

Knowing she was out of time and options, Lizette opened the window and looked out into the darkness.

The sound of metal clanging could be heard, and she saw the man drop to one knee. Lizette turned to see Lady Anne was holding a chamber pot in her hand, a look of satisfaction on her face.

Taking advantage of the situation, Lizette ran towards the door and unlocked it. She threw it open and screamed, "Mr. Westcott!"

Lady Anne dropped the chamber pot and rushed over to her. "It isn't safe here…"

Her words had barely left her mouth when Mr. Westcott appeared, his breathing labored. "What is wrong?" he asked, his voice on the edge of panicking.

Lizette turned towards the window and saw the man was gone. "There was a man that tried to abduct me by knife-point, but he escaped by way of the window."

Mr. Westcott brushed past them and rushed over to the window. He stared out into the night before saying, "I see no sign of him. He is gone now." He closed the window. "How did you manage to avoid being abducted?"

"My aunt saved me with the chamber pot," Lizette explained. "She hit him over the head as he ordered me to leave by way of the window."

Mr. Westcott turned his attention towards Lady Anne. "Well done, my lady," he praised.

Lady Anne huffed. "You seem surprised, young man. This is not my first run-in with a ruffian."

"Do you think you both could describe this man to Mr. Condie?" Mr. Westcott asked, glancing between them.

"I could," Lizette replied. She didn't think she could ever close her eyes again without seeing that man.

Mr. Westcott nodded in approval. "I will have him send for the constable, as well." He stepped closer to them and offered his arms. "I do not want to risk leaving you or Lady Anne alone, for any reason, so we will seek out Mr. Condie together."

Lizette offered him a weak smile as she placed her hand on his arm. "Thank you," she said as she felt herself relax. Now that she was back in his presence, she felt strongly that no harm would befall her.

Chapter Six

From his seated position in the dank hall, Tristan stared up at the cracked ceiling as he leaned his head back against the wall. He was standing guard outside of Lady Lizette and Lady Anne's room, ensuring that no additional harm would come to either one of them. He still couldn't believe that Lady Lizette had almost been abducted, right from under his very nose. He didn't even want to think of the consequences if Lady Anne hadn't been in the right mind to hit the man over the head with a chamber pot.

He had given up on trying to rest hours before as he kept reliving the moment he heard Lady Lizette's panicked voice calling for him. He had never been so afraid. Not just because he risked Lord Ashington's wrath if something happened to his granddaughter, but he couldn't fathom the thought that someone would dare hurt Lady Lizette.

He should have never left Lady Lizette alone, even for a moment, since he knew coaching inns were notorious for a rowdy clientele. This was all his fault, and he was not one to make such careless mistakes. At the least, he should have left a footman to stand guard by the private dining room. But he had gone against his better judgment to appease Lady Anne.

Which would not happen again. He was in charge of protecting the ladies and he would do so at all costs. His pride, his honor, was at stake, and he refused to fail at his assignment.

A rooster crowed outside, and not for the first time. That blasted rooster had been nothing but consistent since the first light appeared over the horizon.

Tristan sat up in his chair and took a moment to stretch his aching back. He was eager to be on the road, leaving this coaching inn far behind. They had made good time yesterday, despite an unplanned stop for a picnic, and they were still on schedule to arrive in Town by the afternoon. With any luck, the ladies would be awake, and they could depart shortly.

Rising, he tipped his head at the footman that was standing guard further down the hall. He made quick work with adjusting his cravat before reaching for his dark grey jacket that hung on the back of the chair. He shrugged it on and knocked on the door. He could hear noise coming from within. That was a good sign, he thought.

The door opened and Lady Lizette stood in front of him. She was still dressed in the same traveling gown, but her hair was neatly coiffed. She looked so beautiful in the morning, but it wasn't only the way she looked, it was what was inside of her, everything from her strength to her intelligence.

Where had that thought even come from, he wondered. Lady Lizette was undoubtably beautiful, but he had been around beautiful women before.

She smiled at him. "Good morning."

"Good morning," he greeted. "Dare I hope that you are ready to depart?"

Lady Lizette glanced over her shoulder and lowered her voice. "Lady Anne is still in bed, but I will inform her that you are ready to leave."

"See that you do," Tristan said. "I want to get on the road soon so we can adhere to our traveling schedule."

She nodded her understanding. "Yes, sir."

"I will see to acquiring some food for our journey," Tristan said.

Lady Lizette placed a hand to her stomach. "That would be much appreciated since I am rather hungry."

"I shall return shortly for you. Do not leave this room for any reason," he ordered.

"You do not need to fear on that account," Lady Lizette said.

He bobbed his head before he proceeded to the rickety stairs. As he descended them, he saw Mr. Condie was in the main hall, trying to arouse a sleeping man at one of the tables.

Tristan approached him and said, "I was hoping to secure a basket of food for our journey."

Mr. Condie turned and gave him his full attention. "I will see to it."

"Thank you," Tristan responded, his eyes straying towards the sleeping man. "It would appear that this man had a rough night."

"Unfortunately, he has had a lot of them lately." Mr. Condie gave him an apologetic look. "I'm afraid the night-watchmen found no signs of Lady Lizette's attacker."

"Have you seen him before?"

"I have not, but we get a lot of travelers cycling through here."

Tristan frowned. "That is what I was afraid of." He turned his head when he saw Lady Anne and Lady Lizette descending the stairs. What in the blazes? Had he not instructed them to stay in their room? Fortunately, a footman was trailing behind them.

"Excuse me," he muttered to Mr. Condie.

He approached them and asked, "Pray tell, what are you doing out of your room?"

Lady Lizette opened her mouth to reply, but Lady Anne

spoke first. "I did not want to spend one more moment in that room. It was much too stuffy for my liking."

"You could have opened the window," he suggested.

Lady Anne smoothed down her wrinkled gown. "I could have, but there was a rooster that was making a commotion outside," she said. "I tried to ignore it, but it was nearly impossible to do so."

Tristan addressed Lady Lizette. "Did the rooster wake you, as well?"

"It did not," she revealed. "We had a rooster at the boarding school I attended, and I learned to sleep through the noise."

"How fortunate for you," Tristan said.

"I suppose so," Lady Lizette murmured.

Tristan watched as Mr. Condie approached them with a basket in his hand. "You are in luck," he said. "My wife had already prepared a basket for you."

He accepted the basket. "You must tell your wife that we are appreciative of her thoughtfulness."

Mr. Condie put his hand up. "It was the least we could do, given the circumstances from last night."

"Yes, quite right," Tristan said, his eyes straying to Lady Lizette. He was concerned how Mr. Condie's comment might affect her.

Lady Lizette's eyes grew downcast, telling him everything that he needed to know.

Tristan held the basket up. "Now that we have sustenance, shall we depart?"

"I think that is a fine idea," Lady Anne replied.

As they walked towards the door, Tristan felt a strong desire to comfort Lady Lizette, which was ludicrous. It wasn't his place to do so. His job was to deliver her to her grandfather. That was all. He didn't want to form any type of attachment with Lady Lizette.

But as he watched her preparing to step into the coach, he

found himself asking, "Would you care to ride this stretch of the road with me?"

Botheration. Why had he just asked that?

Lady Lizette's eyes lit up. "I would like that very much," she said.

Tristan handed off the basket to a footman and retrieved her horse from the back of the coach. Lady Lizette approached him, and he assisted her onto her horse.

Once she was situated, he mounted his own horse.

Lady Lizette glanced over at him and said, "Thank you."

"There is no reason to thank me," Tristan responded.

"I know how much you like your solitude."

The coach started rolling down the road and Tristan urged his horse forward. "I do prefer being alone. It is much more comfortable that way."

"But you will be a marquess one day."

"Do not remind me," he grumbled.

Lady Lizette gave him a curious look. "Do you not want to be a marquess?"

"I do, but I have so much to learn," Tristan replied. "I constantly feel that I am not worthy of such a grand responsibility, especially since my decisions now will affect generations to come."

"I can only imagine the pressures you must be feeling."

"I hope you do not think me ungrateful."

"I do not," Lady Lizette said.

Tristan adjusted the reins in his hands. "My brother had much more time to adjust to being your grandfather's heir."

"How long ago did he die?"

"Three years and one month ago." Tristan hesitated. "He died in a duel."

"A duel?" Lady Lizette asked. "I thought they were illegal."

Tristan sighed. "They are, and I tried to talk him out of it. But it was in vain. My brother was pig-headed."

"May I ask what the duel was about?"

"Thomas was caught kissing Miss Thorpe in the gardens by her brother," Tristan explained. "When he refused to marry her, her brother challenged him to a duel."

"He lost his life over a kiss?"

Tristan winced. "He did."

"That is awful."

Tristan felt his jaw clench as he tried to fight back his emotions. "Thomas asked me to be his second, and I agreed since I knew I couldn't change his mind," he shared. "Had I known what I know now, I would have never let him leave the townhouse."

"His death wasn't your fault."

"A part of me knows that, but I still struggle with it all," Tristan said. "Upon his death, I became your grandfather's heir. I gained so much, and yet, I lost everything that mattered to me."

Lady Lizette's eyes held compassion. "Do you have no other family to speak of?"

"None that I am close with," Tristan replied. "My mother passed away when I was fifteen and Lord Ashington was named as my guardian."

"My grandfather was your guardian?"

"He was, but I spent the majority of my time with my brother, at least when I was home from Harrow," Tristan said. "My brother and I were as thick as thieves, but we were both such different people. After I graduated from Cambridge, I started working my way up in the East India Trading Company and Thomas was heir to Lord Ashington."

Lady Lizette shifted in her saddle. "Did your brother prefer the solitude, as well?"

Tristan chuckled. "No, he enjoyed attending social events. He felt it was important to be seen amongst high Society."

"Did you ever attend social events with him?"

"Some, reluctantly."

Lady Lizette's eyes burned bright. "What were they like?"

"Dreadfully boring," Tristan replied. "Every soiree, ball, or social gathering, has the same goal- to be the event of the Season."

"That sounds exciting."

"I must have said it wrong, then," Tristan joked.

Lady Lizette smiled, just as he had intended. "I find it odd that someone in your position would detest social events."

"Your grandfather would say they are a necessary evil."

The coach came to a stop in front of them, and Tristan reined in his horse. Up ahead, there was a coach tilted to the side due to a broken wheel. A young woman with dark hair was sitting on a trunk and a man stood next to her. Based on their similar appearance, he would wager that they were brother and sister.

Tristan dismounted and handed off his reins to the awaiting footman. "Stay here," he barked up at Lady Lizette.

As he approached the stranded travelers, the young woman rose and inched closer to her brother.

He put his hand up in greeting. "Hello, I am Tristan Westcott," he said. "I mean you no harm, but your coach appears to have had better days."

The man spoke up. "My name is Caleb Bolingbroke, and this is my sister, Miss Bolingbroke," he responded. "Our wheel broke, and we are waiting for our footmen to return with a new one. Then we will continue our journey to London."

Tristan's eyes roamed over the countryside. "This isn't the friendliest stretch of the road since highwaymen are known to frequent it."

Mr. Bolingbroke nodded. "I have a pistol."

"As do I," Miss Bolingbroke interjected.

If Mr. Bolingbroke was displeased by his sister's admission, he didn't make it known.

Tristan knew he had a choice to make. He couldn't leave them out here alone, knowing a highwayman might stumble across them, but he suspected Lady Anne might object to sharing a coach with someone she didn't know.

To his immense displeasure, Lady Lizette came to stand next to him and introduced herself. "My name is Miss Kent... er... Lady Lizette."

Miss Bolingbroke cocked her head. "Which one is it?"

"Lady Lizette," she replied.

Tristan turned towards her and muttered, "I thought I told you to stay on your horse."

Lady Lizette kept her gaze straight ahead. "You did, but I grew tired of waiting."

Shifting his gaze to meet Mr. Bolingbroke's, Tristan said, "We are traveling to London. Would you care to accompany us?"

Lizette watched as Miss Bolingbroke and her brother exchanged a look before Mr. Bolingbroke nodded in the affirmative. "We would be most appreciative to join you on your journey to London," he said. "It is a far better alternative than remaining here."

Mr. Westcott turned towards Lizette and asked, "Would it be permissible if Mr. Bolingbroke rode Moonshine and you rode in the coach with Miss Bolingbroke?"

"I take no issue with that," Lizette replied.

"Good," Mr. Westcott said, glancing up at the sky. "Let us depart so we don't delay our trip any further."

Mr. Bolingbroke led his sister to the coach and assisted her inside. Then he stepped back and approached Moonshine. A footman was in the process of removing the side saddle and replacing it with one that Mr. Bolingbroke could use.

Mr. Westcott gave Lizette an apologetic smile. "I know you would prefer to ride, but I didn't dare leave them here."

"I will manage," Lizette said before she entered the coach.

She sat next to her aunt and Miss Bolingbroke sat across from them. A footman closed the door as they all sat in silence.

It wasn't until the coach started to pick up speed on the bumpy road that her aunt addressed their guest. "What is your name, Child?"

Miss Bolingbroke perked up. "Miss Anette Bolingbroke."

Lady Anne returned her smile. "I must assume that my niece already introduced herself since we are not standing on formalities here."

"She did," Miss Bolingbroke confirmed.

"Very good," her aunt said. "I am Lady Anne Astley."

With a tip of her head, Miss Bolingbroke murmured, "My lady."

Lizette spoke up. "Anette is a French name, is it not?"

"Yes, it is," Miss Bolingbroke confirmed. "I was named after my grandmother."

"It is a great honor to be named after someone," Lady Anne said.

Miss Bolingbroke grew quiet. "I hope one day that I can become the person that my grandmother would be proud of."

"I feel the same way, only it is my mother that I wish would be proud of me," Lizette admitted in a soft voice.

"When did your mother die?" Miss Bolingbroke asked.

"Not long ago," Lizette replied vaguely.

"My condolences," Miss Bolingbroke said. "My grandmother has been dead for many years now, but I do miss her dreadfully."

Her aunt glanced between them. "It has been my experience that people are most proud of you for not giving up even when life feels impossible."

"Life does feel rather impossible right now," Lizette said.

"That is to be expected, but when the pain subsides, you'll

be stronger than you ever thought you could be," her aunt advised.

"Thank you, Aunt Anne," Lizette murmured.

Her aunt turned her attention towards Miss Bolingbroke. "Where do you hail from?"

"Wymondham," Miss Bolingbroke replied, "but my brother was retrieving me from my boarding school. My father wants me to be presented for my first Season."

"How wonderful," her aunt said. "This is to be Lady Lizette's first Season, as well."

Miss Bolingbroke furrowed her brow. "But are you not in mourning?" she asked, perusing her black gown.

"I am—" Lizette started.

Her aunt spoke over her. "We are going to break the rules, given the circumstances."

"Dare I ask what the circumstances are?" Miss Bolingbroke asked.

"Lizette is the granddaughter of Lord Ashington and there will be immense interest in her when she arrives in London," her aunt replied.

Miss Bolingbroke's eyes grew wide. "You are that Lady Lizette?" she asked. "I have heard outrageous rumors about what happened to you and your family over the years."

"I don't understand," Lizette responded with a furrowed brow. "Why would there be rumors about me, or my family?"

"You and Lady Crewe just disappeared one day, and many speculated that Lord Crewe murdered you," Miss Bolingbroke said.

"Truly?"

Miss Bolingbroke bobbed her head. "Many years later, your father died, and everyone thought your family must be cursed."

Lizette shifted in her seat to face her aunt. "Is this true?"

"I'm afraid so," Aunt Anne replied. "The rumors ran rampant after your father's death, and they still linger on the gossips' lips. That is why we must put them to rest by you taking your proper place in Society."

Lizette let out an unladylike sigh. "It sounds impossible."

"Nothing is impossible," Aunt Anne said. "You were born into this life, and I have no doubt you will thrive in it."

The coach dipped to the side as it hit a rut in the road causing Lizette to place her hand up on the side of the coach to steady herself.

"I do wish the driver would slow down," Aunt Anne muttered.

"If he did, then I have no doubt Mr. Westcott would protest," Lizette said. "He is insistent we adhere to the schedule."

Aunt Anne harrumphed. "Him and his schedule. I have not met a more fastidious person when it comes to traveling."

"He appears rather anxious to return to London."

"As am I, but I do not want to make everyone else miserable around me," Aunt Anne said. "Most likely, he wishes to return home to work on the accounts. My father tells me that he is very proficient at running the estates."

"That is good, isn't it?"

"It is, but I do wish he would have some fun," Aunt Anne said. "He is much too serious for my liking."

Lizette glanced out the window and saw Mr. Westcott riding his horse. She had to admit that he cut a dashing figure. He wasn't engaging Mr. Bolingbroke in conversation, which didn't surprise her in the least. She knew he preferred the solitude since he had told her as much.

Her aunt's voice broke through her musings. "What ladies' seminary did you attend?"

"Mrs. Porter's Ladies Seminary," Miss Bolingbroke replied.

"That is a fine school," her aunt said.

Miss Bolingbroke adjusted the sleeves of her grey traveling habit. "It is. My father was adamant that I attend."

"Who is your father?"

"Viscount Oxley."

Her aunt nodded in approval. "I am acquainted with your mother. She is a lovely woman."

"Yes, but she loves to talk." Miss Bolingbroke paused. "I'm sorry. I wasn't quite sure what to say so I just made something up. Please do not tell my mother I said that."

Aunt Anne's lips twitched. "You have my word."

"Thank you," Miss Bolingbroke said. "I have been told that I like to ramble on and on. I have been working on that, but I only do so when I am nervous."

"There is no reason to be nervous," Lizette remarked.

Miss Bolingbroke bit her lower lip. "I know, at least that is what I keep telling myself. My teacher, Miss Anderson, told me to imagine everyone in their undergarments and then I won't feel as intimidated."

"That is the most foolish thing I have heard," Aunt Anne said. "Just be yourself, and everything will work out."

"Miss Anderson told me that I must change everything about myself to fit into polite Society," Miss Bolingbroke revealed.

"What poppycock!" Aunt Anne exclaimed.

"It isn't just my teacher who thinks so," Miss Bolingbroke shared. "My father worries that I will be a spinster since I am such an odd child."

Aunt Anne gave her a knowing look. "There are worse things than being a spinster."

"Not to my father," Miss Bolingbroke said. "He worries that I will be a drain on our family's resources."

"Did your father tell you that you are odd?" Lizette asked.

Miss Bolingbroke shook her head. "No, but he didn't have to," she said. "I knew I was an oddity amongst the other young women at my boarding school."

"Because you ramble on?" Lizette pressed.

Miss Bolingbroke pressed her lips together before sharing, "It is also because I want to write a book."

"A book?" Aunt Anne questioned. "But you are a lady."

"I know, but I wouldn't be the first woman writer," Miss Bolingbroke said. "A book was just published that was written by 'A Lady'."

"A proper lady does not write a book, especially a daughter of a viscount," Aunt Anne pointed out. "It is obscene to even think about."

Miss Bolingbroke leaned back in her seat, looking defeated. "That is what my father says as well."

"Why can't Miss Bolingbroke write a book using an alias?" Lizette asked.

"What if anyone finds out?" Aunt Anne asked. "Her reputation would be at risk."

"But no one will find out," Miss Bolingbroke said.

Aunt Anne let out a bark of laughter. "A tasty piece of gossip such as that won't remain a secret for long."

Miss Bolingbroke's shoulders slumped. "Now you are sounding like my mother."

Lizette felt awful for Miss Bolingbroke, knowing her aunt was discouraging her dreams. But she wasn't wrong. She didn't know much about the *ton*, but she had been told that they pounced on anyone that was different. And Miss Bolingbroke was definitely different. Just as she was. How could she pass judgment on a kindred spirit?

With a kind smile, Lizette said, "I think you should write the book."

Miss Bolingbroke looked at her in surprise. "You do?"

"I do," she replied. "What do you want to write about?"

"I haven't worked out all the particulars yet, but it would be a love story about a lord's son and a vicar's daughter."

"That sounds promising."

Her aunt pursed her lips together. "Lizette—"

Lizette spoke over her aunt. "If more women wrote books, then it would normalize it," she said. "Would it not?"

"It would," her aunt reluctantly agreed. "I just don't want you to get Miss Bolingbroke's hopes up and nothing comes to fruition."

"Hope is a powerful thing. Yes, it can be elusive and difficult to hold on to, but not much is required," Lizette said.

Miss Bolingbroke moved to sit on the edge of her seat. "Do you truly believe I could write this book?"

"I do," Lizette replied. "But it won't matter if you don't believe in yourself."

Her aunt reached into her reticule and pulled out a fan. As she fanned her face, she said, "I see that I am outnumbered, but I urge you not to throw caution to the wind. Your greatest asset will be your anonymity."

A bright smile came to Miss Bolingbroke's face. "What fun this shall be."

"Well, go on, then," her aunt encouraged. "You must tell us more about this story that you wish to write."

Miss Bolingbroke's hands grew animated as she started sharing her story. "It will open at a ball, on a night with no stars in the sky..."

Chapter Seven

The sun was starting to set as Tristan reined in his horse in front of Lord Ashington's townhouse. A few lights flickered from within, but the grand home appeared mostly dark from the street.

A footman rushed down the steps to collect his horse, and Tristan was all too happy to hand off the reins. He had grown tired of being in the saddle, but he didn't dare join the women in the coach. No doubt they would have forced him to engage in useless chatter. Fortunately for him, Mr. Bolingbroke hardly spoke, and he felt no need to fill the silence with polite conversational topics.

They would have arrived earlier but they had seen to ensuring Mr. Bolingbroke and his sister arrived home safely. Luckily, the siblings lived a short distance away from them, so it wasn't much of an inconvenience.

Lady Anne stepped out of the coach and walked up the few steps towards the main door. She stopped at the top step and turned back towards the coach.

"Come along, dear," she ordered before heading into the townhouse.

Lady Lizette slowly exited the coach and came to stand on

the pavement. She stared up at the townhouse with awe in her eyes.

Tristan resisted the urge to smile. Her reaction was very similar to his when he had first seen Lord Ashington's townhouse. It was a three-level building with a brick façade. The sash windows had red-brick window arches that complemented the brown brick and a black iron fence lined the property, adding to its splendor.

He approached Lizette and offered his arm. "May I escort you inside?"

"You may," she replied as she placed her hand on his sleeve.

As he took his first step, he noticed that Lady Lizette did not follow suit. She remained rooted to her spot on the pavement.

He gave her a questioning look. "Is there a problem?"

With vulnerability in her eyes, she asked, "What if my grandfather doesn't approve of me?"

"That is not likely to happen."

"But what if it does?" she pressed.

Tristan turned to face her and dropped his arm. "You mustn't live your life expecting disappointment."

"I don't rightly know why I am so scared, but I am."

"There is no reason to be scared since I am with you," Tristan said.

Lady Lizette smiled weakly. "Thank you."

Tristan glanced over his shoulder at the main door and asked, "Shall we go inside now?"

"I suppose so."

As he offered his arm, he said, "Taking the first step is the hardest, but you never know where it will lead you."

"I know you must think me foolish…"

He spoke over her. "I do not," he replied. "Your entire world has been upended. I think you are brave."

"I am not brave," she rushed to say.

"If you aren't brave, what are you?" he asked as they walked up the stairs.

"I don't know what I am."

Tristan came to a stop at the main door and stood to the side. "Then you must trust me while you figure it out for yourself."

Lady Lizette stepped inside, and he followed her into the entry hall. He watched as her eyes roamed over the expansive hall, from the painted mural on the ceiling to the black and white tiles on the floor.

"It is exquisite, is it not?" he asked. It still seemed surreal that one day this would all belong to him.

Lady Lizette brought her gaze back to meet his. "It is," she agreed. "It is a far cry from where I grew up."

"Me, too," he said.

The tall, white-haired butler stood back, waiting to be acknowledged. Brownell was a man of few words, but he had a pleasant disposition about him.

Lady Anne had removed her hat and extended it towards Brownell. "I would be remiss if I did not inform you that we do not stand idle on the pavement like a vulgarian."

"Yes, Aunt Anne," Lady Lizette responded.

Lady Anne addressed Brownell. "Is Lord Ashington home?"

"He is in his study, my lady," the butler replied.

"Wonderful," Lady Anne said, turning back to face Lady Lizette. "Would you care to meet your grandfather?"

As she opened her mouth to respond, a booming voice came from the other end of the hall. "You are here!"

Lord Ashington crossed the entry hall with a purposeful stride. He came to a stop in front of Lady Lizette and his face softened, something Tristan had never witnessed before. "Just as I suspected; you have turned into a beautiful young woman."

The marquess was not overly tall but was stoutly built. His

dark hair had streaks of white and was thinning along the crown of his head. He had a commanding presence, despite his advancing age.

Lady Lizette dropped into a curtsy. "My lord," she murmured.

Lord Ashington's lips twitched. "Dear child, we do not stand on formalities in this family," he said gently. "I want you to feel at home here."

"Thank you," Lady Lizette murmured.

Tristan felt like an interloper at this moment, and he knew it was time to bow out. Besides, he had more than an ample amount of work to keep him busy for the next few weeks.

He bowed. "I believe that is my cue to leave, my lord."

"Nonsense," Lord Ashington said. "You are a part of this family, whether you want to be or not, and I was expecting you to stay for dinner."

"I'm afraid I have loads of work that I must see to," Tristan attempted.

Lord Ashington gave him a knowing look. "And it will be there for you in the morning."

Tristan reluctantly brought a smile to his lips, knowing that he had no choice but to accept Lord Ashington's invitation to dine with him. It would be rude of him not to.

"I would be happy to dine with you this evening," he said, hoping his words sounded somewhat convincing.

Lord Ashington tipped his head in approval. "Shall we adjourn to the drawing room until the dinner bell is rung?" he asked.

Lady Anne spoke up. "I, for one, need to change before dinner," she said. "One does not simply wear a traveling habit to dine in." She turned her expectant gaze towards Lady Lizette. "Would you care to change, as well?"

Lady Lizette glanced down at her gown. "I suppose it would be nice to get out of these dusty clothes."

"Yes, it most assuredly would," Lady Anne agreed.

"Come, I will show you to your room. It is right down the hall from mine."

Lady Lizette gave Tristan a faint smile. "I am glad that you are staying for dinner," she said before she followed her aunt up the stairs.

Lord Ashington's eyes trailed after his granddaughter's retreating figure. "There is no denying that she is a Kent."

"Did you have any doubts before?"

"None." Lord Ashington gestured towards the drawing room. "Would you care for a drink?"

"I could use one."

After Tristan followed Lord Ashington into the drawing room, he went to stand near the tall windows that overlooked the gardens.

Lord Ashington picked up the decanter and poured two drinks. "I cannot thank you enough for retrieving Lizette for me."

"It is of little consequence."

"To you, perhaps, but I am most grateful." Lord Ashington picked up the two glasses and walked one over to him. "It is hard for me to admit but I am not as young as I once was, and a long carriage ride does not bode well for me."

"You do not need to explain yourself to me."

Lord Ashington took a sip of his drink, then said, "It would appear that you and Lizette have formed some type of attachment."

Tristan tensed. "Nothing untoward happened."

"I am not accusing you of anything," Lord Ashington said. "I am just merely commenting on how at ease you appear to be around one another."

"Lady Lizette is a pleasant enough young woman."

Lord Ashington grinned. "That is high praise coming from you."

Tristan swirled the drink in his hand. "It did take some convincing to get Lady Lizette to accompany me to London."

"I am not surprised. If she is anything like her father, she is stubborn to a fault."

"Fortunately, her mother had written her a letter, confirming her lineage, and she was much more agreeable after that."

Lord Ashington brought the glass up to his lips. "If I had my way, that letter would never have seen the light of day."

"Why is that?"

"The letter was only to be given to Lizette upon the untimely death of her mother," Lord Ashington said. "I can only imagine how hard it was for her to read."

Tristan took a sip before lowering the glass to his side. "She is stronger than she cares to admit."

"I'm glad to hear that since she will be hearing a lot of hard truths soon."

"Do you know why her mother kept the truth of who she was from her?"

Lord Ashington glanced over his shoulder at the empty doorway. "It was to protect her."

"From what?" he asked. "Pardon me for saying so, but growing up as a lady does not seem to be burdensome."

Lord Ashington's face fell. "My son was adamant that Lizette was to be raised in the countryside, far away from the gossipmongers."

"But why keep her identity a secret?" Tristan pried.

"Why, indeed?" Lord Ashington asked. "I think we both know about my son's questionable behavior. He was afraid that his reputation would follow her, wherever she went."

Lord Ashington tossed back his drink and walked over to the drink cart. As he placed the empty glass down onto the tray, he continued. "There are some truths that I hope Lizette will never know."

"Secrets within a family can be destructive."

"I can't risk losing Lizette; not after I just got her back."

Tristan opened his mouth to speak, but Lord Ashington

put his hand up, stilling his words. "Save your breath," he said. "My mind is made up on this one."

Lord Ashington spun on his heel and departed from the room without saying another word, leaving Tristan to wonder how Lady Lizette would respond to her grandfather keeping secrets from her. Based on his limited experiences with her, it would not bode well for him.

Tristan placed his nearly full glass onto the table and sighed. So much for being productive this evening.

———————————————

Lizette trailed closely behind her aunt as she attempted to become familiar with her surroundings. As they turned a corner, she saw portraits with ostentatious gold frames lining both sides of the hall.

Aunt Anne stopped near one and gestured towards it. "This was your great-grandmother," she revealed with pride in her voice. "You would have liked her since she was one to balk at tradition and believed women were capable of great things."

Lizette admired the painting before saying, "She sounds rather progressive."

"She was." Aunt Anne moved down the hall until she stopped in front of another portrait. "This was your great-great grandfather, the first Marquess of Ashington. He served admirably in the Royal Navy, but he did have a penchant for cheating at cards when playing with family and friends." Her words were spoken lightly, as if she were recalling a fond memory.

Aunt Anne continued down the hall until she stopped in front of a portrait that had a black cloth draped over the front.

"This is your mother's portrait," Aunt Anne shared. "Would you care to see it?"

Lizette nodded. "I would."

As she walked towards the portrait, her aunt pushed back the cloth and rested it on top of the frame.

Lizette felt tears starting to form as she stared at the portrait, but she made no effort to wipe them away. It was a perfect likeness of her mother. The artist even managed to show the light that was always prevalent in her eyes.

"This was commissioned right after your parents' wedding," Aunt Anne shared, her eyes remaining on the portrait. "Your mother was a very beautiful woman."

"That she was," Lizette agreed.

Aunt Anne made no attempt at rushing her, and she appreciated the consideration, especially since she didn't think she would ever tire of seeing this portrait. It reminded her of how lucky she was to have as much time as she did with her mother.

Lizette turned towards her aunt and asked, "Did my father commission a portrait as well?"

A smile came to Aunt Anne's lips. "He did, but he was not pleased about it," she replied. "Your father was a restless man, and he grew tired of standing." She took a few steps down the hall before motioning towards a painting. "This was your father."

She walked closer to her aunt and stared up at the portrait of the man- a man that she held no memories of.

Her father was dressed in his finery, but it did little to distract from his thin frame. He had a long face, a bony nose and dark hair.

Aunt Anne spoke up. "Your father loved you very much."

Lizette doubted that to be true. If he had cared for her, then why had he never come to visit her once? Her father was a stranger to her.

"Your father would rather be in his laboratory than anywhere else," Aunt Anne said. "He was obsessed with finding cures to the most basic ailments."

"Was my father a doctor?" Lizette asked.

Aunt Anne gave her a curious look. "He was," she replied. "Were you not aware of that?"

"I'm afraid not. I knew very little about my father."

"It was a great source of contention between your father and grandfather," her aunt shared. "Your grandfather thought it was entirely beneath your father to practice medicine. He would have rather had him focus on running the estates."

Her aunt continued. "We should hurry if we want to change before dinner."

Lizette followed her aunt down the hall and around the corner. Aunt Anne came to a stop in front of a door. "This is your bedchamber," she revealed as she opened the door.

As she stepped inside, she saw a matronly woman, dressed in a maid's uniform, unpacking her trunks.

The maid stopped and turned to face her. "Evening, my lady," she said before dropping into a curtsy. "My name is Libby."

"It is nice to meet you, Libby."

Lizette's eyes roamed over the pale blue papered walls and the floral drapes that were slightly flowing in the breeze of the open window. A four-poster canopy bed sat against a wall, which was piled high with gowns, and a camelback settee was at the base of it, facing the fireplace.

"Would you care to change?" Libby asked.

"Yes, I would," Lizette replied.

Libby walked over to the bed and picked up a black gown. "Shall we dress you?"

It was a short time later that Lizette emerged from her bedchamber, dressed in a muslin black gown, and she was wearing her mother's mourning jewelry. She carefully retraced her steps back towards the entry hall and had only just arrived when she heard the chime of the dinner bell.

The butler stood in the entry hall and tipped his head towards her. "Good evening, my lady," he greeted politely.

She replied in kind before asking, "Where is the drawing room?"

"Allow me to show you." He crossed the entry hall and came to a stop by an open door. "Would you care for me to announce you?"

"That won't be necessary," she assured him as she approached the door.

As she stepped into the drawing room, she saw Mr. West-cott was standing near the window, staring out into the dark night, and his hands were clasped behind his back. He had a solemn look on his face, and she wondered what it would take for him to truly smile. She had seen him smile before, but it never quite met his eyes.

Not wanting to disturb Mr. Westcott's solitude, she retreated a step to leave the drawing room but was stopped by his voice.

"You may stay, my lady," he said as he turned to face her.

Lizette gave him a sheepish smile. "I apologize for not making my presence known but you appeared lost in thought."

"This is your home now and you may come and go as you please."

Lizette's gaze left his as her eyes roamed over the square room. The ivory papered walls contrasted nicely with the ornate woodwork that ran the length of the room. Two uphol-stered settees sat in the middle, facing one another, and chairs were placed on both sides.

Mr. Westcott unclasped his hands and said, "You look... nice." He seemed to trip on that last word.

"Thank you," she replied.

They stared at one another, and before it grew awkward, Lizette found herself asking, "It is a lovely night we are having, is it not?" Drat. What an intolerably stupid thing to say! She could only imagine what he thought of her.

"It is quite lovely," he readily agreed.

Lizette glanced over her shoulder at the empty doorway, wondering where her aunt and grandfather were. She didn't know why she was suddenly nervous around Mr. Westcott.

Mr. Westcott appeared to have no qualms with her presence and asked, "Have you settled in?"

"Not yet, but a maid has been seeing to unpacking my trunks," Lizette replied.

He nodded approvingly. "That is good."

"It is." She clasped her hands in front of her to keep them from fidgeting. "It is a refreshing change to have a maid tend to me."

"Did you not have a lady's maid before?"

Lizette shook her head. "Mrs. Everly tended to me when she was able, but she was usually busy with the household duties," she replied. "I learned to make do on my own."

"That is an impressive feat."

"Many would disagree with you, sir."

"Then they would be wrong," Mr. Westcott said. "I find it refreshing that a young woman of your station can do things for herself."

Lizette grinned. "You seem to forget that I was raised as a country bumpkin."

"You are anything but a country bumpkin," Mr. Westcott argued.

"Mrs. Everly used to chide me for not wearing shoes when I would go outside, but I loved feeling the shafts of grass beneath my feet."

Mr. Westcott looked amused. "I will admit that is odd."

Lizette's gaze grew downcast. "I miss Mrs. Everly," she said. "She was more than just our servant. She was my trusted friend."

"Why didn't you say anything before?" Mr. Westcott asked.

"I didn't wish to burden you with my problems," Lizette replied.

"You may speak plainly to me. Frankly, I would prefer it."

Lizette brought her gaze back up. "Be careful of what you ask for," she joked.

Mr. Westcott's lips twitched. "I will take my chances," he said. "Is there anything else about you that I should know?"

"I love ketchup," she revealed. "Mrs. Everly makes the most scrumptious mushroom ketchup that I have no choice but to devour."

"You do have a choice, actually," Mr. Westcott teased.

"Clearly you have not had Mrs. Everly's ketchup before."

"I shall make note that you have an unnatural love for ketchup."

"See that you do." Lizette turned back towards the empty doorway, wondering why her grandfather and aunt hadn't arrived for dinner yet. "Is the dinner bell more of a suggested time to arrive?"

"In this household, yes." Mr. Westcott motioned towards the settees. "It might take a while. Would you care to sit?"

Lizette walked over to one of the matching blue settees and sat down. Mr. Westcott waited for her to sit before he sat across from her.

To ward off the uncomfortable silence, Lizette asked, "Do you dine with my grandfather and aunt often?"

"Not really," Mr. Westcott replied. "My townhouse is just a few blocks away. It is close enough to be at your grandfather's beck and call, but far enough away to provide me with some space."

"Is your townhouse as grand as this one?"

"Gads, no! I daresay that most townhouses in Town are not as impressive as your grandfather's."

"Oh, I hadn't realized."

Mr. Westcott's eyes held compassion. "My apologies. I forgot that you have never been to Town before."

Before she could reply, her grandfather and aunt walked

into the drawing room. They were both sharply dressed, and she suddenly felt out of place in her black gown.

Her grandfather's eyes crinkled around the edges as his eyes landed on her. "Are you ready for dinner, my dear?"

Rising, she replied, "I am."

Chapter Eight

Tristan had just sat down next to Lady Lizette when Lord Ashington spoke up from the head of the rectangular table.

"I failed to ask- how was your journey to Town?" the marquess asked.

Tristan exchanged a look with Lady Lizette before replying, "It was uneventful."

"Interesting," Lord Ashington muttered. "I would have thought someone attempting to abduct Lizette would have been important enough to mention."

Botheration. Lord Ashington knew, and he had just been goading him. He knew he needed to proceed cautiously or else he might incite the marquess' anger.

However, before he could speak, Lady Lizette said, "Someone attempting to abduct me was not indicative of the care that Mr. Westcott showed me."

"It was not?" Lord Ashington asked.

"No, Mr. Westcott was very attentive, but even he couldn't predict that a drunken man would sneak past him and try to abduct me in our private dining room," Lizette said.

Lord Ashington turned his gaze towards him. "Why did you not post a guard at the door?"

"I should have, but I had planned to be gone for only a few moments," Tristan replied. "Afterwards, I did post a guard in front of their room."

"Too little, too late, if you ask me," Lord Ashington grumbled. "It was most fortunate that my daughter was there to ward off the man."

"Yes, it was," Tristan agreed.

Lady Anne interjected from across the table, "I do believe that you have made your point, Father. Perhaps we could speak of more pleasant things over dinner."

Lord Ashington put his hands up in surrender. "As you wish, dear."

Tristan leaned to the side as a footman placed a bowl of soup in front of him. He retrieved his spoon and began eating. He wasn't in the mood to converse, and he hoped the conversation would go on without him.

But he was not so lucky.

Lord Ashington met his gaze and asked, "Have you had a chance to review the quarterly reports that Mr. Trent prepared?"

"I have not, but I will do so once I return home," Tristan said. He didn't dare mention that his journey to retrieve Lady Lizette had set him back a few days for reviewing the accounts.

"Very good," Lord Ashington remarked before he took a sip of his soup.

Tristan glanced over and saw that Lady Lizette wasn't eating. He gave her a curious look. "Is everything all right with your soup?"

"It is… at least I think it is since I haven't tried it yet," Lady Lizette responded.

"It is a simple process, really," Tristan joked. "You just pick up a spoon, dip it into the soup and place it into your mouth."

Lady Lizette smiled. "Thank you for educating me on how to eat soup."

"You are welcome," Tristan said, returning her smile.

Lady Anne wiped her mouth with her napkin, then remarked, "You need to eat, dear. You are far too thin."

"I just have so many questions and I don't know where to begin," Lady Lizette stated.

Lord Ashington placed his spoon down. "I should have assumed as much."

Lady Lizette shifted in her chair to face her grandfather. "Why did my parents keep my lineage from me?"

"To protect you," Lord Ashington responded.

"From what?"

Lord Ashington sighed. "Your father thought it was the only way to protect you from the harsh realities," he said.

"Which are?" Lady Lizette pressed.

Lady Anne addressed her father. "You may as well tell her the truth."

Lord Ashington nodded. "I suppose it is long overdue." He turned his attention back towards Lady Lizette. "Your grandmother had a rare form of dementia. She just didn't suffer from memory loss, but she also had delirium, depression, tumors, and she lost the ability to walk. For many years, she was bedridden, and we watched her wither away right in front of us."

"That is awful," Lady Lizette murmured.

"By the time she passed, she didn't recognize any of us, and was prone to bouts of anger," Lord Ashington said. "There is no worse feeling than loving someone that doesn't know who you are."

Lord Ashington continued. "My son, William, was obsessed with finding a cure for his mother. Against my direct orders, he became a doctor so he could help her."

"That is admirable," Lady Lizette said.

"Not when he spent every waking moment in that blasted laboratory," Lord Ashington argued. "He thought he could save his mother, and it nearly killed him when she died."

Lady Anne interrupted, "Your father and grandmother always shared a special bond."

"It is true," Lord Ashington agreed. "But we were wholly unprepared for when your father started showing the same symptoms as your grandmother."

"William was always petrified that he would develop this rare form of dementia and took extensive notes on everything. He started noticing that he had a hard time recalling information that he had always taken for granted," Lady Anne explained.

Lady Anne reached for her glass of water before she continued. "Knowing the terrible future that was in store for him, he sent you and Elizabeth away. He was determined not to have you see him wither away, as he did with his mother, and he became even more fanatical with finding a cure," she shared. "He moved his mattress into his laboratory and hardly slept. We would oftentimes have to remind him to eat."

Lord Ashington grew silent. "One morning, we found his body in his laboratory. He had burn marks around his mouth and we believe that he had tried to drink one of his concoctions." He huffed. "One of his so-called cures, that he liked to call them."

Lady Lizette stared at her grandfather in disbelief. "Did he kill himself?" she asked.

"We don't rightly know," Lord Ashington replied. "He wasn't in his right frame of mind, but it wasn't uncommon for him to try his own cures."

Lady Anne gave her niece a look of pity. "We tried to keep his death as quiet as possible, but word got out, and many speculated that he did kill himself."

Tristan glanced at Lady Lizette and saw that her face had gone slightly pale. "Are you all right?" he asked in a concerned voice.

"I will be," Lady Lizette replied.

Lord Ashington leaned to the side as a footman retrieved

his soup bowl. "Your father did manage to scribble his final wishes onto a paper that was discovered on his desk," he said. "He wanted you to remain in the countryside."

"And my mother agreed to this?" Lady Lizette asked.

"By this time, you were happily settled, and your mother didn't want to disrupt your life in such a horrific fashion," Lord Ashington explained. "We decided that you would be told the truth when you reached your majority, but that all changed when I received the letter from your mother on her death bed."

"That still doesn't explain why no one told me that my father was an earl," Lady Lizette said.

Lord Ashington exchanged a look with Lady Anne before sharing, "That was to protect you from the truth. Your father never intended to let the disease consume him like it did his mother and he didn't want you to live with the shame of knowing he took his own life."

"But we don't know that for certain," Lady Lizette pressed. "Does this mean I might inherit this rare disease?"

Lord Ashington shook his head. "No, you have little chance of that."

"How can you be so sure?" Lady Lizette asked. "My grandmother and father both had this disease. It is only logical that I might develop the symptoms later in life."

"Yes, but…" Lord Ashington stopped. "It is different in your case. You must trust me on this."

Lady Lizette let out a puff of air. "Trust you?" she repeated. "You didn't even let me have a say in all of this."

"You would have, but only after you reached your majority," Lady Anne said.

"That is hardly fair," Lady Lizette murmured. "You expect me to be appeased by saying my situation is different. But how is it different?"

"It just is," Lord Ashington replied, his voice growing firm, "and I do not wish to discuss it any longer."

Lady Lizette looked as if she had more to say by the pursing of her lips but she remained quiet.

Lady Anne's eyes held compassion. "You will need to prepare yourself because the gossips can be rather cruel to people in your situation," she said. "Even with the passing of time, your father died in suspicious circumstances."

"Where is my father buried?" Lady Lizette asked.

"In our family plot at our country house," Lord Ashington replied.

"Is he buried head down?"

Lady Anne shook her head. "Heavens, no," she exclaimed. "We would never have done something so distasteful."

Lady Lizette abruptly pushed back her chair. "I… uh… need a moment," she said before she rushed out of the room.

Tristan had risen when Lady Lizette had, and he watched her retreating figure. It only took him a moment to decide he should go after her.

He tossed the white linen napkin onto the table and hurried after her. Once he stepped into the hall, he saw Lady Lizette was staring out of a window, and she was wiping away the stray tears that were sliding down her cheeks

Not wanting to startle her, he said in a low voice, "Lizette." He knew he was being familiar but he thought the situation warranted it.

Lizette turned towards him and gave him a faint smile through her tears. "Mr. Westcott," she said. "You didn't need to come after me."

"I know, but I wanted to see how you were faring after what you just heard."

She bit her lower lip, no doubt in a vain attempt to stop herself from crying. "It was a bit much to take in."

"I can only imagine."

"Do you think my father killed himself?"

He shrugged. "It doesn't matter what I think," he replied. "It only matters what you perceive to be true."

Lady Lizette wrapped her arms around her waist. "Ever since I was a little girl, I wondered why my father wanted nothing to do with me, and now I know why."

"Your grandfather was rather adamant that your father loved you," he attempted.

She huffed. "If he loved me, he would have been there for me," she countered.

"From what I understand, it doesn't appear that your father was in his right mind, especially towards the end."

Tears rolled down Lady Lizette's cheeks and she made no move to wipe them away. "I would have loved him, regardless."

"I know you would have."

"But he didn't give me a chance to," she said with a sob.

Tristan stepped closer and placed a comforting hand on her sleeve. "Your father thought he was doing what was best for you."

"He was wrong," she said. "I should have been with him."

"You can't go back and change the past, but you can move forward, knowing your father loved you very much."

Lady Lizette dropped her hands to her sides. "I just wish I could speak to him, to let him know that I wish things had been different."

Tristan reached up and gently wiped away a tear that was sliding down her cheek. "I do not fully understand why your father did what he did, but I do know that it came from his desire to protect you. And I find that to be honorable."

"Do you truly believe that?"

Lowering his hand to his side, he replied, "You get to decide how you wish to remember your father. No one else gets that right."

Her lips curled into a slow, beautiful smile. "I like that sentiment."

"Then focus on that, and you can handle anything that comes your way."

"You are giving me entirely too much credit."

He offered his arm to her. "You will find that I am an excellent judge of character," he said. "We should return to dinner or else your aunt may come in search of us."

Lady Lizette placed her hand on his. "I am rather famished."

"Then we must remedy that at once."

The first rays of the sun poured into Lizette's bedchamber window as she stared up at the ceiling of her four-poster bed. She knew it was futile to get any additional sleep, despite being up for a few hours. Her mind was bogged down with everything that she had been told about her father.

Why hadn't her mother told her about her father and his desire to heal his mother, and himself? She didn't understand her father's actions, either. He had tried to protect her by sending her away, but he had wasted all those years that he could have had with her.

The worst part is that she didn't know if she would inherit the rare form of dementia that her grandmother and father had. Was she living on borrowed time?

The drapes started blowing haphazardly in the wind, drawing her attention. Her mother's words came to her mind-*with a new day comes a new adventure.* Her mother had always looked for the good in people, which was something she had always greatly admired.

At the thought of her mother, Lizette felt the tears prick at the back of her eyes. Would she ever be able to think of her mother and not grow sad?

The door opened and her aunt glided into the room. "Good morning, Lizette," she said in a cheerful voice.

"Morning," she muttered back.

Her aunt came to a stop next to the bed. "I see that you are not overly pleasant in the mornings," she teased.

"It depends on the day," Lizette replied honestly.

"Well, today, I need you to be lively since the dressmaker is arriving soon with her team of seamstresses."

Lizette moved to sit up on the bed and rested her back against the wall. "I do not think it is wise to forego the mourning period for my mother."

Her aunt waved her hand in front of her. "We can't have you traipsing through London in mourning clothing. It just simply isn't done."

"Do you not worry that people will find me being disrespectful to my mother for not wearing black?"

"It has been over thirteen years since your mother last attended a social event in Town," her aunt said. "Out of sight, out of mind."

"But I will know."

Her aunt's eyes grew compassionate. "Sitting around with no real purpose is the worst thing you can do when mourning a loved one," she revealed. "You need to learn how to live without them."

"I don't think I can."

"I thought the same thing when my Richard died," her aunt said. "I thought my life was over and I prayed for death."

Lizette reached for a pillow and slipped it behind her back. "When did he die?"

"It has been nearly ten years since he passed. He was my everything, and when he passed, I felt as if I had nothing."

"What changed?"

"My perspective, really," her aunt replied. "I do not know how much longer I have on this earth, but I intend to use this time wisely."

"I still cry at the mere thought of my mother," Lizette admitted.

Her aunt moved to sit on the bed. "That is to be expected.

The grieving process is long and hard, but that is the cost for loving someone as much as you did."

Lizette tugged on the sleeves of her white nightgown. "I just feel so alone at times," she said softly.

"I would be going along with my life, and everything seemed right in the world. Then I would go to bed, alone, and the grief would hit me, nearly consuming me," her aunt shared. "But the next morning, I would get up and hope it would be better."

"How long was it before it did get better?"

A sad look came into her aunt's eyes. "I still, on occasion, cry myself to sleep," she revealed.

Unsure of what to say, Lizette settled on, "I'm sorry."

"No one can cheat the grieving process, I'm afraid," her aunt said, her eyes growing reflective. "My father was not pleased that I selected the second son of an earl to marry, and he tried to talk me out of it. Relentlessly, in fact. But it was too late. I had already fallen madly in love with Richard." She sighed. "I just wish that Richard and I were able to have children. I do believe that would have helped with his passing."

Lizette could hear the pain in her aunt's voice, and her heart ached for the woman.

Her aunt blinked the emotions away. "Enough of me and my old people problems," she said lightly. "We need to prepare you for the dressmaker. Your grandfather was generous enough to grant permission for you to receive a whole new wardrobe; one that is worthy of your social standing."

"What if I wore clothing that reflected half-mourning?"

Rising, her aunt replied, "I propose we come to a compromise. You can wear half-mourning colors around the townhouse but will change to more fashionable gowns when you attend a social event."

Lizette didn't think that sounded like much of a compromise, but as she started to voice her opinion, a knock came at the door.

"Enter," her aunt ordered.

The door opened and Libby stepped into the room. She curtsied before saying, "Madame Auclair has arrived, and she is setting up in the parlor."

Her aunt nodded approvingly. "Will you see to preparing Lady Lizette for the day?"

"Yes, my lady," Libby said.

After her aunt departed the room, Libby walked over to the wardrobe and pulled out a black gown. She draped it over the back of the settee before coming to a stop by the dressing table, giving Lizette an expectant look.

Lizette tossed off the linens and put her feet over the side of the bed. As she rose, she said, "I can manage doing my own hair."

Libby looked at her, aghast. "But what will you have me do?"

Lizette sat down in front of the dressing table and picked up a brush. "You can tidy up my bedchamber while I brush my hair."

Libby remained rooted to her spot. "Did you take issue with me styling your hair last night?" she asked in a hesitant voice.

"Not at all, but I can pull my own hair up into a chignon."

"But, my lady, I was told that one of my responsibilities was to style your hair," Libby said.

Lizette removed the cap from her head and placed it onto the dressing table. "That isn't necessary."

"As you wish." Libby walked awkwardly over to the bed and went to fluff the pillows.

Lizette brushed her hair and placed the brush down. Then she twisted her hair into a chignon that rested at the base of her neck.

The moment she had finished with her hair, Libby came to stand next to her with the dress in her hand.

"Shall we dress you?" Libby asked.

Lizette could hear the eagerness in the maid's voice, and she murmured her approval. She didn't have the heart to tell Libby that she could dress herself, as well.

Once she was dressed, Libby stepped back and asked, "Will there be anything else, my lady?"

"Not at this time."

Libby bobbed her head in response and picked up the discarded white nightgown from the floor.

Lizette exited her bedchamber and headed towards the stairs. As she descended them, a knock came at the main door and the butler crossed the entry hall to open it.

Brownell opened the door wide and said, "Good morning, Mr. Westcott."

Lizette watched as Mr. Westcott stepped inside the townhouse and he held a large book in his hand.

Mr. Westcott's eyes landed on hers and he gave her a polite smile. "Good morning, my lady."

"Good morning," she greeted as she closed the distance between them. "You are out and about early."

"Is it early?" Mr. Westcott asked. "I have been up for hours."

She gestured towards the book. "Have you been reading anything of note?"

"I have, but not in the way you are thinking," Mr. Westcott replied, holding up the book. "I have been reviewing the ledger."

"That sounds… interesting."

Mr. Westcott chuckled. "It is much more fun than you are imagining."

"I don't think it is."

"There is something oddly satisfying with balancing the

accounts," Mr. Westcott said. "I should mention that I have always been good with numbers."

Her aunt stepped out of the parlor and caught Lizette's attention. "Madame Auclair is waiting for you," she announced before disappearing back into the room.

"Wonderful," Lizette muttered under her breath.

Mr. Westcott lifted his brow. "You do not seem pleased by that prospect."

"I'm not," Lizette replied. "I should be mourning my mother for at least three months before I start wearing half-mourning clothing. My aunt wants me to start wearing more fashionable colors."

"The world does not stop moving when someone dies," Mr. Westcott said. "I have known many debutantes that were presented to Court right after they suffered a death in their families."

"I just want to mourn my mother properly."

Mr. Westcott gave her an understanding look. "Clothing is only an outward expression of mourning. There is nothing stopping you from mourning your mother inward, which is more important, in my mind, at least."

"I would agree with you."

The corner of his mouth quirked up suddenly. "Remember what we said about agreeing with one another."

"I do believe we agreed we wouldn't make it a habit," she said with a smile.

Mr. Westcott's eyes dropped down towards her lips and he cleared his throat. "Well, I should be going," he remarked in a hoarse voice. "I have a meeting with Lord Ashington, er, your grandfather."

"I am well aware of who my grandfather is," she said, feeling a need to tease him.

"Yes, you do now, especially since you are here, with him, at his townhouse."

Lizette didn't know why she found his stammering to be

oddly charming, but she did. It made him seem much more approachable.

Mr. Westcott held up the ledger. "I don't want to keep Lord Ashington waiting."

"And I do not want to keep Madame Auclair waiting."

"Would you like me to escort you to the parlor?" Mr. Westcott asked.

Lizette glanced over her shoulder at the parlor door. "That won't be necessary since it is just right there."

Mr. Westcott stepped back and bowed. "In that case, I wish you a good day, my lady," he said before he headed towards the rear of the townhouse.

Once he disappeared down a side hall, she walked over to the parlor door and stepped inside. She saw her aunt was conversing with a fashionably dressed, tall woman with black hair.

They stopped speaking as she approached them and the black-haired woman, who she assumed was Madame Auclair, spoke up.

"You are a tiny little thing, but your skin is flawless," the dressmaker said.

Her aunt came to stand next to her. "Lady Lizette requires a whole new wardrobe and accessories."

Madame Auclair bobbed her head. "I can see this since you look much too drab in black."

She opened her mouth to protest, but her aunt spoke first. "I think she would look much better in pale colors."

"As do I." Madame Auclair snapped her fingers, and her two assistants came to stand behind her. "We have much to do."

Lizette tried to put on a brave face, but she knew this was going to be a very long, tedious process. And she hadn't even had breakfast yet.

Chapter Nine

As Tristan walked towards Lord Ashington's study, he chided himself on what a fool he had just made of himself around Lady Lizette. Why had he just turned into a blabbering idiot around her? And when she had smiled, his eyes were drawn to her lips. Her perfectly formed lips.

Blazes. What was wrong with him? He should not be noticing Lady Lizette's lips, for any reason. His job had been to retrieve her for Lord Ashington, and he had done just that. She was no longer his responsibility and he intended to keep his distance from her. Not just her, but every woman in high Society. He had no desire to be shackled to a wife. He had the freedom to do as he pleased and that was a luxury he did not want to lose.

Tristan walked into the study and saw Lord Ashington hunched over his desk, reviewing the papers in front of him.

"Good morning," Tristan said.

"What is good about it?" Lord Ashington muttered, not bothering to look up.

Tristan walked over to the desk and sat in an upholstered armchair. He had grown accustomed to Lord Ashington's grumpy mood in the morning. It usually wore off after breakfast, but until then, Tristan would be forced to endure his moodiness.

Lord Ashington placed a paper down onto the desk and brought his gaze up. "It is entirely too early for whatever it is that you brought me."

"I just have a question."

"Just one?" Lord Ashington asked.

Tristan nodded.

"Proceed, then."

He opened the ledger and found the entry that he found concerning. "I was reviewing the past ledgers and I noticed a recurring expense that was logged in every year with no description as to what it was for. It is in the amount of two thousand pounds, and from what I can tell, it has been going on for many years."

"You do not need to concern yourself with that charge," Lord Ashington said dismissively.

"It is a substantial sum, though."

Lord Ashington leaned back in his seat. "Pray tell, why are you going through past ledgers?"

"I thought it would be beneficial to become even more acquainted with our accounts," Tristan replied.

"It is a waste of time."

"Not in my mind."

Lord Ashington frowned. "Regardless, let my solicitor handle that charge. He will send word when it has been paid."

Tristan wasn't about to let the issue go. He needed to be familiar with all aspects of Lord Ashington's business dealings.

"But what is it for?" Tristan pressed.

Lord Ashington's eyes grew guarded. "You will learn the truth of it, in due time."

"Why can't I learn the truth now?"

"Because the fewer people that know the truth, the better."

Tristan furrowed his brow. "What truth?"

Lord Ashington huffed. "You are being far too inquisitive this morning."

"You wanted me to run the estates while you immersed yourself in politics, and I am doing just that," Tristan said.

"You are, and you are proving to be proficient at the task."

Tristan closed the ledger and placed it down onto the desk. "In order for me to do a thorough job, I need to be privy to every expense that is logged into this book."

Lord Ashington pressed his fingers to the bridge of his nose. "Perhaps I won't find you as irritating once I have had some coffee."

Tristan did not take offense at Lord Ashington's remark since there was no harshness to his words. "Some prefer tea in the morning," he said.

"I am not one of those people," Lord Ashington griped. "My cook has managed to make the perfect cup of coffee."

"That is most fortunate."

Lord Ashington pushed back his chair. "Speaking of which, I could use some coffee right now. Would you care to join me for breakfast?"

Tristan resisted the urge to look at his pocket watch. He had his day planned out and he didn't have time to waste. Although, he still needed Lord Ashington to explain the line item to him. It was enough money that caused him pause.

Coming around the desk, Lord Ashington said, "Your schedule can wait."

Rising, Tristan picked up the ledger and brought it to his side. "I will join you, but only because you still haven't answered my question yet."

"You are going to leave disappointed, then."

"We shall see," Tristan said as he turned to follow Lord Ashington out of the study.

They didn't speak as they approached the dining room and Tristan sat at the right of Lord Ashington at the table.

A footman promptly placed a coffee cup in front of Lord

Ashington before turning towards Tristan. "Would you care for some coffee, sir?"

"I would," Tristan replied.

The footman retrieved a coffee cup from a side table and placed it onto the table.

Tristan reached for the cup and took a sip of the luke-warm drink. He grimaced before glancing down at the drink.

"Is it not to your liking?" Lord Ashington asked.

"I prefer my coffee with more cream," Tristan replied.

Lord Ashington grinned. "That is not coffee, then," he said. "I prefer it strong, and I avoid the cream and sugar."

A footman approached with a serving dish in his hand. "Would you care for cream, sir?" he asked.

Tristan held his coffee cup up so the footman could pour fine cream into it.

Once the footman stepped back, Tristan took another sip. "Much better," he declared, placing the coffee cup onto the table.

Lord Ashington leaned to the side as another footman placed a plate down on the table. He picked up his napkin and draped it onto his lap. Then he picked up a fork to begin eating.

Tristan followed suit and they started eating their break-fast in relative silence. Once he had finished eating his eggs, he asked, "Do you intend to go to the House of Lords today?"

"I do," Lord Ashington replied. "There is much work that needs to be done and there are too many fools in Parliament."

"I can only imagine."

Lord Ashington placed his fork down and motioned towards the plate, indicating that he was done. A footman retrieved the plate and stepped back.

"I do want to speak to you about something," Lord Ashington said.

Tristan gave him an expectant look.

Lord Ashington leaned forward and said, "I need you to be attentive to Lady Lizette."

"I beg your pardon?" He had not been expecting that. Nor did he want to shower any attention upon Lady Lizette.

"We need to show the members of high Society that we are united as a family," Lord Ashington explained.

"But, why me?" he asked.

Lord Ashington grew solemn. "I know you are against all social events, but you need to take your rightful place in Society, as my heir."

"I know what is expected of me——"

"Do you?" Lord Ashington asked, speaking over him. "I hardly see you at any social gatherings, and when I do, you look as if you just ate something that disagreed with you."

"What is it that you want me to do?"

Lord Ashington glanced at the empty doorway before saying, "It would go a long way if you would accompany us to Lady Maria Rundell's ball this evening."

He decided to point out the obvious fact that was being overlooked. "Even if I did agree to this, Lizette is new to Town, and I doubt that she has anything appropriate to wear to a ball."

"The modiste has assured us that this would not be an issue and guaranteed a ballgown will arrive within the day," Lord Ashington said.

Tristan stifled the groan on his lips. He no more wanted to go to a ball than to a hanging fair in the square. He had learned long ago that social events were insufferable and he tried to avoid them at all costs. No one had cared about him when his brother was Lord Ashington's heir, so why should he care about those people now that he was the heir?

Putting his hand up, Lord Ashington said, "Before you say no, just think of Lady Lizette and the impossible position she has been put into."

As if Lord Ashington's words had conjured her up, Lady

Lizette stepped into the room and pressed her back against the green-papered walls.

Tristan shifted in his seat to face her. "What is—"

Lady Lizette put a finger up to her lips. "Shh, you must keep your voice down," she said in a hushed voice. "I'm hiding from Aunt Anne and Madame Auclair."

"Pray tell, why are you hiding from them?" Tristan asked, matching her low tone.

"I am tired of being poked and prodded," Lady Lizette replied.

Tristan found her antics to be amusing and a smile formed on his lips. "So naturally you run away and hide."

"I told them I needed to make use of the water closet," Lady Lizette revealed as she turned to peek out the door.

Lord Ashington chuckled. "Your plan is far from flawless."

"I know," Lady Lizette sighed, "but it was the only thing I could come up with on such short notice."

Tristan gestured towards the window along the opposite wall. "Why not go out the window and hide in the gardens?"

Lady Lizette's eyes lit up. "That is brilliant."

As she walked towards the window, Lady Anne stepped into the room and let out an exasperated sigh. "There you are, Child," she said. "Madame Auclair does not like to be kept waiting, for anyone."

Lady Lizette's shoulders drooped. "So close," she muttered under her breath.

With a wave of her hand, Lady Anne said, "Come along. We still have much to do."

Tristan watched as Lady Lizette walked slowly towards Lady Anne as if her boots were made from irons. He felt a twinge of pity for her, but there was nothing that could be done to help her.

After the ladies left the room, Tristan turned back towards Lord Ashington and saw that he was smiling.

"My granddaughter is a delight, is she not?" he asked as he brought his coffee cup up to his lips.

Tristan was a smart enough man not to answer that question. If he answered in the affirmative, it might give Lord Ashington the impression he cared for Lady Lizette. Which he didn't. They were hardly acquaintances. But if he answered negatively, then he would risk Lord Ashington's ire. No, there was no good response to the posed question, so he remained silent.

Lord Ashington lowered his cup to the table. "Will you come this evening, for Lizette's sake?"

Tristan didn't respond right away. He was trying to think of an excuse as to why he couldn't come, but his mind was blank. His evenings usually consisted of him eating dinner and retiring to his study to do some work on his accounts.

Shoving back his chair, Lord Ashington rose and said, "I do apologize if I made it seem like you have a choice in the matter. I will expect to see you this evening at Lady Maria's ball."

Lord Ashington didn't bother to wait for his reply before he walked out of the dining room. Drats. He didn't dare defy Lord Ashington so he had no choice but go to a ball this evening.

Saints above, how he hated mingling with people.

***

The afternoon sun streamed through the windows as Lizette sat in the drawing room, working on a watercolor painting of an idyllic countryside. She found the pastime to be relaxing and it allowed her to retreat to her own thoughts as she worked.

Her aunt walked into the room, holding up a piece of paper. "I have the best news."

Lizette lowered her paintbrush and asked, "The war is over?"

"How would I know such a thing?" her aunt asked with a baffled expression. "I am referring to Madame Auclair sending word that she has managed to secure you a ballgown for this evening."

"How is that possible?" Lizette asked.

"Someone didn't show up to collect their ballgown and Madame Auclair was able to alter it to fit you," her aunt shared. "Isn't that wonderful?"

Lizette shrugged. "That isn't the best news I have ever heard, but it is adequate."

"Adequate?" her aunt repeated with a wave of her hands. "Do you know how fortunate you are? It usually takes weeks to commission a ballgown."

"I still contend it is too soon after my mother's death to attend a ball."

"We have been over this, repeatedly," her aunt said. "It will do you good to have some fun and get your mind off your mother."

Lizette brought the brush back up and started touching up the clouds on her painting. There was no use in arguing with her aunt over this since she would only be wasting her breath. Her aunt was insistent that she attend the ball and, truth be told, she was rather eager to see what a ball was like in Town. She just wished it was under difference circumstances.

Her aunt came to stand next to her and remarked, "You are very talented, my dear."

"Thank you," Lizette said. "My teacher at the boarding school thought I could one day sell my paintings."

"I do believe she is correct in her assumption."

Lizette placed her paintbrush down onto the tray. "Do you paint?"

"Not for many years, I'm afraid."

Brownell stepped into the room and announced, "Lady

Oxley and her daughter, Miss Bolingbroke, have come to call. Are you receiving visitors?"

Her aunt moved towards the center of the room as she replied, "We are. Please send them in."

Brownell tipped his head. "Yes, my lady."

Lizette rose and removed the apron that she had been wearing to protect her gown while she was painting.

As she placed the apron down on the chair, Miss Bolingbroke walked in with her mother, and she had a bright smile on her lips. "Hello, again." Her eyes strayed towards the watercolor painting, and they widened in response. "Did you paint that?"

"I did," Lizette confirmed.

Miss Bolingbroke approached the painting and acknowledged, "It is breathtaking."

"Thank you," Lizette said.

"I am a terrible painter," Miss Bolingbroke admitted. "My mother assures me that my strengths lie elsewhere, but I wish I could paint as well as you."

"Everyone is talented in their own unique way," Lizette encouraged.

Miss Bolingbroke blew out a puff of air. "I am still trying to discover what I am good at. Last I heard, eating biscuits with one's toes is frowned upon."

Lizette gave her an odd look. "Do you eat biscuits with your toes?"

"Heavens, no," Miss Bolingbroke rushed out. "I'm sorry. I am terrible at making polite conversation. It is just one of the many things I am not good at."

Lady Oxley interjected, "You will have to excuse my daughter. She tends to say the first thing that comes to her mind, without thinking it through."

"There is nothing to excuse," Lizette said. "I find it endearing."

Lady Oxley gestured towards the painting. "I must agree

with my daughter. That is a lovely picture of a windmill and the sheep grazing next to it."

"It reminds me of where I am from," Lizette shared.

"And where is that, dear?" Lady Oxley asked.

"Bridgwater."

Lady Oxley smiled kindly at her, immediately setting her at ease. "You are immensely talented at painting, just as your mother was."

"You knew my mother?"

"I did," Lady Oxley said. "I counted her as one of my friends until she just up and disappeared one day. I have often thought of her over these years."

Lizette smoothed down her black gown. "I'm afraid she just recently passed."

Lady Oxley's voice held an undeniable sadness to it. "That pains me to hear but I assumed as much since you are in mourning."

Her aunt stepped over to the settees and asked, "Would you care to sit and enjoy some refreshment?"

"We do not mean to impose," Lady Oxley replied.

"You could never impose," her aunt said as she sat down. "Besides, it has been far too long since we chatted over a cup of tea."

"Yes, it has," Lady Oxley agreed as she sat down, her back remaining perfectly straight. A straw hat rested atop her head and her blonde hair peeked out from underneath. She was fashionably dressed in a blue gown and she had a netted reticule around her right wrist.

As her aunt poured the tea, Lady Oxley continued. "I did have a purpose for my visit. I wanted to thank you for the kindness that you bestowed upon my daughter and son when you saved them from the side of the road."

"It was the least we could do," her aunt said, placing the teapot down.

"I shudder to think of what could have happened to them,

broken down, alone..." Lady Oxley's voice trailed off. "I believe we have all heard the stories of the highwaymen that haunt that stretch of road."

Miss Bolingbroke sat down next to her mother and said, "I would have welcomed a chance to speak to a highwayman."

"Good heavens, why would you ever wish to speak to one?" her aunt asked as she extended a cup to Miss Bolingbroke.

"I am curious as to how they pick their victims," Miss Bolingbroke said, accepting the cup. "Surely, they cannot rob every coach they encounter. They must have a system."

"For what purpose do you wish to know this?" her aunt pressed.

Miss Bolingbroke gave a half-shrug. "Highwaymen have always intrigued me."

"They are criminals," Lady Oxley declared. "It is not just a passing whim to these men. They steal to line their own pockets."

"What if they are stealing from the rich to give to the poor?" Miss Bolingbroke asked.

Lady Oxley shook her head. "These highwaymen are not Robin Hood. Furthermore, I thought we decided to not discuss folklores when we are calling upon people."

"Yes, Mother," Miss Bolingbroke said, bringing the cup up to her lips.

There was a lull in the conversation as everyone took a sip of their tea, but Lizette knew she couldn't let Lady Oxley leave without asking her a few questions about her mother.

"How did you become acquainted with my mother?" she asked.

Lady Oxley brought her cup and saucer to her lap. "We met at a ball," she replied. "Your mother and I bonded over our love of books."

Lizette smiled at that thought. "My mother did love to read."

"Your mother was a very private person, but she would grow quite animated whenever she spoke about a book that she was passionate about," Lady Oxley shared. "A group of us used to meet once a week to discuss the books we read, and we called ourselves 'The Brazen Bluestockings'."

"The Brazen Bluestockings?" Miss Bolingbroke repeated.

"It was a silly name, but we all grew to be great friends," Lady Oxley said.

Miss Bolingbroke gave her mother a curious look. "Who else was in this group?"

"We had one rule," Lady Oxley replied. "We never spoke about 'The Brazen Bluestockings', especially who was a member. We had our reputations that we had to consider."

"But surely you can speak of it now," Miss Bolingbroke pressed.

"I only mentioned it for Lady Lizette's sake," Lady Oxley said.

Lizette leaned forward and placed her empty cup and saucer onto the tray. "I am glad that you did. Sometimes, I forget that my mother had a life before she had me."

"I do remember how much your parents loved one another," Lady Oxley remarked. "They only seemed to have eyes for one another, at least until you were born. After that, I would only see your mother when I came to call."

"Why was that?" Lizette asked.

"Your mother stopped going to social events, opting to stay home with you, and your father…" She stopped. "Well, that is in the past."

Lizette wanted to know what Lady Oxley had intended to say, but when she opened her mouth to ask, her aunt spoke first.

"Do you intend to go to Lady Maria's ball this evening?"

Lady Oxley bobbed her head. "We are," she replied. "Dare I hope you will be coming, as well?"

"We intend to," her aunt said.

"We?" Lady Oxley asked, glancing between them.

Her aunt gestured towards her. "Lizette will be joining Lord Ashington and myself this evening."

Lady Oxley's brow furrowed. "I do hope she will not be attending in her mourning clothes."

"Heavens, no," her aunt said. "We were most fortunate that Madame Auclair was able to secure a ballgown for her this evening."

"That is quite the accomplishment since Lady Lizette has only arrived in Town," Lady Oxley remarked.

"Madame Auclair did owe me a favor," her aunt shared.

Lady Oxley nodded in approval. "I have no doubt that Lady Lizette will be the belle of the ball this evening." She placed her teacup on the tray. "We should be going."

"So soon?" her aunt asked.

Lady Oxley rose. "The ball is in a few hours, and I daresay that it will take that long for me to look presentable."

"We both know that isn't true," her aunt said. "I do recall that you were once a diamond of the first water."

"That was many, many years ago," Lady Oxley stated.

Rising, her aunt asked, "Where has the time gone? I feel as if I blinked, and I turned into an old woman."

"You are hardly old," Lady Oxley contended.

"But I am. It is a simple fact," her aunt said.

Lady Oxley let out a heavy sigh. "If you are old, that means I have to admit that I am old, too, and I am not ready to do so yet."

Her aunt laughed. "What a pair we make."

Miss Bolingbroke leaned closer to Lizette and asked, "Do you think we will sit around and complain about our age when we are older?"

Lady Oxley interrupted, "Just you wait! Every woman does it."

"It's true," her aunt confirmed. "You will change your tune when you discover your first white hair."

Lizette laughed. "My mother used to have me pull them out, at least until they grew too plentiful."

Lady Oxley beamed at her. "You are a good daughter, and I am pleased that I have finally made your acquaintance."

Lizette dropped into a curtsy. "Likewise, Lady Oxley."

Miss Bolingbroke's eyes returned to the watercolor. "Do you think you can teach me how to paint like that?"

"I can try," Lizette said

"I would like that. My last painting was of my dog and my father thought I had drawn a dinosaur," Miss Bolingbroke shared.

"Oh, my," Lizette murmured.

Miss Bolingbroke waved her hand in front of her. "Sadly, it wasn't my worst attempt. At least he was able to tell it was an animal."

Lady Oxley spoke up from the doorway. "Come along, Anette. We do not wish to overstay our welcome."

After they had departed from the room, her aunt walked over to her and ran a discerning eye over her. "You should start getting ready for the ball."

"Now?" she asked. "But it is in a few hours."

"It is a very important night for you, and I want you to look your best."

Lizette conceded, knowing it would save a considerable amount of time. Some things were worth the fight, but this was not one of them. "As you wish," she said. "I could use a good soak."

"Enjoy."

Chapter Ten

Tristan sat in the darkened coach as it traveled to Lady Maria's townhouse. How he dreaded this evening. He was in no mood to engage in polite talk with members of the *ton*. He would have rather remained at home, reviewing the accounts. But Lord Ashington was adamant that he attend this evening for Lady Lizette.

An image of Lady Lizette came to his mind, and he found himself smiling. She was unique. There was something different about her, and it was that difference that made her fascinating.

The coach came to a stop in front of a whitewashed townhouse and a footman stepped off his perch to open the door. After he exited the coach, he followed the steady stream of patrons that were heading inside.

He bypassed the receiving line, knowing it was a waste of his time, and went in search of the ballroom. It didn't take long before he had a drink in his hand and was leaning against a column in the back of the long, rectangular hall.

His eyes roamed over the red-papered walls and ornate woodwork that ran the length of the room. Lighted sconces hung on the walls and an ostentatious gold chandelier sat in the middle, over the chalked dance floor.

Tristan took a sip of the champagne and wished he was anywhere else but here. A few young women were glancing his way and offering him coy smiles, but he was not interested in conversing with any of them. He was only here to offer support to Lady Lizette. Nothing more, nothing less.

A servant walked past him with a tray of discarded flutes of champagne and he placed his nearly full glass onto it. He had no desire to drink this evening and risk putting himself in a compromising situation.

A welcoming voice came from behind him. "As I live and breathe, I never thought I would see you at a ball."

Tristan turned around and saw his friend, Lord Roswell Westlake. "I am here under protest," he grumbled.

"That doesn't surprise me in the least," Lord Roswell said. "How did Lord Ashington manage to convince you to come this evening?"

"He ordered me to do so."

"I see. But it wouldn't be such a terrible thing if you did have some fun while you were here," Lord Roswell said with a knowing look.

Tristan's eyes roamed over the patrons and saw a few young women batting their eyelashes at him. How predictable these women were. "I shall pass."

Lord Roswell smiled. "More for me then."

"I wish you luck with that," Tristan said. "I have no desire to get caught in the parson's mousetrap."

"Neither do I." Lord Roswell tugged down on the ends of his black jacket. "Although my mother would no doubt be pleased. She has been rather eager for me to secure a bride this Season."

Tristan sobered. "How is your mother faring?"

"She is resting this evening," Lord Roswell replied. "I'm afraid she didn't quite feel up to coming to the ball."

"That is understandable, considering her condition."

Lord Roswell's eyes grew reflective. "I consider every day with her a gift. The doctor isn't sure how much time she has left."

Tristan placed a comforting hand on his friend's shoulder. "I'm sorry," he said, knowing his words were wholly inadequate.

The orchestra started warming up in the corner and Tristan dropped his hand. He thought it was best if he changed topics. "Do you intend to dance this evening?"

"I do," Lord Roswell responded. "After all, I do not wish to deny the ladies the pleasure of my company."

Tristan vaguely heard Lord Ashington and Lady Anne being announced over the noise in the ballroom. However, when Lady Lizette was announced, the room went eerily quiet. The only noise that remained was the orchestra.

He shifted his gaze towards the door that Lady Lizette had entered. She was dressed in a silver ballgown with a square neckline that highlighted her comely figure. Her hair was piled high on her head and small curls framed her face. To say she looked beautiful would be an understatement since the entire ballroom seemed brighter now that she was here.

Lord Roswell followed his gaze. "That is Lady Lizette?" he asked with a low whistle. "In my mind, I had pictured a younger, female version of Lord Ashington."

"I shudder to think what you imagined."

"It wasn't pretty," Lord Roswell admitted.

Tristan kept his gaze on Lady Lizette as she walked further into the room. She kept her head held up high, despite the blatant stares that were being directed at her.

"If you will excuse me, I need to go see to Lady Lizette," Tristan said.

"Can I get an introduction?"

Tristan nodded. "Follow me," he ordered as he went to intercept Lady Lizette.

As he approached them, Lady Lizette's eyes lit up. Or had he just imagined that? He came to a stop in front of her and bowed. "You are looking lovely this evening, my lady," he said.

Lady Lizette dropped into a curtsy. "Thank you, sir."

He gestured towards Lord Roswell. "Lady Lizette, allow me the privilege of introducing you to my friend, Lord Roswell Westlake."

Lady Lizette's lips quirked into a smile. "I thought you didn't have any friends."

"I have friends," he defended.

"So say you," Lady Lizette teased.

Lord Roswell chuckled. "You are truly a delight, my lady," he said with a bow.

Lady Lizette tipped her head. "It is a pleasure to meet you, Lord Roswell."

"The pleasure is all mine," Lord Roswell responded with a flirtatious smile.

If Lady Lizette was affected by his friend's attempts to charm her, she hid it well. She brought her gaze back to meet his. "Why is everyone staring at me like I'm a public spectacle?"

Lady Anne interjected, "Do not fret. These busybodies will find something else to gossip about soon enough."

"But why are they even gossiping about me?" she asked. "They don't know me."

"That means very little to the gossipmongers," Lady Anne replied. "They think they know you, and that makes all the difference."

Lord Ashington placed a hand on his granddaughter's sleeve. "Why don't you dance the first set with Mr. Westcott and do try to enjoy yourself?"

Lady Lizette glanced his way as she pursed her lips. "I do believe it is customary for the gentleman to ask permission to dance."

Tristan put his hand out and said, "I would be honored if you would dance with me for this set."

Lady Lizette looked unsure. "You don't have to do this."

"I assure you that I had every intention of asking you to dance, but your grandfather spoke up first."

Lady Anne nudged her forward. "Go on, then," she encouraged.

Lady Lizette hesitantly brought her hand up and slipped it into his. "Thank you, sir," she murmured.

Tristan started to lead her towards the dance floor and noticed that she was visibly tense. "Is everything all right?" he asked.

"You will think me terribly foolish, but I have never danced a set with a gentleman before," she said as she averted her eyes.

"I have no doubt that you will rise to the challenge."

Lady Lizette brought her eyes to meet his. "What if I step on your feet?"

"I'm wearing boots so that won't be an issue."

"What if I fall?"

"Then I will be there to catch you," Tristan replied.

Lady Lizette smiled up at him. "I believe you."

Tristan felt his chest puff out with pride at the thought that Lady Lizette trusted him- without a hint of hesitation. It might have been a simple admission on her part, but it had a profound impact on him.

He led her to where she was to line up before he took his place with the men. They were to dance the quadrille and it had been some time since he had executed the dance.

The music started up and they started dancing. Tristan noticed that Lady Lizette was counting her steps and he found it endearing. As the dance progressed, so did Lady Lizette's confidence, and by the end, she had a bright smile on her face.

The music came to an end and Tristan approached Lady Lizette. "You dance superbly," he praised.

"Thank you," she said. "I can't recall the last time I have had so much fun."

"I am glad that you enjoyed it." He offered his arm. "May I escort you back to your grandfather?"

As she accepted his arm, she asked, "Would you mind terribly if we stepped outside for a moment?"

"I would prefer it, actually."

Tristan led her out the French doors and onto the veranda. He dropped his arm and took a step back. He turned his attention towards the sky. "It is a lovely evening we are having." Good gads, did he truly just comment on the weather?

"It is," Lady Lizette murmured.

The way she spoke her words caused him pause. "Are you all right?"

Lady Lizette pressed her lips together, then asked, "Do you think I am a terrible person?"

"I do not," he replied. "Where is this coming from?"

"My mother just died, and I am dancing at a ball, as if I don't have a care in the world," Lady Lizette said in a hushed voice.

It was obvious that Lady Lizette felt her words deeply so he knew he needed to choose his response very carefully. He didn't want to upset her more than she already was. To grow emotional at a ball simply wasn't done. A reputation could be ruined for far less.

Tristan took a step towards her, but was still mindful to maintain proper distance. "Would your mother have faulted you for coming this evening?"

Lady Lizette shook her head. "She would not have."

"The truth of the matter is that you will grieve your mother forever, but you will learn to live with it," Tristan said.

"How is that possible?" Lady Lizette asked, her eyes searching his.

"I promise that one day you will be whole again, but you

will never be the same. Nor should you want to be," Tristan replied. "After all, I am not the same man I was before my brother died."

Lady Lizette's face softened. "You are a good man."

Tristan was about to disagree with her when Lord Roswell's voice came from next to them. "I apologize for interrupting, but I was hoping to dance the next set with Lady Lizette."

Blazes. How had he not seen his friend approach? He had been so distracted by his conversation with Lady Lizette that he had failed to notice what was going on around him.

Lady Lizette addressed Lord Roswell. "I would be honored, my lord."

Lord Roswell stepped forward and extended his hand. "Shall we, my lady?"

As his friend escorted Lady Lizette to the dance floor, Tristan found his mood grow sour. He didn't like the fact that Lord Roswell had asked Lady Lizette to dance. He took no issue with him as a person, but he was in no way worthy of Lady Lizette.

But neither was he.

Not that it mattered. He had no interest in pursuing a courtship with Lady Lizette. Although, the thought wasn't as abhorrent as it once was.

Lizette couldn't seem to wipe the smile off her face as she descended the stairs. She had the most wonderful time at the ball last night. She had danced every set and had been introduced to the most extraordinary gentlemen.

The entry hall was filled with bouquets of flowers and she eagerly went to read the cards. She knew it was customary for gentlemen to send flowers after they danced a set, but that didn't curtail her excitement. She had never been sent flowers before and she was going to savor the moment.

Brownell stepped into the entry hall with a vase of pink roses. "Another bouquet arrived for you, my lady," he said as he placed it down onto a side table.

Her eyes became fixated on the pink roses. "Do you know who sent that one?"

"It was from Mr. Westcott," he answered before he walked away.

Lizette approached the roses and took in the heavenly scent. For the briefest of moments, she felt as if she were back in her home, breathing in the scent of the roses in the garden.

She reached for the card and read, "*You are stronger than you were yesterday.*"

As she placed the card down, her aunt's voice came from the stairs. "Who sent the lovely roses?"

"It was Mr. Westcott."

Her aunt nodded in approval. "That was most thoughtful of him."

"It was," she agreed.

"May I ask what the note said?"

Lizette turned towards her aunt and replied, "'You are stronger than you were yesterday'."

"That is an odd thing to say in a card."

"I disagree," she said. "It reminds me of the conversation that we had last night after we danced."

"I daresay that I have never seen Mr. Westcott smile so much as he did when he danced with you."

"I scarcely believe that to be true."

Her aunt smiled. "Regardless, it would appear that your first ball was quite the success."

The words had just left her mouth when her grandfather stormed into the entry hall, holding up the newssheets.

"I am going to ensure the whole lot is fired," her grandfather grumbled.

Her aunt lifted her brow. "Who do you want fired?"

"Whoever authorized this article," her grandfather replied, extending the newssheets towards Lady Anne.

As she read the article, her eyes grew wide. "Good heavens, why would they print such rubbish?"

"Precisely! I am going down there right now to demand a retraction," her grandfather said.

"We both know that won't do any good," her aunt remarked. "Quite frankly, this is not entirely unexpected. We knew that Lizette's presence would dredge up past rumors about William."

Her grandfather furrowed his brow. "You expect me to sit quiet when his name is dragged through the mud... again, taking Lizette's name with him."

Lizette interjected, "What does the article say?"

Her aunt lowered the paper to her side. "After your mother disappeared from high Society, many people speculated that she had fled to France with you."

"Why would they believe that?" Lizette asked.

"Why, indeed? But the gossips could speak of little else," her aunt said. "It was better than the rumor that your father killed your mother and hid her body under the floorboards."

Her grandfather crossed his arms over his chest. "It did not help that William grew more of a recluse with each passing day."

"He did cause the scene at Lady Richard's soiree," her aunt pointed out.

"That he did," her grandfather said.

Lizette glanced between them. "What happened at the soiree?"

Her aunt frowned. "He claimed he saw Napoleon's army outside of the townhouse and he started pushing furniture in front of the doors. Whenever someone tried to approach him, he grew combative, claiming that he was attempting to save them all."

"Fortunately, William stopped attending social events after that, preferring to spend his time in his laboratory," her grandfather shared.

Her aunt extended her the paper. "The newssheets were rather complimentary to you, my dear," she said. "You were toasted as the belle of the ball."

"That is good, is it not?" Lizette asked as she started to peruse the article.

"It is, for now," her grandfather grumbled. "Just know that the *ton* is a fickle lot. You can be in their good graces until you aren't."

Lizette brought her gaze up. "That sounds petrifying."

Her aunt gave her a pointed look. "Now you know what is at stake," she said. "We should eat breakfast before your suitors come to call."

"I don't have any suitors," Lizette argued.

"You will after last night," her aunt responded confidently.

Lizette wasn't quite sure what to make of that. She did want to get married, but the thought of picking a suitor terrified her.

Her grandfather leaned forward and kissed Anne on the cheek. "If you will excuse me, I have work that I need to see to."

As her grandfather walked off, her aunt said, "My father gets so riled up when he sees our family in the newssheets. He just wants to protect us."

"That is honorable."

"It is unrealistic, though," her aunt responded. "There are always going to be people that will criticize you no matter what. It is important that you develop a thick skin."

"I have yet to develop that."

"You will, in due time. One cannot belong to the highest echelons of Society and not have one," she said as she started walking towards the dining room.

Lizette followed behind as she continued to read the

Society page. It referenced what she wore to the ball, who she spoke to, and even posed the question of where she had been hiding all of these years.

Once she sat down at the table, a footman placed a cup of chocolate in front of her. She eagerly reached for it.

"I haven't had chocolate in so long," she admitted before taking a long, unladylike slurp of the warm drink.

"Dear heavens, Child," her aunt admonished. "I assure you that the cook can make more, if you so desire it."

Lizette placed the cup back onto the saucer. "The last time I had chocolate was for my sixteenth birthday. It was a luxury that we could scarcely afford."

"You don't ever have to worry about that again."

"I know, but now I have new worries."

Her aunt waved her hand in front of her. "Worrying is a waste of time. It doesn't change anything, and it keeps you very busy doing nothing."

Lizette leaned to the side as a footman placed a plate in front of her. "It is not that simple," she said. "How am I to go on with my life, knowing I might succumb to the same illness that killed my father and grandmother?"

"You mustn't worry about that."

"How can I not?"

As her aunt picked up her fork, she replied, "You cannot live your life in fear. That isn't living, but, rather, you are just surviving."

Lizette sighed. "I just hate not knowing what the future holds for me."

"Life would be boring if we knew precisely how things would turn out in the future," her aunt said. "It is far better to live your life as you see fit."

"Is it selfish of me to want to get married and have a family?"

"I don't think it is."

Lizette reached for her cup of chocolate. "At what age did my father start showing symptoms?"

"I don't know the exact age since he wasn't forthcoming with that information, but I started noticing the signs when he was thirty-five or so."

After a long sip, Lizette placed the empty cup back down onto the table. "I used to think thirty-five was so old, but now I realize how truly young that was."

Her aunt smiled. "It is just a drop in the bucket," she said. "Besides, I have yet to show any symptoms of dementia and I am much older than your father."

Lizette felt hope well up inside of her at her aunt's remarks. It wasn't a given that she would develop dementia.

Placing her fork down, her aunt continued. "If I had put my life on hold, I would have lost out on marrying Richard. He brought so much joy into my life."

"I wish I could have met my uncle."

A reflective look came into her aunt's eyes. "Your uncle was acquainted with you and he loved nothing more than holding you when you were a baby," she said. "Richard wanted a large family, but that was one thing I was unable to give him."

"That was hardly your fault."

"A woman's role is to bear her husband's children." Her aunt pushed back her chair and rose. "Shall we adjourn to the drawing room to receive our callers?"

Lizette could hear the pain in her aunt's voice and she didn't dare press her. "I think that is a splendid idea," she replied, rising.

They walked in silence as they departed from the dining room and headed towards the drawing room.

As they stepped into the entry hall, a knock came at the door and Brownell went to open it.

"Good morning, sir," the butler greeted before opening the door wide, revealing Mr. Westcott.

Lizette took the briefest of moments to admire Mr. West-cott's handsome face. She shouldn't be noticing such things about him, but she did. Every time.

Mr. Westcott stepped into the entry hall and bowed. "Good morning, ladies."

Lizette dropped into a curtsy. "Mr. Westcott," she murmured.

Their eyes met and, together, they stared at each other. It was a fleeting, lasting moment, where something passed between them. She just wasn't sure what that was.

Her aunt spoke up. "What brings you by today?"

Mr. Westcott shifted his gaze towards Lady Anne. "Lord Ashington sent word that he needed to speak to me."

"Very well, then," her aunt remarked with a wave of her hand. "I presume that my father is in his study."

"Then I shall go see him at once," Mr. Westcott said.

Lizette found that she wasn't ready to say goodbye to Mr. Westcott yet. He was a welcome reprieve, and she would rather speak to him than any suitor that came to call. She just needed to find something to say that would keep him here. As she debated what to say, her eyes landed on the bouquet of pink roses. "Thank you for the flowers you sent," she rushed out.

"You are most kindly welcome," he said.

"They remind me so much of the roses we had in my mother's garden."

"That was my intention," Mr. Westcott shared. "I remembered seeing the roses from the drawing room window at your manor."

"That was most thoughtful of you."

Mr. Westcott's eyes crinkled around the corners. "I can be observant when the situation warrants it." His gaze left hers and roamed over the entry hall. "It would appear that you have many admirers."

Dare she hope that Mr. Westcott was one of her admirers?

She chided herself on thinking something so preposterous. He had never shown her any attention, and she was most grateful for that. She considered him a friend, even if he didn't feel the same.

Knowing that Mr. Westcott was still waiting on her response, she replied, "That is not true. The gentlemen were just being courteous and sent flowers as Society dictates."

"I do believe you are selling yourself short, my lady." Mr. Westcott bowed. "If you will excuse me, I do not want to keep Lord Ashington waiting."

As Mr. Westcott walked away, her aunt stepped closer to her and lowered her voice. "You could do far worse than him."

Fearing she misunderstood her aunt, she asked, "Pardon?"

Her aunt grinned. "Mr. Westcott will be a marquess one day."

"I am well aware, but if I do marry, I want a love match," Lizette stated.

"As well as you should." Taking a step back, her aunt said, "We should adjourn to the drawing room to receive our callers now."

As Lizette followed her aunt into the drawing room, her thoughts strayed towards Mr. Westcott. She did hold him in high regard, but that was a far cry from having affection towards him. Wasn't it? Perhaps her emotions were just befuddled since he had shown her such care and consideration over the past few days. But he had sent her pink roses, knowing their special significance to her. Was it just a thoughtful gesture on his part or could it mean that she meant more to him than he was letting on?

Regardless, she would need to be mindful to safeguard her heart from making such a foolish mistake as falling for the one man who merely seemed to tolerate her existence.

Chapter Eleven

As Tristan walked towards Lord Ashington's study, he resisted the urge to glance over his shoulder for one last parting look at Lady Lizette. Why was he drawn to someone that was inherently different from himself?

Lady Lizette smiled, as if she never knew any pain. Which was ludicrous. She had just lost her mother and she was dealing with the truth about the death of her father. She had every reason to be miserable, but she wasn't. Quite the opposite, in fact.

Botheration. Even if he was interested- which he wasn't- he would never make his intentions known to Lady Lizette. He wasn't worthy of her, and he never would be.

Tristan stepped into the study and saw Lord Ashington was hunched over his desk. Not wanting to startle the marquess, he remained back and cleared his throat.

Lord Ashington's head shot up. "It is about time you got here," he grumbled.

"I came straight away, my lord," Tristan said.

The marquess frowned. "I have asked you, repeatedly, to call me Adam. Family does not make use of titles."

"My mother would have boxed my ears if I was so informal with you," Tristan said.

"You are my heir, and I was your guardian for many years," Lord Ashington pointed out. "I believe you have earned the right to address me by my given name."

"Fair enough," Tristan said. "I will start calling you... Adam."

Lord Ashington gave him an amused look. "That was a terrible first attempt."

Tristan walked further into the room and asked, "May I ask why you sent for me?"

The humor disappeared from Lord Ashington's expression. "Did you review the documents that Mr. Trent sent over?"

"I did, and they have all been signed."

"Very good," Lord Ashington replied.

Tristan knew that Lord Ashington hadn't summoned him to ask him about the accounts, so he waited for Lord Ashington to continue.

The marquess leaned back in his seat. "I would like you to take Lizette on a carriage ride through Hyde Park."

The thought of spending more time with Lady Lizette sounded pleasant enough, but he had a question of his own. "May I ask why?"

"I was pleased that Lizette was praised in the newssheets, but we all know how fickle the *ton* can be," Lord Ashington replied. "I want her to be seen in Society, and often."

"I am sure that Lady Lizette will be inundated with requests for carriage rides. Why not let one of her suitors take her?"

"Because I want someone that I trust." Lord Ashington pushed back his chair and walked over to the drink cart. "Would you care for something to drink?"

"No, thank you," Tristan replied.

Lord Ashington picked up the decanter and poured

himself a drink. Then he retrieved his glass. "I have decided to set Lizette's dowry at forty thousand pounds."

Tristan's brow shot up. "That is a generous sum."

"It is, but I don't want fortune hunters or rakes anywhere near her," Lord Ashington said. "I want my granddaughter to marry for love."

"Love doesn't exist, at least not in our circles," Tristan huffed.

"That is not true. I fell in love with my wife right away. The moment I saw her, I knew I wanted to spend the rest of my life with her."

"You are an exception."

Lord Ashington sighed. "I know your brother's wayward behavior affected you deeply, but you mustn't let his past define you."

"Thomas was always searching for the perfect woman, but he never did find her."

"He was looking in all the wrong places."

"Perhaps, but that quest cost him his life."

Lord Ashington shook his head. "No. It was Thomas' pride that killed him. He should never have engaged in that duel."

"He had little choice because he refused to marry Miss Thorpe, and her brother demanded satisfaction."

"This is precisely why you can't go around kissing young women and not expect repercussions to your actions."

Tristan nodded. "I wholeheartedly agree."

Lord Ashington took a sip of his drink, then lowered it to his side. "Promise me that you will look after Lizette."

"I... uh..." His voice stopped. That was the last thing he wanted to do. She wasn't his responsibility, and he didn't think he could go on resisting her if he spent more time with her. "Do you think that is wise?"

"When I die, and you take my place, I need to know that you will see to the care and comfort of Lizette and Anne."

"You aren't going to die anytime soon," he attempted.

"Just promise me," Lord Ashington asserted.

Tristan knew Lord Ashington wouldn't let the matter drop until he uttered those words. "I promise," he said, knowing he had little choice in the matter.

Lord Ashington bobbed his head approvingly. "Thank you."

"Although, I daresay that Lady Anne won't be pleased to know that I will be responsible for her upon your death." He glanced back at the open door. "I do not think she cares much for me."

"Why do you say that?"

"She is very abrupt with me and chides me for the simplest infractions."

Lord Ashington grinned. "That is just Anne. Do not let it bother you. If she didn't care for you, she would just ignore you," he said. "William threw mud at Anne's dress when they were younger, and she didn't speak to him for a whole week."

"A whole week?"

"By the end of the week, William was following Anne around, begging her to forgive him," he shared. "They made up quickly after that and William never threw mud again."

Tristan smiled. "My brother and I used to roll around in the mud and my mother would be mortified when we arrived home. I still can remember my mother scrubbing the dirt off my skin."

"It has been my experience that boys love nothing more than to get dirty while they have too much idle time on their hands."

"You would be correct in that assessment."

Lord Ashington put his empty glass down onto the tray. "You should go collect Lizette for your carriage ride. I took the liberty of having the carriage brought around to the front."

"What if she is surrounded by her suitors?"

"Then make your presence known," Lord Ashington advised. "You will be the Marquess of Ashington one day. That is nothing to scoff at."

"What if she doesn't want to go on a carriage ride with me?"

Lord Ashington looked at him as if he hadn't considered that as a possibility. "Ask nicely and she will go. I'm sure of it."

Tristan knew there was no use in arguing with him, so he was about to turn to leave when he stopped. He needed to tell Lord Ashington one more thing. "Your solicitor notified me that the mysterious payment has been paid."

"Good, good," Lord Ashington muttered.

"I don't suppose you will tell me what it was for," Tristan pressed.

"In due time."

Tristan didn't feel the need to confide in Lord Ashington that the solicitor had let the name of the receiver slip- Mrs. Jane Hendre. Now he just needed to discover where she lived, and he could go sort out this mystery on his own.

As he turned to leave, Lord Ashington said, "Do try to enjoy yourself on the carriage ride, but not too much."

"Yes, Adam."

Lord Ashington chuckled. "That was much better than your first attempt."

"I assure you that I can be taught," he joked.

After he departed from the study, he walked towards the drawing room and could hear male voices drifting out into the entry hall. He resisted the urge to groan as he stepped into the room. Four gentlemen were sitting around Lady Lizette and Lady Anne, and they all had enamored looks on their faces.

His eyes landed on Lord Roswell, who was engaging in conversation with Lady Lizette. She laughed at something he said, and the sound was like music to his ears.

What had Lord Roswell said that was so amusing? He wasn't that funny.

Lady Lizette's eyes shifted towards him, and a smile came to her lips. "Mr. Westcott, please join us," she encouraged.

Tristan walked further into the room and tipped his head at Lord Roswell. Then he found an upholstered armchair and repositioned it towards Lady Lizette.

He had just sat down when Lady Lizette shared, "Lord Roswell was just sharing the most interesting story."

Tristan went to address his friend. "Were you now?"

Lord Roswell puffed out his chest. "It was nothing but a story about my sister, Octavia," he shared. "She decided to purchase peacocks for our garden, but the male peacock chases her around all the time. It is almost as if he has a grudge against her."

"Peacocks can be temperamental," Tristan remarked.

"That is precisely what my sister has discovered," Lord Roswell said. "I'm afraid she didn't think the peacocks through."

A dark-haired gentleman spoke up. "Do you like peacocks, my lady?" he asked, addressing Lady Lizette.

"I do," she replied. "I think peacocks are beautiful, especially when they display their feathers."

"When they show off their feathers, it is largely considered a mating ritual and courtship displays," Tristan said. Why had he just said that? It was not polite to speak about such things in front of a lady.

Lady Lizette's lips twitched. "Thank you for that, Mr. Westcott."

Tristan felt like an imbecile. He wanted to excuse himself and be on his way, but he had told Lord Ashington that he would take Lady Lizette on a carriage ride.

Lord Roswell spoke up. "Mr. Westcott was speaking true," he said. "The peahens will pick their mates based upon the size of the feathers."

"Well, now we know how peacocks mate," Lady Anne interjected. "It might be best if we speak of something else."

Tristan shot his friend a grateful look. He knew what Lord Roswell had been trying to do. He had been helping him save face.

A pale-skinned gentleman leaned forward in his chair and asked, "Is it true that you were in France until your mother passed away?"

Lady Lizette visibly stiffened. "I was not in France," she vaguely responded.

"But why did your father send you away?" the gentleman pried. "Or did your mother take you and flee from him?"

"No, that is not at all what happened," Lady Lizette replied.

"Then what did happen?" the gentleman pressed.

"I... uh..." Lady Lizette shifted her gaze towards Tristan, and he could see the panic inside of them, causing him to act.

Tristan rose and held his hand out towards Lady Lizette. "Would you do me the grand honor of taking a carriage ride with me through Hyde Park?"

"I would," she said as she slipped her hand into his.

As he assisted her in rising, the other men in the room stood. Neither of them spoke as he led her towards the entry hall.

It wasn't until they stepped outside that Lady Lizette said in a low voice, "Thank you for what you did back there for me."

"It was nothing."

"To you, perhaps," Lady Lizette murmured. "I must admit I wasn't expecting to be peppered with questions about my past."

"You have an aura of mystery around you and that fascinates people."

"The truth isn't very exciting."

Tristan came to a stop in front of the open carriage. "It rarely is," he said as he assisted her inside.

Once Lady Lizette was situated, he sat across from her. He

would take her to Hyde Park and then he would go home to finish his tasks. It seemed simple enough, so why did he think it was a terrible mistake?

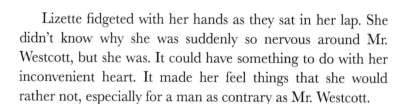

Lizette fidgeted with her hands as they sat in her lap. She didn't know why she was suddenly so nervous around Mr. Westcott, but she was. It could have something to do with her inconvenient heart. It made her feel things that she would rather not, especially for a man as contrary as Mr. Westcott.

Perhaps she was just confused since he had saved her on more than one occasion. That must be it. After all, it was preposterous that she was developing feelings for Mr. Westcott. He was far too serious for her.

But he did have a kind heart.

The carriage wheel hit a rut in the cobblestones and dipped to the side. Lizette reached out and steadied herself.

Mr. Westcott spoke up, drawing her attention. "It shouldn't be much longer until we arrive at Hyde Park."

"Thank you for suggesting the carriage ride."

"It wasn't my idea," Mr. Westcott said. "Your grandfather thought it would be best if you were seen in public."

"I see." Lizette tried to hide her disappointment from Mr. Westcott. How she wished that he wanted to spend time with her and not at her grandfather's behest.

Mr. Westcott's eyes roamed over the grand townhouses. "I haven't been on a carriage ride through Hyde Park since…" His voice stopped. "I don't think I have ever been on a carriage ride through Hyde Park."

"Well, I am glad that we are doing this then."

"As am I," Mr. Westcott responded. "Hyde Park shouldn't be too crowded since it isn't the fashionable hour yet. With any luck, we can be home before our midday meal."

"Are you in a hurry?"

Mr. Westcott gave her an apologetic smile. "I'm afraid I have a lot of work I need to see to," he revealed. "It occupies my mind, unceasingly."

"What do you do for fun?"

"Work is fun for me."

Lizette cocked her head. "What else?"

"On occasion, I go boxing with Lord Roswell."

"Anything else?"

Mr. Westcott shook his head. "I have too much work to do, and I don't have time to lollygag around."

"Do you not worry that you will get tired of working all the time?"

"People are waiting for me to fail, and I refuse to give them that satisfaction."

"Are you one of those people?"

Mr. Westcott furrowed his brow. "I suppose so, but I haven't thought of that before," he said. "I have so much at stake, and I can't let anyone down, including myself."

"You should do one fun thing every day."

"I don't have time for games. I am a very busy man."

Lizette clasped her hands in her lap. "I just worry that you will wake up one day and realize that your life has passed you by."

"I am not even thirty years old."

"Precisely, you should be out in Society, enjoying yourself."

Mr. Westcott grew solemn. "I wasn't truly accepted into Society until I became Lord Ashington's heir. Until then, I was merely a blight at social gatherings." He paused. "Besides, why would I wish to mingle with the same people that watched my brother's downfall with enjoyment?"

"I doubt that people could be as cold and unfeeling as that."

"It is true," Mr. Westcott said. "After Mr. Thorpe shot my brother, he was hailed as a hero for protecting his sister. The newssheets made my brother out to be a rake of the highest order and even had the audacity to imply his death was his own fault."

"That is awful."

Mr. Westcott's jaw clenched. "I won't give them the satisfaction of watching me fall into the same trappings as my brother."

"You and your brother are two different people."

"We are, but my brother had so much to live for, and he threw it away for a tryst with a woman."

Lizette could hear the anguish in Mr. Westcott's voice. He had placed so much responsibility on his shoulders that she was afraid the weight of his burdens would cause him to topple over.

Mr. Westcott's gaze roamed over the trees that lined one of the many paths in Hyde Park. "We should speak of something much more pleasurable."

"The weather, perhaps?" she joked.

"I would prefer not to," he said. "How are you settling in?"

Lizette let out a sigh. "I miss Mrs. Everly," she admitted. "I didn't think I would this much, but I do. She has been around for as long as I can remember, and she has always treated me with such kindness."

Mr. Westcott shifted on the bench. "I have never had a servant that showed me such care before."

"That is most unfortunate."

"Is it?" Mr. Westcott asked. "Servants have a job to do, and I would hate to distract them from their tasks at hand."

"My mother always treated our staff as if they were part of the family."

"That is foolishness," Mr. Westcott said. "They have their own family. They are just paid to tend to you."

Lizette arched an eyebrow. "Servants have feelings, too."

"I don't dispute that, but I do not have time to coddle

anyone," Mr. Westcott asserted. "They do their jobs, get paid and the transaction repeats."

"That is a sad way to look at it."

Mr. Westcott shrugged. "I think it is the practical way to look at it."

"Are you always so practical?"

"I try to be," he replied. "I don't have time to live in the clouds. My feet are firmly on the ground."

"But you don't have any fun," she pointed out.

"I work. That is all the fun I need."

Lizette knew she was fighting a losing battle with Mr. Westcott since she doubted they would ever see eye to eye on this issue.

Mr. Westcott frowned. "You must think me a terrible ogre but wait until you get older. You will discover that common sense is not that common. That is why I have to work as hard as I do."

"I don't think of you as an ogre, but I would like a chance to prove you wrong."

"How do you propose that?"

Lizette considered him for a moment before saying, "Try to have a conversation with one of your servants."

"For what purpose?"

With a disbelieving look, Lizette replied, "To get to know them."

"You seem to think that I feel as if I am better than my servants, but that is the farthest thing from the truth," Mr. Westcott said. "I respect them and the work that they render for me."

"Yet you know nothing about them and their lives."

Mr. Westcott put his hand up in surrender. "You win. I will converse with one of my servants when the situation presents itself."

"Thank you."

He grinned. "You will find that I can be reasonable when it is warranted."

Lizette felt herself relax. "I don't dispute that, but it did take a rather long time to come to a consensus."

"I take it that you usually get your way."

She gave him a smug smile. "I do."

"I pity the man that you marry then," Mr. Westcott joked.

Her smile slipped. "Do you, pity him?"

Mr. Westcott leaned forward and said, "Any man that is lucky enough to capture your heart is a fortunate man, indeed."

"Do you mean that?" she asked in a soft voice.

"Wholeheartedly."

Lizette glanced down at her hands in her lap. "That is kind of you to say, but I have yet to decide if I wish to marry."

"Why wouldn't you marry?"

"My grandmother and father both had a rare form of dementia and I fear that I will inherit the disease."

"So you stop living?" he asked. "You give up all hope of a normal life?"

Bringing her eyes up, she replied, "It wouldn't be fair of me to marry, knowing that I would become a burden to my husband."

"No one knows what the future holds for us."

"But can I risk it?"

Mr. Westcott grew solemn. "I daresay that the greatest risk is doing nothing."

"You make it sound so simple."

"It can be," Mr. Westcott said. "Worrying doesn't take away tomorrow's troubles. It just makes today unbearable."

Lizette reached up and tucked a piece of errant hair behind her ear. "My aunt said something similar."

Mr. Westcott sighed. "I do not mean to preach at you, but I think it would be foolish of you to put your life on hold for a disease that may or may not present itself."

"The disease is so awful that my father spent his lifetime trying to find a cure."

"True, but you could die before you ever even contract the disease."

"That is a morbid thought," Lizette muttered.

Mr. Westcott gave her a knowing look. "Life has a funny way of working itself out. You may not end up where you thought you'd be, but you'll end up right where you're meant to be."

"You sound as if you speak from experience."

"I do," Mr. Westcott said. "I should have never been Lord Ashington's heir, but here I am. I went from working at the East India Trading Company with a small income to being responsible for grand estates that will one day be mine."

"Most people would consider you fortunate."

"I am, but what was the cost?" he asked, his voice growing strained. "I lost my brother."

Lizette held his gaze and said, "You did nothing wrong."

"Then why do I feel as if I did?"

"It was your brother's choice to engage in a duel."

"I should have tried harder to stop him."

"Would that have made a difference?"

Mr. Westcott shook his head. "I don't believe so."

"You should take comfort in knowing you did all that you could."

His face showed no emotion as he watched her. "You make it sound so simple," he said, using her own words against her.

Lizette gave him a sheepish smile. "I'm sorry. Now it is me that is preaching to you."

"I don't mind," Mr. Westcott said.

Lizette's eyes left his and she looked over the trees that lined the road. A movement in the distance caught her attention and she saw a man was leaning up against one of the trees. A black top hat sat low on his head and his hand was on the brim, angling it downward.

As the carriage drove past him, the man looked up, revealing his face, and he winked. It only took her a moment to recognize this man as the person who had attempted to abduct her from the coaching inn.

Her heart began to pound within her chest as she turned to Mr. Westcott. "That man…" she started.

Mr. Westcott gave her a baffled look. "What man?"

Lizette gestured towards the tree where he had been standing, but he was gone. "It was the man from the coaching inn, the one who tried to abduct me," she revealed. "But he is not there anymore."

His alert eyes shot towards the trees. "Do you see which way he went?" he asked, his voice taking on a sharpness that she was unaccustomed to.

"I did not," she replied. "I assure you that he was right there by the tree."

"I believe you."

Lizette felt her hands shaking as she thought about that terrible man. "I would like to go home now," she said, pleased that her voice was somewhat steady.

"I think that would be for the best," Mr. Westcott agreed.

Chapter Twelve

The carriage came to a stop in front of Lord Ashington's townhouse and Tristan didn't bother to wait for the footman. He opened the door and stepped onto the pavement. Then he reached back to assist Lady Lizette down the step.

Once her feet were on the ground, she withdrew her hand and took a step back. "Thank you," she murmured.

They hadn't spoken much since Lady Lizette had seen her attacker in Hyde Park. He could tell that she had been shaken up by it so he didn't want to upset her further by peppering her with questions. But he was worried. The man had some audacity to make his presence known to Lady Lizette and in such a public place. But for what purpose? Surely the man wouldn't be foolish enough to attempt to abduct her again, especially in such a crowded place as London.

Tristan offered his arm to Lady Lizette and she placed her hand on his. After he escorted her inside, he dropped his arm but remained close.

"You need not fear," he said. "Your grandfather and I will keep you safe."

Lady Lizette didn't appear convinced. "Why would this man follow me to London?" she asked.

"I don't know, but he can't get to you."

With a glance at the stairs, Lady Lizette said, "I hope you don't take offense, but I would like to be alone for a while."

"I understand that feeling all too well."

Lady Lizette started walking towards the stairs but stopped. She turned around and said, "Thank you for taking me on a carriage ride. It was fun until..." Her voice trailed off.

"I agree."

She gave him a grateful smile. "I hope you have a pleasant day."

He bowed. "Likewise, my lady."

Tristan watched as Lady Lizette walked up the stairs and disappeared as she turned a corner. He had to admit that he didn't enjoy it when Lady Lizette wasn't very talkative. At first, her talking had grated on his nerves, but now, he missed hearing the soothing sound of her voice. It had an effect on him that he didn't quite understand. Her voice seemed to silence all his demons, even for but a moment.

He turned towards Brownell, who was standing guard in the entry hall. "Is Lord Ashington in his study?"

"He is not, sir," Brownell replied. "He left for the House of Lords no more than an hour ago."

"Very well. Will you send word once he returns home? I have a pressing matter I wish to discuss with him."

Brownell tipped his head. "As you wish."

Tristan departed the townhouse and started walking down the pavement. He should return home, but he wasn't in the mood to work. A trip to the club might clear his head or at least make him forget that panicked look on Lady Lizette's face when she had seen her attacker.

It was a short time later when he arrived at the doors of White's. A liveried servant opened the door and he stepped into the hall. Small, round tables filled the room and men were sitting around them, speaking in hushed tones. He walked over to an empty table in the corner and sat down.

A server approached his table and asked, "Would you care for something to drink?"

"Brandy."

"Yes, sir," the server said before he left to do his bidding.

Tristan's eyes searched over the room, and they landed on Mr. Bolingbroke. He was conversing with a group of men, a drink in his hand, and a smile on his lips. Mr. Bolingbroke must have sensed that he was being observed because he turned his head and met Tristan's gaze.

To his great disappointment, Mr. Bolingbroke pushed back his chair, rose and approached his table. "Good morning, Mr. Westcott."

"Good morning," he muttered off the greeting.

Mr. Bolingbroke placed his glass down onto the table and pulled out a chair. "I haven't seen you in here before."

"I am here now."

"That you are," Mr. Bolingbroke said as he sat down. "Can I buy you a drink?"

Tristan shook his head. "That isn't necessary."

"I think it is since you saved me and my sister from being stranded on the road."

"It was nothing."

A server stepped forward and placed the glass in front of Tristan. "Will there be anything else, sir?"

"Not at this time," Tristan said.

Mr. Bolingbroke took a sip of his drink, then asked, "Are you meeting someone here?"

"I am not."

"Would you care to join my group of friends?"

"I would not."

Mr. Bolingbroke gave him an amused look. "You are a man of few words. I can respect that."

Tristan reached for his glass and said, "I am just having a quiet drink before I return to my work."

As he said his words, he saw Lord Roswell was approaching the table with a smirk on his lips. Botheration. Perhaps he had made a mistake coming to the club and being forced to interact with other people.

Lord Roswell came to a stop at the table. "I had to look twice before I was convinced that it was you."

Tristan held up his glass. "I'm just here for a drink and then I am going home."

"I didn't even think you had a membership to White's," Lord Roswell said.

"Lord Ashington was insistent that I have one," Tristan shared.

Lord Roswell acknowledged Mr. Bolingbroke with a tip of his head. "Caleb," he said. "I hadn't realized that you were acquainted with Tristan."

"I wasn't until Mr. Westcott saved me and my sister from the side of the road when our coach's wheel broke," Mr. Bolingbroke explained.

"That was most kind of him," Lord Roswell acknowledged. "And it doesn't sound at all like my friend."

Tristan frowned. "What is it that you want, Roswell?"

Lord Roswell chuckled. "I am just having some fun at your expense." He sat down. "I was going to have a drink and then call upon Lady Lizette."

"Again?" Tristan asked.

"I am going to ask if she would like to go on a carriage ride with me during the fashionable hour," Lord Roswell responded.

"I wish you luck with that," Tristan said, bringing the glass to his lips.

"Is there a particular reason why?" Lord Roswell asked.

Tristan lowered the glass to the table. "I just departed

from Lady Lizette's townhouse, and she informed me that she wished to be alone for the time being."

"You do seem to have that effect on women," Lord Roswell joked. "I am sure that she will receive me."

"How can you be so sure?" Tristan asked.

Lord Roswell grinned a crooked smile. "Because I am incredibly handsome."

"And humble, too, I see," Tristan said.

"I cannot help it if women fawn over me."

Tristan tossed down his drink before saying, "Good gads, I am going to need another if I am going to be able to stomach this conversation."

Leaning back in his seat, Lord Roswell asked, "Perhaps there is another reason why you don't want me to call on Lady Lizette?"

"Whatever reason could that be?" Tristan asked, feigning uninterest.

Lord Roswell shrugged. "It could be that you fancy her for yourself."

"I think not."

Mr. Bolingbroke spoke up. "There would be no shame in that because Lady Lizette is a beautiful young woman."

Tristan stifled the groan on his lips. So Mr. Bolingbroke had also noticed how beautiful Lady Lizette was? This did not sit well with him.

Lord Roswell caught the eye of a passing server and indicated he wished for a drink. Then he said, "I have never known Tristan to show favor to any young woman before."

"That is because I do not wish to marry," Tristan grumbled.

"So you have said, repeatedly," Lord Roswell said, "but I do believe that Lady Lizette has caught your eye."

"You would be wrong."

"Then why did you ask her to dance and take her on a carriage ride through Hyde Park?" Lord Roswell asked.

"Both times were at Lord Ashington's behest," Tristan shared.

"And you clearly did not enjoy yourself," Lord Roswell teased.

Tristan wanted to leave and stop this ridiculous conversation, but to do so would be rude of him. But when had that stopped him before?

He was about to shove back his chair when Lord Roswell put his hand up and said, "Don't go. I promise, I won't tease you about Lady Lizette anymore."

"How did you know I was about to leave?" Tristan asked.

Lord Roswell placed a hand to his heart. "You insult me. I have known you for a long time and I do not want a woman to come between us. You may press your court with Lady Lizette."

"I have no intention of courting Lady Lizette," Tristan asserted.

"Well, neither do I, at least not anymore," Lord Roswell said.

Mr. Bolingbroke interjected, "Can I court her?"

Tristan and Lord Roswell both turned their heads towards him and said in unison, "No."

Putting his hands up, Mr. Bolingbroke smiled. "Understood."

A server placed three drinks onto the table before walking away.

As Tristan reached for a glass, he said, "The only reason why I am spending any time with Lady Lizette is because she is Lord Ashington's granddaughter."

"That is the only reason?" Lord Roswell pressed.

"Yes." He took a sip of his drink. "Lord Ashington asked me to keep her away from rakes and fortune hunters."

Lord Roswell leaned in and asked, "Is it true that her dowry is forty thousand pounds?"

"It is," Tristan confirmed.

Mr. Bolingbroke let out a low whistle. "That is a hefty sum and is enough money for people to be willing to overlook her father's delicate situation."

Tristan turned to face Mr. Bolingbroke and asked, "What do you know about Lord Crewe's delicate situation?"

"Lord Crewe committed suicide after he turned mad," Mr. Bolingbroke said.

"Who told you that?" Tristan asked.

Mr. Bolingbroke gave him a blank expression. "I thought everyone knew that. I have heard rumors about it for years."

"Well, I don't believe it to be true," Tristan stated.

"My apologies, I meant no offense," Mr. Bolingbroke said.

Tristan pushed away his nearly full glass and rose. "I have tarried long enough," he declared. "I have work that I need to see to. I bid you good day."

He didn't bother to wait for their replies before he walked away from the table. The last thing he needed to do was keep talking about Lady Lizette, especially since he was starting to think about her entirely too much.

Lizette laid on her bed as she stared up at the ceiling of her four-poster bed. She was still reeling from the fact that her attempted abductor had followed her to London. What if he tried to abduct her again? Mr. Westcott had assured her that she was safe, and she believed him... for the most part. But she was afraid.

When had her life gotten so complicated? Although, she already knew that answer. It was the moment when Mr. Westcott had showed up on her doorstep, declaring her to be the daughter of an earl. Her life had felt like a whirlwind since then.

She felt alone, despite the townhouse being filled with

servants. How she wished her mother were here to offer her up some advice. She would know precisely what to say to her; she always did.

A knock came at the door.

"Enter," Lizette ordered.

The door opened and Mrs. Everly stepped into the room with a smile on her face.

Lizette's eyes grew wide at the sight of her housekeeper. "Mrs. Everly." She hurried off the bed and went to throw her arms around her. "How are you here?"

Mrs. Everly released her and explained, "Mr. Westcott sent the coach for me. He said that my presence was needed here in Town."

"He said that?"

"Was he wrong?" Mrs. Everly asked.

Lizette shook her head. "He was not," she replied. "I am most grateful that you are here, but I thought you were caring for my manor."

Mrs. Everly waved her hand dismissively in front of her. "Mr. Stockton and his wife can handle the manor. I am much more concerned about you."

"I am fine," Lizette said, hoping her words were convincing.

Mrs. Everly gave her a look that implied she didn't believe her. "Try again, Child."

"I don't know what to feel anymore." Lizette felt her shoulders slump slightly. "I have such a myriad of emotions and I can't seem to quell any of them."

"Just as I thought," Mrs. Everly said, gesturing towards the settee that sat at the end of the bed. "Perhaps we should sit and you can tell me everything."

Lizette walked over to the settee and dropped down in an unladylike fashion. "I don't even know where to begin. Should I start with my attacker following me to London or how my father may or may not have killed himself?"

Mrs. Everly blinked. "Dear heavens, let's start with the fact that you were attacked. When was this?"

"Someone attempted to abduct me at the coaching inn but my aunt was able to stop him by hitting him over the head with a chamber pot," Lizette explained. "He ran out shortly after that and I had assumed I would never see him again. But he was at Hyde Park when Mr. Westcott took me on a carriage ride."

"What did Mr. Westcott do?"

"He could do very little since the man disappeared before I could point him out," Lizette said. "The man even had the audacity to wink at me."

Mrs. Everly reached for her hand. "You poor thing. But you must know that you are safe here."

"That is what Mr. Westcott told me, as well, but I am afraid."

"There is no shame in admitting that."

Lizette sighed. "If my mother was here, she would tell me to be brave."

"Most likely, she would have, but do you want to know a secret?"

"I do."

Mrs. Everly's voice held a hint of mirth as she revealed, "Your mother wasn't always brave, either."

"I doubt that."

"It is true," Mrs. Everly responded. "She worried about you constantly when you were away at your boarding school. You were her whole world."

Lizette ran a hand over her blue gown. "And yet, I am not even mourning for her properly. She would be terribly disappointed in me."

"Not true. Your mother was known to balk at tradition."

"That she was," Lizette agreed.

Mrs. Everly released her hand and sat back. "Be patient with yourself. You were thrust into circumstances that were not of your own making. I have no doubt that your mother is proud of you."

"I hope that is the case, because I don't want to let her down."

"Just be true to yourself. That is all that your mother ever wanted for you." Mrs. Everly's eyes surveyed the bedchamber. "This is a lovely room."

"It is, but I miss my small bedchamber at home. This townhouse is much too grand for my liking. After all, I am just a country bumpkin."

"You are many things, but a country bumpkin is not one of those things."

"I was told about my father and how he died by drinking one of his own concoctions. Many speculate that he killed himself."

"Is that what you believe?"

With a slight shake of her head, she replied, "I want to believe that he didn't intentionally leave us."

"Then hold on to that."

Lizette gave her a weak smile. "Mr. Westcott said something similar, but I am still struggling with it all."

"It would seem that Mr. Westcott has been most attentive to you these past few days."

"He has, but nothing untoward has happened."

"I assumed as much."

Lizette felt a slight breeze drift into the room and she turned her face towards the window. "Behind Mr. Westcott's gruff exterior, there lies a kind heart."

"It almost sounds as if you have developed feelings for Mr. Westcott."

She shook her head vehemently. "No, you misunderstood me. We are just friends." She didn't dare admit what she had been feeling, despite Mrs. Everly being a trusted friend. To utter that she cared for Mr. Westcott would make it real, and she didn't want it to be real, at least, not yet.

Mrs. Everly didn't look convinced but thankfully she let the matter drop. "While I am here, I will be acting as your lady's maid."

"I am most grateful for that, but are you not accustomed to running a household?"

"I care little for what my title is as long as I am getting paid accordingly," Mrs. Everly said. "And I was assured that my pay would not be deducted."

"I am glad to hear that."

Mrs. Everly rose and cast her eyes around the room. "I was told that I was to dress you to receive your callers this afternoon."

"I assume that my aunt issued that decree."

"It was," Mrs. Everly confirmed.

Lizette rose and smoothed down her gown. "What is wrong with the dress that I have on?"

Mrs. Everly's eyes looked Lizette over carefully. "It is terribly wrinkled. It almost appears that you slept in it."

"I tried to take a nap, but I'm afraid my mind wouldn't shut off long enough for that to happen."

"You poor thing," Mrs. Everly said, "but you must look presentable when you are residing in London, especially since you don't know who will come to call."

"I tire of constantly changing my gowns."

Mrs. Everly grinned. "If you want me to feel sorry for you, then you will be sorely disappointed."

Lizette rose. "I am sorry. I'm afraid I am out of sorts today."

"There is no reason to apologize," Mrs. Everly said as she walked over to the dressing table. "You have had a rough go of it lately and, knowing you, entertaining suitors is not a high priority for you."

"That is true," Lizette agreed.

Mrs. Everly patted the back of the chair. "Why don't you tell me about your father while I style your hair?"

Lizette closed the distance between them and sat down, her back to Mrs. Everly. "From what I have been told, my father was an eccentric man and dedicated his life to finding a cure to a debilitating disease for his mother, then himself."

"What disease?" Mrs. Everly asked as she started removing the pins from her hair.

"It is a rare form of dementia that causes a multitude of issues," Lizette said. "Not only did my father deal with memory loss but he also had hallucinations."

"That is most unfortunate."

Lizette sighed. "What if I develop this disease?"

"What if you don't?" Mrs. Everly countered. "You mustn't put your life on hold or else you will start having regrets."

"I just don't want to be a burden to anyone."

Mrs. Everly started brushing her hair as she said, "Sitting around, moping about it, won't do you any good. You are young and vigorous. Do not let worry consume you."

"Everyone is telling me that, but no one truly understands the impossible situation that I have been placed in."

"What did Lady Anne say about it?"

"She said something similar to you, as did Mr. Westcott."

"Great minds think alike," Mrs. Everly teased as she placed the brush down. "You have always been more concerned about others than yourself. What is it that *you* want?"

Lizette grew silent as she considered Mrs. Everly's words. "I want to fall in love and marry the man of my choosing."

"Then so be it."

An image of Mr. Westcott came to her mind, but she quickly banished the thought. She may hold him in high regard, but that was a far cry from wanting to marry the man.

Mrs. Everly continued as she started styling her hair. "I was told by the other servants that your first ball was a great success."

"It was," Lizette said. "It was brilliant."

"Did you dance with Mr. Westcott?"

Lizette nodded. "We danced the first set together," she said. "He even sent flowers the next day that resembled the roses from the garden back home."

Mrs. Everly gave her a knowing look. "That was most thoughtful of him, and it causes me to wonder how close of friends you and Mr. Westcott are."

Lizette did not like where this conversation was heading so she attempted to change the subject. "Did you have a pleasant carriage ride to Town?"

"Don't think I don't know what you are doing," Mrs. Everly said.

"What am I doing?" Lizette asked innocently.

Mrs. Everly laughed. "You win. We won't talk about Mr. Westcott anymore."

"Thank you."

A knock came at the door before it was opened, revealing her aunt.

Lady Anne let out an exasperated sigh. "Dear heavens, are you not ready to receive callers yet?"

"I am not," Lizette replied. "I have been chatting with Mrs. Everly."

"Where is your other lady's maid that was assigned to you?" Lady Anne asked.

Once Mrs. Everly placed the last pin in her hair, Lizette rose and turned towards her aunt. "I don't rightly know but Mrs. Everly was the housekeeper at my manor in Bridgwater."

"I thought she looked familiar, but why is she here?" Lady Anne asked, glancing between them.

Mrs. Everly spoke up. "Mr. Westcott sent a coach for me and informed me that my presence was requested here."

"Interesting," Lady Anne muttered. "He mentioned none of this to me."

"Well, I, for one, am glad that Mrs. Everly is here," Lizette said.

Lady Anne smiled kindly. "Then she must stay," she responded. "But you must not dally any longer if you want to meet with your callers this afternoon."

Mrs. Everly walked over to the wardrobe and started sorting through the gowns. Her hand stilled on one and she pulled out a pale yellow gown with a net overlay of blue flowers.

"What of this gown?" Mrs. Everly asked.

"That is perfect, and it is one of her newest gowns that has just arrived for her," Lady Anne said. "Madame Auclair has had her seamstresses working around the clock to ensure her wardrobe is prepared as quickly as possible."

"That one is much too bright," Lizette contested. "I thought we decided on dark colors."

"You decided on that, but Madame Auclair and I thought you would look perfectly beguiling in pale colors," Lady Anne said.

Mrs. Everly walked the gown over to Lizette and held it up for her inspection. "What would you care to do, my lady?"

Lizette ran her finger over the fine muslin material as she admitted to herself that the gown was exquisite. Perhaps it wouldn't be too much of a burden to wear it, but only for the afternoon.

"I will wear it, but I would like to change into something more somber for dinner," Lizette said.

Lady Anne bobbed her head. "That sounds like a fine compromise." She walked over to the door. "Hurry up and change. You don't want to keep your suitors waiting."

"I have no suitors," Lizette said.

"Yet," Lady Anne corrected as she opened the door. "You could have suitors, but you haven't shown any of your callers any favor."

After her aunt departed from the room, Mrs. Everly asked, "Shall we dress you?"

"I suppose that would be for the best," Lizette replied.

Mrs. Everly started to assist her in undressing and Lizette felt a smile come to her lips. She was beyond pleased that her housekeeper was here with her, and she owed a debt of gratitude to Mr. Westcott. He had heard what she had said and, frankly, didn't say, and had sent for Mrs. Everly, a woman that meant everything to her. How could she even repay such kindness?

Chapter Thirteen

The sun had begun to set as Tristan signed the final document that his man of business had left for his review. He leaned back in his chair and rubbed his temples. He had been working for hours, and yet, he felt that he had accomplished very little. Every time he started focusing on work, his thoughts would stray towards Lady Lizette.

Botheration.

He didn't have the time or luxury to spend time thinking about Lady Lizette. He had multiple estates that he had to oversee, and people's livelihoods were dependent on him. He couldn't sit back and let his thoughts be taken over by a woman that he had no right to even think about.

Furthermore, he had no intentions of marrying, but if he did fall prey to the parson's mousetrap, it would be to a sensible woman that understood his priority was to ensure his legacy would never be tarnished. What he accomplished now would affect generations to come and that was a sobering thought. He couldn't risk making a mistake, especially by falling in love.

Love. He didn't have time for love. It was much more practical to marry someone that he had mutual toleration with. His wife could see to raising the children while he focused on his work. He paused at the thought of children. He did need an heir and the thought of children underfoot was enticing. But first, he had to marry. Perhaps taking a wife wouldn't be the worst thing in the world, but now he just had to find one that would suit him.

The problem was that he detested the games that most of the women in high Society played with their coy smiles and come-hither looks. They had never given him the time of day when his brother had been Lord Ashington's heir, so why should he give them any attention now?

Lady Lizette sprung to his mind. Her beauty was only outshined by her sweet soul. She was nothing like the other women of the *ton*, which made her so enticing. She had the courage to be vulnerable around him and showed him a side of herself that made him even more intrigued.

Tristan shook his head. Hadn't he just decided he didn't have time to think about Lady Lizette? She was starting to get past his defenses and that would not do. He needed to find a way to banish Lady Lizette from his mind, once and for all.

His dark-haired butler stepped into the room with his usual stoic expression. "Pardon the interruption, sir, but we just received word that Lord Ashington has arrived home," Tolstead revealed.

"Very good," Tristan said.

"Would you care for me to bring the coach around?"

"That won't be necessary," Tristan replied. "It would be much faster if I just walked the few blocks to Lord Ashington's townhouse."

As Tolstead turned to leave, Lady Lizette's voice came to Tristan's mind about how she had encouraged him to have a conversation with his staff.

"Before you go," Tristan said, rising, "how are you faring?"

Tolstead gave him an odd look. "I am well."

"Have you settled in?"

"I have."

"How long has it been since you started working for me?"

"Six months, sir."

Tristan came around his desk and walked over to the drink cart. "Can I offer you something to drink?"

Tolstead's face blanched. "No, thank you, sir," he said. "Will there be anything else?"

Not responding to his question, Tristan asked one of his own. "Do you have a family?"

"I do."

"Will you tell me about them?" Tristan prodded as he picked up the decanter. He felt a little absurd in his line of questioning, but he wanted to inform Lady Lizette that he had made a valiant effort.

Tolstead glanced over his shoulder before saying, "I have a mother and two sisters."

"Are they in servitude as well?"

"They are not," Tolstead replied, looking deucedly uncomfortable. "My two sisters are married and have their own families."

"And your mother?"

"My income goes to help support her," Tolstead replied. "She has gotten rather frail in her older age."

Tristan poured himself a drink. "Do you enjoy working as a butler?"

The lines around Tolstead's lips tightened. "I do," he replied.

"Did you always want to be a butler?"

"Yes. I watched my father work at grand estates as a butler and I knew I wanted to follow in his path."

"That is admirable." Tristan paused. "What preoccupies your time when you are not at work?"

"I whittle wood."

"That is a fine pastime."

Tolstead nodded. "My grandfather taught me how when I was young, and it has just stuck with me."

"I have never whittled wood," Tristan admitted.

Tolstead shifted in his stance. "Do you take issue with my work?"

"Not at all," Tristan said. "I am merely just trying to make conversation."

"Conversation, sir?"

Tristan put down the decanter and picked up his glass. "Lady Lizette encouraged me to have a conversation with someone from my staff," he explained.

Tolstead visibly relaxed. "I see," he said. "I thought you were going to fire me."

"Fire you? For what?" Tristan asked.

"I know not, but I am not used to engaging in polite conversation with my employer."

Tristan took a sip of his drink, then said, "I did not mean to give you that impression, but I did learn a thing or two about you."

"Do you still wish to converse, or may I go about my tasks?" Tolstead asked.

"You are dismissed."

"Thank you, sir." Tolstead sighed with relief.

Tristan watched as his butler departed from the room and he felt like an absolute fool. That is not how he intended the conversation to go, but he had done what he had set out to do. Now, he could report to Lady Lizette that he had accomplished his task.

The long clock in the corner chimed as Tristan placed his glass down. He needed to speak to Lord Ashington and it would be best to do so at once. Besides, if he went now, there was a chance that he would be invited to dinner, allowing him to see Lady Lizette once more.

Blazes. He needed to stop looking for opportunities to see

Lady Lizette. No good would come out of spending more time with her. He was sure of that.

Tristan picked up his black top hat from his desk and placed it on his head. Then he proceeded out of his townhouse and onto the pavement. Lord Ashington's townhouse was only a short distance away and it was ridiculous to drive in a coach.

As he approached the main door, it opened and he was greeted by Brownell. "Good evening, sir."

"Good evening," he responded as he stepped into the entry hall. "Is Lord Ashington in his study?"

"Aye," Brownell greeted. "Would you care for me to announce you?"

"That won't be necessary."

Tristan headed towards the rear of the townhouse. The only noise was the clicking of his heels on the polished marble floor. He stepped into the study and saw Lord Ashington sitting in an upholstered armchair with a drink in his hand.

Lord Ashington met his gaze. "I understand that you wished to speak to me."

"I do," Tristan said as he sat across from Lord Ashington, "and it is of the utmost importance."

Leaning to the side, Lord Ashington put his drink down onto a table. "Proceed, then."

"When I took Lady Lizette on a carriage ride through Hyde Park, she claims she saw her attacker near a tree along the side of the road."

Lord Ashington's brow shot up. "Did you alert the constable?"

"I did not."

"Whyever not?" Lord Ashington demanded.

"I wanted to speak to you first before I did anything too hasty."

Lord Ashington frowned. "The time to act is now," he

declared. "I will send for a constable, and I will make sure she doesn't go anywhere without being escorted."

"I think that is wise."

"I won't let anything happen to my granddaughter, especially since I just got her back," Lord Ashington said.

Tristan leaned back in his seat. "I have no doubt that you can keep her safe."

Lord Ashington gave him a curious look. "Besides the unwanted visitor, how was the carriage ride through Hyde Park with Lizette?"

"It was..." His words trailed off as he tried to think of the right word. He had enjoyed himself immensely, but he didn't dare admit that to Lord Ashington. No, it would be best to appear indifferent about it. Knowing the marquess was still waiting for his response, he settled on saying, "It was uneventful."

"I see," Lord Ashington said. "Do you not enjoy spending time with Lizette?"

Drats. How did he answer that question without giving away that he held Lady Lizette in high regard?

"She is a pleasant enough young woman," Tristan said.

"That she is," Lord Ashington agreed. "I have no doubt that she will marry this Season, assuming that is what she wants to do."

The way the marquess spoke his words caused Tristan to pause. "Is that what *you* want?" he asked.

Lord Ashington looked at him in surprise. "Why do you ask?"

"It just appears you are not eager to let her go."

"I want to ensure she marries someone that is worthy of her," Lord Ashington said. "I want her to be happy."

"Lady Lizette deserves a lifetime of happiness."

"That she does," Lord Ashington agreed.

A dinner bell rang in the distance and Tristan rose. "If you will excuse me, I do not wish to intrude on your time a moment longer."

"You are never an intrusion," Lord Ashington said. "Would you care to stay for dinner?"

Tristan felt elated by the question, but he kept his face expressionless. "I would like that very much."

Lord Ashington nodded in approval. "I had anticipated your response, so I already informed Brownell to set an additional plate."

Was he so predictable?

"Should we adjourn to the drawing room to wait for the ladies?" Tristan asked.

"I need to see to a few things before dinner, but I would like you to go on ahead of me."

Tristan didn't need to be told twice. He hoped he would be able to speak to Lady Lizette alone, even if it was for only a moment.

As he headed for the drawing room, he was rewarded with seeing Lady Lizette descending the stairs in a maroon gown. Her hair was styled nicely in an elaborate chignon and two small curls framed her face. How was it that he noticed the little things about her, like the style of her hair?

He stopped at the bottom of the stairs and waited for Lady Lizette to do the same. She came to stand in front of him and a smile appeared on her lips.

"I hadn't expected to see you this evening," she said.

"I had some business with your grandfather and he invited me to dine with you," he shared. "I hope that is all right with you."

"Need you ask?"

Tristan gestured towards the drawing room. "Shall we wait for your family in the drawing room?"

"I think that is a splendid idea."

Tristan followed closely behind Lady Lizette as she crossed the entry hall and stepped into the drawing room. He was grateful for a moment to catch his breath from seeing her this evening. Was it his imagination or had she grown even more beautiful since he had last seen her?

Perhaps dinner wasn't the best idea, but it was too late to back out now.

Lizette gracefully lowered herself onto the camelback settee and tried to appear at ease. She was acutely aware that she was alone with Mr. Westcott and she felt fluttering in her stomach. She had been alone with him before, but with every interaction, every touch, she felt her feelings growing deeper for Mr. Westcott. She couldn't deny those feelings any longer, but that didn't mean she had to act on them.

What if she was so lonely that her heart was playing tricks on her? Mr. Westcott had shown her no attention, but he had sent for Mrs. Everly. Did that grand gesture mean he cared for her or did he do so out of obligation?

Mr. Westcott met her gaze and gave her a brief smile. "I hope we haven't run out of things to say to one another."

"I most certainly hope not," Lizette said.

"We could discuss the weather."

"That sounds intolerably boring."

"It does, but it is far preferable to silence."

Lizette cocked her head. "I thought you detested useless chatter."

Shifting in his seat, Mr. Westcott revealed, "I have found my opinion has changed on that matter."

"That is good." She hesitated and she hoped her next words were filled with the gratitude that she was feeling. "Thank you for sending for Mrs. Everly. That means more to me than you will ever know."

"You are most welcome."

"May I ask why you sent for her?"

Mr. Westcott's face softened. "I could hear in your voice how much you cared for her, and I thought it was for the best if you two weren't parted."

"It was quite a surprise today when she walked into my bedchamber."

"Everyone should be surrounded by people that care for them and are rooting them on," Mr. Westcott said.

The way Mr. Westcott said his words caused her to prod. "Do you have that?"

He cleared his throat. "It is not necessary in my case."

"Why is that?"

"I don't have any choice but to succeed," Mr. Westcott said.

"Aren't you lonely?"

Mr. Westcott's eyes grew reflective. "Loneliness is a constant companion of mine," he said. "After I lost my brother, I didn't find as much contentment being around other people."

"I can understand that. No matter how much it hurts, no matter how broken my heart is, the world doesn't stop for my grief."

"Precisely."

"But that doesn't mean I stop trying to move forward."

"As well you should," Mr. Westcott said. "But it is different for me. The path I have chosen is a lonely one."

"Can you not alter your path?"

"For what purpose?"

Lizette held his gaze as she said, "So a friend can join you."

"None of my friends would be foolish enough to accompany me."

"I daresay that you underestimate them."

Mr. Westcott let out a dry chuckle. "I know you are trying to help, but you do not need to concern yourself with me."

"Why is that?"

"You know nothing about me."

"I know more than you realize."

"Is that so?" he asked.

Lizette bobbed her head. "I believe you have resigned yourself to being alone because you are afraid to open up to anyone," she said. "And the simple reason is because you don't trust anyone to accept you for who you truly are."

"And who is that?" Mr. Westcott asked in a bored tone.

Moving to stand, she said, "A man that has a generous heart, but hides it behind a gruff exterior."

"You would be wrong."

"I don't think I am," Lizette pressed. "You proved that to me when you sent for Mrs. Everly."

"You are giving me far too much credit." He stood up to face her. "Some people are past hope and they don't wish to be saved."

"No one is past hope," she murmured.

"Regardless, you can't barge into someone's life and disrupt everything that they have been clinging to. It isn't fair of you to do so."

Lizette was close enough to Mr. Westcott that she saw deeply into his brown eyes. She heard what he was saying, but his eyes told an entirely different story. She could see the words that they held within them.

"Lizette," Mr. Westcott said in a hoarse voice. "I assure you that I am not worthy of your time or notice."

"I disagree." The sound of her name on his lips caused her heart to take flight.

Mr. Westcott's eyes roamed over her face. "It would be better if you kept your distance from me."

"Why?" she asked, her eyes dropping to his lips.

He took a ragged breath. "I can't give you what you seek."

"How do you know what I seek?" she asked in a whisper.

Mr. Westcott moved closer to her, his face just inches away

from her. They stood motionless as they stared deep into each other's eyes.

"I am trying to be a gentleman, but my resolve is weakening with every breath I take," he said.

Lizette could sense the struggle that Mr. Westcott was having deep within himself, partially because she was having the same emotional turmoil. As much as she wanted to kiss him, to feel his lips on hers, she knew that there was no going back if they did this. Their relationship would forever be altered, and she didn't know if they should risk what they did have.

But what did they have?

She was so lost in the moment that she almost didn't hear her aunt's shrill voice... almost.

"Good gracious, what do you think you are doing?" her aunt demanded.

Lizette and Mr. Westcott both jumped back with guilty expressions on their faces.

Her aunt advanced into the room. "Pray tell, what was about to happen here?" she asked in a hushed voice.

"We were just talking, and it got away from us," Lizette said as she avoided catching Mr. Westcott's eyes.

Her aunt huffed. "I should say so!"

Mr. Westcott spoke up. "It was entirely my fault, my lady."

"That is very gentlemanly of you to say so, but I surmise you were both equal conspirators," her aunt remarked. "Do you know what would have happened if my father had walked in on you both?"

Lizette bit her lower lip. She knew full well the consequences of being caught in a compromising position.

The silence in the room was deafening as her aunt stared at them with a pointed look.

Her grandfather stepped into the room with a perplexed look on his face. "Whatever is the matter?" he asked.

Lady Anne turned towards her father and Lizette feared

what she would say. To her pleasant surprise, her aunt said, "We were just discussing the weather."

"I hadn't realized the weather was such a gloomy topic," her grandfather said with a smile.

"That was terrible, Father," her aunt stated.

Her grandfather laughed. "I thought it was quite clever." He offered his arm. "May I escort you to dinner?"

Her aunt stepped back. "It might be best if you escorted Lizette to dinner."

Without skipping a beat, he said, "It would be my pleasure." Her grandfather approached her and offered his arm. "Shall we?"

Lizette placed her arm on his and allowed him to lead her from the room.

As they walked across the entry hall, her grandfather said, "Mr. Westcott informed me that you saw your attacker in Hyde Park today and I want you to know that I notified the constable. I have no doubt that he will come around tomorrow to speak to you."

Her grandfather continued. "From now on, you will be escorted by no less than four footmen and a maid. At least until this blackguard is no longer a threat to you."

"Thank you," she murmured.

"I do not want this to ruin your Season."

"It won't," she rushed to assure him.

Her grandfather seemed pleased by her response. "You have come too far to give up now," he counseled.

They walked into the dining room and her grandfather led her to her seat. He pulled out the chair for her and waited until she sat down before pushing it back in. Then he claimed his seat at the head of the table.

Mr. Westcott sat down next to her but was mindful to avoid her gaze. What must he think of her? She had been entirely too brazen, and she feared that she might have pushed him away forever.

Lizette reached for her glass as she attempted to will herself to disappear. When that failed, she wondered if she could feign a headache and slink off to her bedchamber.

As the soup was served, Brownell stepped into the room with a solemn look on his face. "There is a caller for Lady Lizette."

"Well, send him away," her grandfather ordered.

Brownell winced. "I'm afraid he is insistent on speaking to Lady Lizette."

"Who thinks he is important enough to interrupt our dinner?" her grandfather growled.

"Her fiancé, Mr. Slade," Brownell replied.

Her grandfather's disbelieving gaze turned towards her. "Are you engaged?" he demanded, tossing his napkin onto the table.

Lizette shook her head vehemently. "I am not."

"Then why is this man here, in my home, claiming you are?" her grandfather pressed.

"I know not, but I assure you that we are not engaged," Lizette asserted.

Mr. Westcott interjected, "I met Mr. Slade when I was in Bridgwater and I can attest that he is not an honorable man."

Her grandfather pushed back his chair. "I will deal with this."

Rising, Lizette said, "If you don't mind, I would like to speak to him first."

"For what purpose?" her grandfather asked.

"We were friends once and I owe it to him to speak to him," Lizette replied.

Her grandfather looked unsure. "I do not want you to be alone when you speak to him—"

"I will go with her," Mr. Westcott said, speaking over him.

Picking up his napkin, her grandfather returned to his seat. "Very well, but make it quick. I am famished."

Lizette walked over to the door and Mr. Westcott followed

closely behind. Once they left the dining room behind, she said, "Thank you for agreeing to come with me."

"I find myself curious as to what game Mr. Slade is playing," Mr. Westcott remarked in a low voice.

"As am I, especially since he asked me to be his mistress the last time we spoke," Lizette said.

When they stepped into the entry hall, Mr. Westcott placed a hand on her sleeve and gently turned her to face him. "About what happened earlier…"

She put her hand up to stop him from speaking. "Please, I do not care to discuss that." That was the last thing she wanted to talk about.

"I think we must."

As she stared into his eyes, she saw that they sparked with vulnerability, but she didn't trust herself to say what needed to be said. Frankly, she didn't know what needed to be said. All she did know was that she was falling in love with Mr. Westcott and she didn't dare admit that to him, or anyone for that matter.

Lizette found herself nodding. "I understand, but I would prefer to wait until after we rid ourselves of Mr. Slade."

Mr. Westcott withdrew his hand. "As you wish, my lady."

With a boldness she scarcely knew she had, she said, "I would prefer if you called me by my given name."

His eyes shone with approval. "I would like that, but only if you call me by mine."

"I can agree to that, Tristan."

With a broad smile, he offered his arm and said, "Let us go dispatch Mr. Slade- together."

Chapter Fourteen

Tristan was smiling as he led Lizette to the drawing room. He shouldn't be, but he was. He had managed to properly embarrass himself earlier with Lizette when he had almost kissed her. He wanted to feel her soft lips on his. Heaven knows that he would have if Lady Anne hadn't walked in when she did.

He had never let his guard down with a woman before. To do so could mean that he would be forced into an unwanted marriage or end up in a duel, as it had with his brother. But it was different with Lizette. He trusted her not to be careless with his feelings, even the ones that once would have shamed him.

Blazes.

What was happening to him? He had never in his life ever felt this way towards anyone. He could feel the barriers around his heart starting to crack, and he wasn't as afraid as he once was.

Lizette's feet faltered by the door and she looked up at him. "Thank you for accompanying me," she said.

"It is my pleasure."

"I do hope the conversation will go better than it did the last time I spoke with Mr. Slade."

"It will."

"How can you be so sure?"

Tristan placed his other hand over hers. "Because this time, I am here with you, and I won't let Mr. Slade treat you with any disrespect."

Lizette gave him a grateful smile before she continued on into the drawing room.

Mr. Slade had been pacing in the small room, but he had stopped when they entered the room. His eyes narrowed slightly at the sight of Tristan.

"What are you doing here?" he demanded.

Tristan dropped his hand to the side. "I have been tasked with accompanying Lady Lizette to speak to you."

"That isn't necessary," Mr. Slade said with a wave of his hand. "I would like to speak to Lizette privately."

"I'm afraid that is not possible," Tristan responded.

"Why is that?" Mr. Slade asked.

"Because I don't trust you," Tristan said plainly.

Mr. Slade scoffed before turning his attention towards Lizette. "Is his presence truly required here?"

Lizette nodded. "It is. My grandfather requested it," she replied. "What is it that you want, Mr. Slade?"

With a frown, Mr. Slade asked, "Since when did you stand on formalities?"

"I suppose it was around the time you asked me to be your mistress," Lizette shot back.

Mr. Slade had the decency to look ashamed. "I was wrong to do so, and I have come humbly to ask for your forgiveness."

Lizette clasped her hands in front of her. "Thank you for that, but I must ask why you announced yourself as my betrothed?"

"Your butler wouldn't let me see you otherwise and what I had to say was of utmost importance," Mr. Slade said as he retrieved a gold band from his jacket pocket. "I came to ask you to marry me."

Lizette stared at the ring. "I beg your pardon?"

Mr. Slade dropped down to one knee in front of her and held the ring up. "I know this is rather sudden, but after you left, I realized that I loved you."

"You love me?" Lizette repeated.

"I do," Mr. Slade replied. "And when I read that you were Lord Ashington's granddaughter in the newssheets, I knew it was a sign for us to be together."

Tristan stifled the groan on his lips. So that is what this was about.

"Mr. Slade…" Lizette started.

He cut her off. "It is Colin, if you don't mind."

Lizette pressed her lips together. "Colin, I'm sorry, but I can't marry you," she said. "I don't love you."

Mr. Slade looked up at her in disbelief. "You are turning me down?"

"I am," she replied.

"But I know you care for me," Mr. Slade pressed.

"I did, but that was a long time ago. We are both such different people now."

"We are not so very different," he argued. "I am still that boy that declared his love before I went off to school."

"I will always look back at those memories with much fondness, but our futures are not entwined. Not anymore."

His voice took on a hard edge as he asked, "Is this because I am not a member of your precious high Society?"

"That has nothing to do with it," Lizette replied.

Mr. Slade lowered the ring but remained on his knee. "I must admit that this went very different than I had imagined," he said. "With your elevated status, I am finally in a position to marry you."

"I bet her dowry meant nothing to you," Tristan muttered.

Mr. Slade looked the epitome of innocence. "I want to marry Lizette because I love her."

"And when did you decide this?" Tristan asked. "Before or after you were flirting with the barmaid?"

Mr. Slade glared at him. "You turned my Lizette against me," he said, rising.

"She was never yours to begin with," Tristan challenged. "Besides, I only have the utmost respect for Lady Lizette."

With his finger wagging, Mr. Slade seethed, "This was all part of your plan. You want Lizette for yourself."

"I have no such plan."

"I won't let you get away with this," Mr. Slade declared.

"I tire of your baseless accusations. There is no truth to any of it," Tristan said.

Mr. Slade took a step towards Lizette. "Don't you see what Mr. Westcott is trying to do?" he asked with a hint of a plea in his voice. "He is trying to keep us apart."

Lizette sighed. "There is no 'us', Colin," she said. "Furthermore, Mr. Westcott has done nothing nefarious. He has only treated me with kindness."

"Surely you can't be that naïve?" Mr. Slade asked. "He only wants you for your dowry and lands."

"You are wrong. Mr. Westcott and I have no understanding between us," Lizette informed him.

Mr. Slade reached out and grabbed her sleeve. Then he walked her a short distance away. He leaned closer and whispered something to her.

Lizette's eyes darted towards Tristan before she responded in a hushed tone to Mr. Slade. It was evident that he did not like what was being said because he dropped his arm and took a step back, his nostrils flaring.

"You will regret this," Mr. Slade growled.

"I don't think I will," came Lizette's quick response.

"I loved you when you were nothing, but now you think you are better than me."

"I think no such thing, Colin."

Mr. Slade turned his heated gaze towards Tristan. He

approached him, coming to a stop in front of him, and saying, "You think you are so clever, but we both know what this is about."

"Please enlighten me. Because for the life of me, I have no idea what you are talking about," Tristan remarked in a bored tone.

"You are just trying to lift her skirt," Mr. Slade growled.

Tristan tensed. "How dare you speak so crassly in front of a lady."

"You don't deny it, then?"

Tristan balled his hands into tight fists. "I will not dignify that with a response," he said. "It is time for you to leave. You are no longer welcome here."

"This is not your home," Mr. Slade mocked. "You have no authority here."

Lord Ashington's voice came from the doorway. "You are right, but it is *my* home, and I am asking you to leave."

Mr. Slade took a step back and shifted his gaze to Lord Ashington. "I apologize for the intrusion, my lord. I assure you that it won't happen again."

"See that it doesn't," Lord Ashington said.

Turning towards Lizette, Mr. Slade dropped into an exaggerated bow. "Good evening, my lady," he drawled.

No one spoke as Mr. Slade stormed out of the drawing room.

Once the main door was slammed closed, Lord Ashington muttered, "What an insufferable man."

Tristan approached Lizette and asked, "Are you all right?"

"I am," she replied. "Although, I have never seen that side of Colin before."

"He had no right to say such things to you," Tristan said.

"He was just angry."

"No one should speak to you in such a horrific manner."

Lizette gave him a weary smile. "I'm sorry he took his

anger out on you, as well. He tried to convince me that you wanted me as your mistress."

Tristan reared back slightly. "That is not the least bit true."

"I know," Lizette said. "I told him that was not indicative of the man that I have come to know."

"Regardless, I can handle Mr. Slade," he stated. "It is you that I am worried about."

"There is no reason to worry about me, but I think it might be best if I retired for the evening," Lizette said, her eyes drawing down to the floor. "I fear that I might not make the best company."

Tristan reached out and placed his hand on her sleeve. "Must you go?" he asked. "I would prefer if you stayed."

Bringing her gaze up, she asked, "You would?"

"I don't know why you sound so surprised," he replied. "You always make the evening much more bearable."

A slow smile erased the creases between her brows. "That almost sounded like you were complimenting me."

"That was my intention."

"Then I have no choice but to stay for dinner," Lizette said.

Tristan returned her smile. "Wonderful."

Lord Ashington cleared his throat. "Now that we have that resolved, shall we return to our supper?"

With great reluctance, Tristan lowered his hand to his side. "I think that is a fine idea."

Lizette walked over to her grandfather and accepted his proffered arm. "Poor Aunt Anne might think we have forgotten about her."

"I do hope our soup hasn't gotten cold," Lord Ashington said as he started leading his granddaughter out of the drawing room.

Tristan trailed behind as he listened to them converse.

Once they arrived outside the dining room, Lord

Ashington kissed Lizette on the cheek and said, "Go on ahead. I need to speak to Tristan for a moment."

Lizette nodded before she headed into the dining room.

Lord Ashington turned to face him, a solemn look on his face. "I thought you were going to come to blows with Mr. Slade."

"I was tempted."

"I imagine so," Lord Ashington said. "He made some rather disparaging comments to Lizette and you."

"It was nothing that I couldn't handle, but I do hope Lizette doesn't take his words to heart. They were just the words of a desperate man."

Lord Ashington placed a hand on Tristan's shoulder. "Thank you for taking such great care of Lizette. You are a good friend to her."

Friend? Is that what Lord Ashington thought he was to her?

Tristan tipped his head. "It has been my honor, sir."

"You are a good man," Lord Ashington said before he removed his hand.

As he followed Lord Ashington into the dining room, Tristan's eyes landed on Lizette and she rewarded him with a bright smile. In that moment, he knew he didn't just want to be friends with her. But what did he want?

Love.

Where had that thought even come from? He didn't love Lizette. He couldn't. But the more he thought on it, the more of a possibility that it might be true. Which both terrified and excited him at the same time.

"You are being awfully quiet this morning," Mrs. Everly

commented as she stepped back and scrutinized Lizette's appearance.

Lizette smoothed down her jonquil gown and said, "I'm afraid I have a lot on my mind."

"Anything you wish to share?"

Did she dare admit the pesky feelings that she had developed for Mr. Westcott? She knew she could confide in Mrs. Everly, but she thought it might be best if she kept her thoughts to herself, at least for the time being. She needed to sort them out on her own before she admitted it out loud. Frankly, they were too discombobulated anyways.

Knowing that Mrs. Everly was still waiting for a response, she replied, "Not at this time."

"Well, if you change your mind, I am willing to listen."

"Thank you," Lizette said.

Mrs. Everly smiled, as if she were privy to a secret. "Now, you best hurry if you want to eat breakfast in the dining room," she encouraged.

"I believe I shall."

As Lizette walked over to the door, Mrs. Everly's cheery voice stopped her. "Do try to avoid kissing Mr. Westcott today."

Her head whipped around. "Pardon?"

Mrs. Everly's smile grew. "Surely you didn't think your actions would have gone unnoticed by the household staff of this grand townhouse."

She groaned. Did that mean her grandfather knew? Would he force Mr. Westcott and her into an arranged marriage because of the compromising situation they were caught in?

Lizette went to sit on the settee and asked, "Am I ruined?"

"Hardly," Mrs. Everly said. "Although, if you were caught by anyone other than Lady Anne, I do worry about the repercussions of your actions."

"We didn't even kiss," Lizette shared.

"But you were about to, and an almost kiss can be just as scandalous."

Lizette bit her lower lip as she dared to admit, "I wish he had kissed me."

Mrs. Everly considered her response for a moment before asking, "May I offer some advice?"

"Please do."

Mrs. Everly's voice started off slow. "Love is patient. Do not rush into anything that you want to last forever."

"I said nothing about love."

"You didn't have to," Mrs. Everly said.

Lizette's shoulders slumped. "I am just afraid of making a misstep, considering Mr. Westcott has given me no indication that he favors me."

"He did almost kiss you," Mrs. Everly pointed out.

Lowering her gaze to her lap, Lizette said, "Perhaps I made a mistake in coming to Town."

"Why do you say that?"

"I should be mourning my mother, not traipsing around like a love-craved debutante," she said.

"You are doing no such thing."

Lizette huffed. "Aren't I?" she asked. "I almost let Mr. Westcott kiss me last night and I am hoping that he will try again."

Mrs. Everly came to sit down next to her on the settee. "There is no shame in exploring your feelings for Mr. Westcott."

"I don't even know what I am feeling for him," she admitted. "He just keeps drawing me in and I should be pushing him away."

"Why do you want to push him away?"

"Because what if I develop the same disease my father and grandmother had?"

"Then so be it."

Lizette jumped up from her seat. "No, I refuse to shackle Mr. Westcott to a broken woman."

"You are most assuredly not broken, my dear, and, furthermore, you don't know the future," Mrs. Everly said. "You might not even start to develop symptoms."

"But what if I do?" she asked. "Would that be fair to Mr. Westcott?"

"I daresay that you aren't giving Mr. Westcott enough credit."

"It is better for me to push him away now than continue down this path."

Mrs. Everly sighed. "Be careful what you push away. I would think hard before you walk away from Mr. Westcott."

Lizette's attention was drawn to the birds that were chirping merrily on a tree that was just outside of her window. They were being entirely too cheerful for such an early hour.

Mrs. Everly continued. "Promise me that you won't do anything too hasty right now. Just try to enjoy the moment."

She knew Mrs. Everly's advice was sound, but her heart was just as befuddled as her thoughts were.

Lizette bobbed her head. "I can agree to that."

"Good," Mrs. Everly said, rising. "Now, go enjoy your breakfast while I clean up your bedchamber."

As if on cue, her stomach growled, causing her to laugh. "I am rather famished this morning." She walked over to the door and stopped. "Thank you, Mrs. Everly."

"You don't need to thank me."

"But I feel as if I should," Lizette said. "I am most grateful that you decided to make the trek to London."

"It hardly felt like a trek, considering Mr. Westcott gave the direction that I was to sit inside the posh coach."

Lizette smiled. "That was most thoughtful of him," she acknowledged before she stepped into the hall.

She headed towards the dining room on the main level and tipped her head at Brownell as she passed by him in the entry hall. As she stepped into the dining room, she saw her grandfather was sitting at the head of the table and he was reading the newssheets.

He placed the paper down and rose. "Good morning," he said.

Lizette waved him back down and greeted him in kind before sitting down to his right. "Anything of note in the morning newspaper?"

"I'm afraid not," her grandfather replied. "The war is wreaking havoc on the Continent, but it should be over in due time."

"I hope so."

Her grandfather picked up the paper and folded it, placing it back down onto the table. "Forgive me. I should not have brought up the war to you."

"Why is that?"

"It is unsavory to speak of the war in front of a lady."

"But I am your granddaughter."

"You are still a lady."

A footman placed a cup of chocolate in front of her and Lizette immediately reached for it. After she took a sip, she said, "I have not had my head under a bushel. I know there is a war going on and I find that I am most curious about it."

"There is nothing 'curious' about a war. It is a terrible plight that we find ourselves in and our own people are suffering because of it."

"I am sorry. I did not mean to make light of the situation."

Her grandfather's face softened. "It is I who should apologize," he said. "I'm afraid I can get passionate about certain topics. You should see how I speak about water."

Lizette placed her cup back onto the saucer. "I read about how you lobbied for clean water in the rookeries, and I find that admirable."

"Sadly, not everyone shares your opinion. It is an uphill

battle in Parliament because of the enormous cost associated with such an undertaking."

"Doing the right thing isn't always easy."

"No, it is not," her grandfather agreed. "But I do believe we could save lives by giving the poor access to clean water. Your father was the one who convinced me of that."

At the mention of her father, she grew solemn. "I hadn't realized he was passionate about clean water, as well."

"I hate to admit it but William was a remarkable doctor. I had wished he would have followed in my footsteps and managed the estates, but he was determined to make his own path," her grandfather shared. "He was going to find a cure for his mother or die trying." He winced. "I'm sorry. Those were a poor choice of words."

"It is all right," Lizette assured him. "Besides, I can't fault you for stating the truth."

Leaning back in his chair, her grandfather said, "Your father did love you very much. I hope you know that."

"That is what I have been told, but he sent me away."

"To protect you."

"I would have rather had a father," Lizette admitted.

As a footman placed a plate in front of her, Brownell stepped into the room and announced, "The constable has arrived, my lord."

"Send him in," her grandfather ordered.

Brownell departed and it was only a moment before a portly man stepped into the room. He had red hair, bushy sideburns and his nose was abnormally large.

The constable bowed. "My lord," he murmured. "I apologize for arriving at such an early hour but your note said it was of the utmost importance."

"That it is." Her grandfather gestured towards her. "Allow me the privilege of introducing you to my granddaughter, Lady Lizette."

The constable turned his gaze towards her. "My lady," he

said. "From what I surmised from the note, the man you saw in Hyde Park was the same person who tried to abduct you from a coaching inn."

"That is correct," Lizette confirmed.

"Can you describe this man?"

"He was tall with dark hair," Lizette started. "He had a scar above his right eye and he had these beady eyes that seemed to bore into your soul."

The constable seemed to acknowledge her words before asking, "Is there anything else that would help distinguish this man from others?"

Lizette grew silent. "He had terrible breath."

Frowning, the constable said, "Based upon your description, it will be difficult to find this man and arrest him."

Her grandfather spoke up. "But it isn't impossible."

"Nothing is impossible, but I would recommend hiring a Bow Street Runner to investigate this case," the constable advised. "My case load is nearly full, and I don't have the time to go around smelling people's breaths."

"You forget yourself," her grandfather said, his voice growing stern.

The constable put his hand up. "I did not mean to insult Lady Lizette, nor do I intend to make light of the situation, but I just wanted to be upfront, so you don't have unrealistic expectations."

"There is nothing that you can do?" Lizette asked.

"I could have one of my men stand outside of your townhouse but that seems wholly unnecessary since there are more than enough servants that can protect you," the constable replied.

"You are dismissed," her grandfather abruptly stated.

The constable tipped his head. "Good day, my lord."

After the constable departed from the room, her grandfather muttered a few curse words under his breath at the expense of the lawmaker.

"It will be all right," she attempted. "He was right in the assumption that there are enough servants to watch over me."

"I had been warned that constables were useless, but I didn't think he would be so dismissive of your situation."

"He appears to be a busy man."

"Or he is incompetent at his job," her grandfather countered. "Regardless, I do think I will take his advice and hire a Bow Street Runner."

Lizette perked up in her seat. "I have read the most fascinating stories about Bow Street Runners in the newssheets."

Her grandfather looked amused. "I doubt that their lives are that exciting."

"How could they not be?" Lizette asked. "They solve crimes and arrest criminals."

As he pushed back his chair, her grandfather said, "I will be sure to introduce you to the Bow Street Runner when he comes to meet with me."

"I would like that very much."

Her grandfather rose. "Do you have any plans for today?"

"I'm sure Aunt Anne has a host of things to do today, including waiting in the drawing room for callers."

"I wish you luck with that." Her grandfather leaned in and kissed her on the cheek. "I am glad that you are here, Lizette."

"As am I."

With an approving nod, her grandfather departed from the dining room, leaving her to her own thoughts. She had meant what she had told him. She was glad that she was here, with him and Lady Anne, but she did miss the quiet life of the countryside. Life wasn't nearly as complicated there.

Chapter Fifteen

Tristan sat at his desk as he reviewed a ledger. He had to get work done, but his mind kept straying towards Lizette... again. This would not do. She had found a place in his thoughts, holding him captive. But this was not the time or place to dwell on Lizette. His first priority was, and always would be, his legacy, and he needed to prove to Lord Ashington- and himself- that he could proficiently manage the estates.

Lord Roswell's voice came from the doorway. "Good morning," he greeted.

"Good morning," Tristan said as he closed his book. There was no point in trying to pretend that he was working now.

His friend walked further into the room. "I was hoping to persuade you to join me for a round of boxing at Gentleman Jackson's."

"I find that I am amenable to that," he replied. "I could use the break." Perhaps boxing would help clear his head and he would be able to stop constantly thinking about Lizette.

Lord Roswell's eyes roamed over his desk. "You work entirely too much."

"Estates don't run themselves," Tristan said.

"Or you can be the second son, the spare, and do as you please," Lord Roswell joked.

Tristan leaned back in his seat. "You seem to forget that I used to live in the shadow of my brother."

Coming to sit down in a chair that faced the desk, Lord Roswell said, "Yes, but now you are the heir, and you will be a marquess one day."

"I hope that day won't come for many years," Tristan stated. "I still have loads to learn from Lord Ashington."

Lord Roswell glanced over his shoulder and asked, "Do you want to explain why your butler seemed relieved when I waved him off from announcing me?"

Tristan groaned. "He has been acting standoffish since I tried to have a conversation with him yesterday."

"Why would you want to converse with your butler?"

"It was Lady Lizette's idea," he replied. "She encouraged me to learn more about the lives of my servants."

"That seems odd."

Tristan nodded. "I tried the same thing with a maid and now she avoids me whenever we meet in the hall."

Lord Roswell chuckled. "I would have liked to witness those conversations."

"They did not go well."

"I would imagine not," Lord Roswell said. "Servants like to go about their jobs, keeping their heads down and trying to avoid drawing too much attention to themselves."

"That is what I tried to explain to Lady Lizette, but she tried to convince me otherwise."

Lord Roswell gave him a knowing look. "Lady Lizette seems to have a hold on you."

"I disagree," Tristan lied. "We are just friends."

"You are friends now?" Lord Roswell asked. "That is disconcerting, because I have been your only friend for many years."

"I have more friends."

Lord Roswell put his hands up. "I have yet to see any," he teased.

"I am just too busy to lollygag. I have work I need to see to."

Lowering his hands, his friend replied, "Which is a problem. You need to step away from the demands on your time and learn to enjoy yourself."

"Did I not just agree to go boxing with you?"

"It is much more than that," Lord Roswell replied. "I hope, one day, that you will discover there is more to life than work."

"Not for me."

Lord Roswell smirked. "Why do I feel as if I talk in circles with you?"

Tristan rose from his desk and walked over to the drink cart. "Would you care for something to drink?"

"I would, but only one drink. I need to have a clear mind when I wallop you in boxing."

As he picked up the decanter, Tristan decided to share, "I did something intolerably stupid last night."

"That doesn't sound like you."

Tristan poured two glasses and placed the decanter down. "I almost kissed Lady Lizette," he admitted.

"Where? How?" Lord Roswell asked. "I need more details."

He picked up the glasses and went to hand one to Lord Roswell. "We were having a frank conversation and I felt drawn to her in a way that I have never felt for another woman."

"That is good, but what stopped you from kissing Lady Lizette?"

"Lady Anne," Tristan said. "She walked in right before we kissed in the drawing room, and proceeded to chastise us for the compromising situation she found us in."

"She wasn't wrong."

Tristan frowned. "Whose side are you on?"

"There are no sides," Lord Roswell admonished. "You are lucky she didn't demand you marry Lady Lizette."

"I don't think Lady Anne likes me enough to marry her niece."

"Regardless, you can't go about kissing women, and not expect some sort of repercussions for your actions," Lord Roswell advised. "I thought you would have learned your lesson from your brother."

"I am not my brother," Tristan said firmly.

"No, you are not. But in this one instance, you are similar," Lord Roswell remarked.

Tristan tightened the hold on his glass. "If Lady Anne had demanded that we should marry, I would have agreed."

Lord Roswell lifted his brow. "Would you have been happy in an arranged marriage?"

"With Lady Lizette, I believe I would."

"That is not a good way to start off a marriage," Lord Roswell said. "It is far better to marry the woman of your choosing."

Tristan didn't dare admit that a marriage to Lady Lizette didn't sound terrible, but hadn't he decided he wanted a woman that he wouldn't be able to fall in love with?

Lord Roswell took a sip of his drink, then asked, "Unless Lady Lizette is the woman of your choosing?"

"She is tolerable, I suppose."

"I contend that Lady Lizette is more than tolerable, and it doesn't hurt that she is incredibly beautiful."

Tristan knew that his friend was trying to bait him but he refused to confess his feelings for Lady Lizette.

His butler stepped into the room and announced, "Mr. Greydon Campden would like a moment of your time, sir."

"Send him in—"

His words had barely left his mouth before his butler disappeared into the hall to do his bidding.

Lord Roswell chortled. "I think it might be best if you stop trying to converse with your staff."

"I agree."

Rising, Lord Roswell said, "I should go."

"You are welcome to stay," Tristan encouraged. "It shouldn't take long and then we can depart for Gentleman Jackson's."

Lord Roswell returned to his seat. "Who is this Mr. Campden anyways?"

"He is a Bow Street Runner."

His friend's brow shot up. "Why on earth do you need to speak to a Bow Street Runner?"

"You will see."

A tall, burly man walked into the room and he was wearing a red waistcoat, which was indicative of his position as a Bow Street Runner. His alert eyes searched the room before landing on Tristan.

"I presume you are Mr. Westcott." Mr. Campden spoke in a deep voice.

"I am," Tristan said as he gestured towards a chair. "Would you care to sit?"

"I would prefer to stand." Mr. Campden reached into his jacket pocket and pulled out a piece of paper. "I was able to ascertain the information you requested."

"Very good."

Mr. Campden glanced down at the paper. "Mrs. Jane Hendre is from Bracknell, and she passed away a few months ago. She is survived by a daughter, aged eighteen, and a sister."

"Did you discover any indication as to why Lord Ashington would be sending yearly payments?" Tristan asked.

"I did not, but I spoke to her neighbors. They all said that

Mrs. Jane Hendre was a pleasant enough woman, and no one had any disparaging words about her." The Bow Street Runner shoved the paper back into his pocket. "I did dig deeper and discovered that the manor she lived at was purchased by Lord Crewe."

Tristan stared back at the man in disbelief. Was it possible that Mrs. Hendre was, in fact, his mistress?

Mr. Campden smirked. "I know what you are thinking, and I had the same thought. But no one remembers Lord Crewe visiting Bracknell."

"Lord Crewe did die many years ago, and recollections could vary."

"Perhaps, but why guard that secret so fiercely?" Mr. Campden asked.

"Mr. Crewe might have wanted to spare his wife the embarrassment of keeping a mistress," Tristan suggested.

Mr. Campden shrugged. "I do not pretend to know about matters of the heart. The only thing I can confirm was that her sister, a Mrs. Everly, was her only known visitor."

Tristan gave the Bow Street Runner an odd look. "Did you say Mrs. Everly?"

"I did."

Surely that couldn't be a coincidence.

With a curious look, Lord Roswell asked, "What is it?"

"I know Mrs. Everly," Tristan replied. "At least, I believe I do."

"How is that possible?"

Tristan pointed towards the ceiling. "Lady Lizette's house-keeper, and now lady's maid, is named Mrs. Everly."

"Are you sure it is the same one?" Lord Roswell asked. "Everly isn't an entirely uncommon surname."

Mr. Campden crossed his arms over his wide chest. "I don't believe in coincidences."

"Neither do I," Tristan said. "I believe it is time I have a frank conversation with Mrs. Everly and I hope I can get to the truth of the matter."

"I can speak to her," Mr. Campden offered.

"That won't be necessary." Tristan worried that Mr. Campden wouldn't be as gentle with Mrs. Everly as he would be. Furthermore, he didn't want word to get back to Lady Lizette that she had been mistreated at his direction.

"Very good, sir," Mr. Campden said.

"Did you have any success on the other matter at hand?" Tristan asked.

"I did not," Mr. Campden replied, "but I will continue to monitor Lord Ashington's townhouse and look for any signs of Lady Lizette's attacker."

Tristan truly hoped this wouldn't be a cat and mouse game, where Lady Lizette's attacker had the advantage. "Please do. Lady Lizette's safety is of the utmost importance."

Mr. Campden tipped his head before he departed from the study.

Tristan picked up his glass and took a long, lingering sip. Who was this Mrs. Hendre and how did Mrs. Everly play into all of this? There were too many questions and Lord Ashington was being tight-lipped about it all. What would happen if he confronted Lord Ashington with what he did know? Would the marquess fill in the gaps or would he keep silent?

Lord Roswell rose and asked, "Dare I ask what is going on?"

"Trust me, you don't want to know," Tristan replied, putting his glass down. "But I could really use the excuse to hit something."

Lord Roswell grinned. "That is only if you get a shot in."

"I most assuredly will."

Lizette's back was starting to ache as she sat rigid on the settee. She was growing tired of Lord Simon prattling on and on about his last hunting trip. At least, that is what she thought he was still speaking of. Frankly, she had lost interest ages ago and her mind continuously strayed to Tristan. She hoped that she would be able to see him today. Just one glimpse of him always raised her spirits.

Her aunt nudged her arm and asked, "Don't you agree, Lizette?"

"I do," Lizette replied, not entirely sure what she had just agreed to.

Lord Simon smiled broadly. "Wonderful," he said. "I will be looking forward to our carriage ride through Hyde Park tomorrow."

Lizette forced a smile to her face. "As will I." It was her own fault for woolgathering and ignoring the boring lord.

Rising, Lord Simon said, "I shall return tomorrow during the fashionable hour." He bowed. "Good day, ladies."

After the lord had departed, her aunt shook her head and said, "You must be present when gentlemen come to call on you."

"I grow tired of them talking about themselves and their many accomplishments," Lizette admitted. "Besides, I daresay that Lord Simon didn't even notice- or care- that I was wool-gathering."

"Lord Simon would be an advantageous marriage for you."

"I could never marry someone so utterly boring and pretentious."

"You need to give your suitors a chance to woo you."

"I will pass."

Her aunt sighed. "You are stubborn, much like your father was," she said. "Dare I ask what you are looking for in a suitor?"

An image of Tristan came to her mind. Not only was he

devilishly handsome, but he listened to the things she said and didn't say. And she loved the way he looked at her, with a genuine interest for who she really was. No one else had looked at her quite like that.

"I shall know it when I find it," Lizette said.

"That didn't entirely answer my question."

Lizette reached for her teacup and took a sip to delay her response. She didn't dare admit her feelings out loud for Tristan, especially to her aunt. She would see right through her and know that she had deep feelings for him.

Her aunt gave her a knowing look. "I see that you have no intention of expanding on your response."

"Is it so obvious?" Lizette asked as she returned the cup to the saucer.

"To me, but I must wonder if this is all because of Mr. Westcott."

Lizette tensed. "Why do you say that?"

"I would be blind if I did not notice the growing attraction between you and Mr. Westcott, and I did catch you in a compromising situation in the drawing room."

"Nothing happened."

"But it would have if I had not arrived when I did," her aunt said.

Lizette did recognize that her aunt had a point, but she didn't want to continue this conversation.

Fortunately, Brownell stepped into the room and announced, "Miss Bolingbroke and Lady Esther Harington have come to call."

"Send them in," her aunt ordered.

After the butler departed, it was only a moment before Miss Bolingbroke and a blonde-haired young woman stepped into the room.

Lizette perked up at the sight of her friend. "Good morning, Miss Bolingbroke," she greeted.

Miss Bolingbroke smiled. "I hope it is all right, but I

brought along Lady Esther," she said as she gestured towards the young woman. "Since you are new in Town, I thought you would like to meet one of my friends."

"That was most thoughtful," Lizette remarked before turning her attention towards Lady Esther. "It is a pleasure to meet you."

Lady Esther dropped into a curtsy and murmured, "Likewise."

Her aunt waved a hand over the tea service. "Would you care for a cup of tea?"

Miss Bolingbroke bobbed her head. "I would," she said as she sat down across from them. "I do not think I could ever tire of tea."

"That is the way I feel about chocolate," Lizette remarked.

"I must admit that I am not a fan of chocolate," Miss Bolingbroke shared. "It has just never appealed to me."

Lizette feigned outrage. "I am not sure if we can be friends, then," she joked.

Miss Bolingbroke laughed. "I hadn't realized that was a deciding factor on whether or not we could be friends."

Lady Esther sat down in an upholstered armchair. "I like chocolate," she shared in a soft voice. "I drink it every morning with my breakfast."

"As do I," Lizette said, "at least since I arrived in Town."

"But not before?" Miss Bolingbroke asked.

Lizette shook her head. "My boarding school did not serve chocolate and it was a commodity that my mother and I could scarcely afford."

"Which boarding school did you attend?" Lady Esther asked.

"It was a small school that was near Bridgwater, which is where I grew up," Lizette replied. "It only had ten students, but we received a thorough education."

"How lovely," Miss Bolingbroke said. "My parents sent me to a boarding school in Ponders End, Middlesex, and Mrs.

Tyler was relentless in ensuring we were properly prepared to enter Society."

Her aunt interjected, "That is a fine school."

"It is, but I would have preferred to be educated by a governess as Lady Esther had been," Miss Bolingbroke remarked.

"I had no choice in the matter," Lady Esther said. "My father thought it would be best if I remained at home."

"Your father recently married, did he not?" her aunt asked.

Lady Esther grimaced, but quickly schooled her features. "He did, and my," she hesitated, "stepmother is expecting."

"That is wonderful news," her aunt said as she extended her a cup of tea.

Lady Esther accepted the cup and responded, "I suppose it is."

Miss Bolingbroke spoke up. "Lord Mather married one of Esther's friends," she shared before taking a sip of her tea.

"Truly?" Lizette asked.

Lady Esther frowned. "Susanna was many years older than me, mind you, but we grew up together since our parents had neighboring estates. As you can imagine, it has been rather difficult to come to terms with."

"I'm sorry," Lizette said, unsure of what she should say.

"There is no reason to apologize," Lady Esther responded. "Everyone else has been elated by the marriage, especially now that Susanna is increasing. My father has made no secret that he hopes it is a boy."

"Would he be terribly disappointed if it was a girl?" Lizette inquired.

Lady Esther bobbed her head. "He wants an heir, so my cousin doesn't inherit," she said. "My father is worried that Daniel would run the estate into the ground, if given the chance."

"That is unfortunate," her aunt remarked.

"It is," Lady Esther agreed. "Daniel has always been somewhat lazy in his endeavors, and he has a fondness for betting on the horse races."

"Sadly, that isn't an uncommon vice for gentlemen," her aunt expressed.

"No, it is not," Lady Esther said. "But my father uses that as a further example that he needs to have more children, specifically, males."

A silence descended over the room and Lizette took that opportunity to take a sip of her tea. She could hear the pain in Lady Esther's voice, and it saddened her. She had so many questions, but she didn't dare bring them up now.

Brownell stepped into the room and announced, "Lord Roswell has come to call for Lady Lizette." He met her gaze. "Are you receiving callers at this time?"

Her aunt answered for her. "She is."

After Brownell departed, Lizette couldn't help but notice that Miss Bolingbroke had smoothed out her pale blue gown and was now fidgeting with her hands in her lap.

Lord Roswell stepped into the room and his gaze landed on Miss Bolingbroke. "Anette?" he asked. "I hadn't expected to see you here."

"I could say the same of you," Miss Bolingbroke said with a tightness to her words.

He stared at Miss Bolingbroke for a moment longer than what would be considered proper before turning his attention towards Lizette. "I do hope I am not intruding."

"You are doing no such thing," Lizette rushed to assure him. "Would you care to sit down and join us?"

"It would be my pleasure," Lord Roswell said as he went to sit down next to Miss Bolingbroke on the settee.

Miss Bolingbroke shifted on the settee, creating more distance between them.

Lizette picked up the teapot and asked, "Would you care for some tea, my lord?"

"I would, thank you," Lord Roswell replied.

No one spoke as she poured the tea and extended a cup to Lord Roswell.

Knowing what was expected of her as a host, Lizette addressed Lord Roswell. "Are you acquainted with Lady Esther Harington?"

Lord Roswell turned his attention towards Lady Esther and tipped his head. "I have not had the privilege."

A blush formed on Lady Esther's cheeks as she ducked her head.

Miss Bolingbroke abruptly rose, causing Lord Roswell to awkwardly stand with his teacup in his hand. "I just remembered that I have an appointment that I am unable to miss." She turned her attention towards Lady Esther. "Shall we?"

Rising, Lady Esther said, "That would be for the best."

After the two ladies departed from the room, Lord Roswell sat down and placed his teacup onto the table in front of him.

Lizette found herself curious about one thing. "May I ask how you are acquainted with Miss Bolingbroke?"

"I attended Cambridge with her brother, and I spent most of the holidays with their family," Lord Roswell shared.

"I see," she murmured, even though she didn't see. That didn't explain Miss Bolingbroke's odd behavior around Lord Roswell.

Her aunt spoke up. "Will you be in attendance at Mrs. Bremerton's soiree this evening?"

"I will," Lord Roswell replied. "I was hoping to persuade Lady Lizette to sit next to me during the musical number."

"She would be honored to," her aunt said.

Why did her aunt keep answering for her? It was quite vexing. She had been hoping to sit next to Mr. Westcott, assuming he came, but now she was committed to Lord Roswell.

To Lord Roswell's credit, he shifted his gaze towards Lizette and gave her an expectant look. He most likely wanted to hear that she was in agreement, and not just take Lady Anne's word for it.

Lizette brought a smile to her face. "I will be looking forward to it."

A boyish grin came to Lord Roswell's lips. "Wonderful," he said, rising. "I will see you this evening."

"Yes, you will," Lizette responded.

Lord Roswell glanced over his shoulder at the doorway before asking, "Do you know if Miss Bolingbroke will be in attendance?"

"I do not."

His smile slipped, but only for a moment. "I was just curious, but that is neither here nor there." He bowed. "Good day, ladies."

Once Lord Roswell left, her aunt said, "That was interesting."

"It was," Lizette agreed. "It would appear that Lord Roswell's interest lies elsewhere."

"That is what I assumed as well."

A yawn slipped past Lizette's lips, and she brought her hand up to cover her mouth. "Pardon me, but I do believe I could use a nap."

Her aunt glanced at the long clock in the corner. "That is most inconvenient since you will no doubt have more suitors come to call."

"I doubt that."

"Very well. Go rest for now and I will inform Brownell that you are not available for callers at this time."

Rising, Lizette said, "Thank you."

"I believe I would benefit from a nap as well."

"Doesn't everyone?" Lizette joked as she waited for her aunt to rise.

"I can't sleep for too long or else I will never be able to fall asleep this evening," her aunt shared.

Lizette nodded her understanding. But she was having an entirely different problem than her aunt. She couldn't seem to sleep because she woke up and fell asleep thinking about Mr. Westcott, and almost every thought in between was of him.

Chapter Sixteen

The hackney came to a stop in front of Lord Ashington's townhouse and Tristan opened the door. Once he stepped onto the pavement, he took in a deep breath, grateful to leave the foul-smelling coach behind.

The door to the townhouse opened and Brownell greeted him. "Good afternoon, sir," he said.

Tristan acknowledged him with a tip of his head before he entered. "Is Lord Ashington in his study?"

"I'm afraid not," Brownell replied. "He has yet to return home from the House of Lords."

That was what Tristan had presumed, so it came as little surprise. But he had one more hurdle he had to overcome.

Glancing towards the drawing room, he asked, "Is Lady Lizette receiving callers?"

"Not at this time. She is resting."

Tristan could not have planned a more perfect time to come speak to Mrs. Everly. He had a few questions to ask her, and he didn't want to be interrupted.

"Will you inform Mrs. Everly that I wish to speak to her in the parlor?" Tristan asked as he removed his top hat.

Brownell gave him a curious look. "You wish to speak to Mrs. Everly- Lady Lizette's lady's maid?"

"Yes, I do."

The butler quickly recovered and schooled his features. "I shall see to it," Brownell said before he walked off.

Tristan placed his top hat onto a table and proceeded towards the parlor. It was a private enough room and was rarely used by the family. He stepped into the dark room and opened the drapes that covered the large windows. After he shoved the drapes aside, the room was flooded with light. He glanced out the windows and saw the gardeners were busy tending to the rose bushes.

It was a long moment before Mrs. Everly stepped into the parlor. She wasn't dressed in a maid's uniform but wore a grey dress.

There was no hesitancy in her voice as she said, "Brownell informed me that you wished to speak to me."

"I do," he responded. "Would you care to sit down?"

"No, thank you," she replied.

This was not a good way to start the conversation, but he was determined to find the answers that he was seeking.

Tristan smiled, hoping to disarm her, but it did nothing to soften her stance. Perhaps he should just say what needed to be said and be done with it.

Mrs. Everly lifted her brow. "Is there something you need, Mr. Westcott?"

He found her directness to be refreshing. "I do," he replied. "I was hoping you could help me by answering a few questions."

"What kind of questions?"

Tristan walked over to the door and closed it. He wanted to ensure this conversation stayed private, given the sensitivity of the subject.

He turned to face Mrs. Everly and asked, "Do you know a Mrs. Jane Hendre?"

Mrs. Everly stared at him for a moment, but her expression gave nothing away. Finally, she replied, "I do."

Tristan waited for her to elaborate but no more information was forthcoming. So, he continued. "Is she your sister?"

"Yes, at least she was," Mrs. Everly replied. "She passed away a few months ago."

"My condolences for your loss," Tristan said.

"Thank you," Mrs. Everly murmured. "May I go now?"

"I have a few more questions, if you don't mind."

Mrs. Everly frowned. "But I do mind," she remarked. "I have tasks that I need to see to before Lady Lizette wakes up from her nap."

"I shall strive to be quick in my questions," he said. "Do you know why Lord Ashington has been paying your sister a hefty sum each year?"

"I do."

"Will you tell me why that is?"

Mrs. Everly looked unsure. "Have you asked Lord Ashington?"

"I have, but he is not forthcoming with the information."

"There you have it, then."

Did Mrs. Everly think he was going to give up so easily? "I was hoping you could tell me," he pressed.

"It is not my place to do so."

"Whyever not?" he asked. "She was your sister."

"I am aware of that, sir," Mrs. Everly said dryly.

Tristan sighed. This was not going the way he had intended. "I am just looking for answers."

"The answers that you seek are better left undiscovered."

"How can you say that?"

Mrs. Everly pressed her lips together. "If you continue down this path, it will hurt the people you care about the most."

"I doubt that."

"It is true. Leave the past well enough alone."

"So am I to continue paying an enormous sum every year to Mrs. Hendre's daughter?" he asked. "When will it end?"

Mrs. Everly's face paled. "You know too much."

"I don't know anything."

In a soft voice, she asked, "How did you even discover Mrs. Hendre had a daughter?"

"I hired a Bow Street Runner."

"That was foolishness on your part," Mrs. Everly said as she glanced over her shoulder at the closed door. "You need to stop prying into other people's business."

Tristan put his hand up. "Please don't go. I just want to get to the truth of the matter."

Mrs. Everly huffed. "Trust me, you do not want to know the truth."

"Isn't that for me to decide?"

With a tilt of her chin, Mrs. Everly replied, "If you care for Lady Lizette, as I believe you do, you will not continue down this impossible path."

"What does this have to do with Lady Lizette?" Tristan asked.

Mrs. Everly's eyes widened and he suspected she hadn't meant to say those words. She started backing up towards the door. "You have been warned, Mr. Westcott. Lives are at stake here."

As he went to reply, Mrs. Everly opened the door and departed from the room without a parting glance.

What in the blazes was that? What had he stumbled upon? All he wanted to know was why Lord Ashington had been paying Mrs. Hendre for years. It shouldn't be so complicated, but it was. And what did Lady Lizette have to do with Mrs. Hendre? The only connection that they shared was Mrs. Everly, who was being incredibly tight-lipped on the matter.

Tristan decided it was time to visit Bracknell and meet with Mrs. Hendre's daughter. Perhaps she could shed some light on all of this. If he left now, he could arrive at the village before nightfall. But it might be best if he left at first light tomorrow.

Lizette's voice came from the doorway. "Hello, Tristan," she greeted. "May I ask why you are loitering in the parlor?"

"I am not loitering."

"What exactly are you doing then?" she asked, her eyes sparkling with mirth.

Tristan didn't dare admit that he was just conversing with Mrs. Everly so he decided to change subjects and hoped she didn't press him. "How was your nap?"

"It was delightful," she replied.

"I can't recall the last time I have taken a nap."

Lizette smiled. "What a shame."

Tristan couldn't help but notice that Lizette became more lovely when she smiled and seemed to enliven everything about her. Not that she wasn't already fascinating. To him, she was the most extraordinary person he knew.

"Will you be attending Mrs. Bremerton's soiree this evening?" Lizette asked.

Drats. Was that tonight? He would never have even entertained the thought of going if it wasn't for Lizette. He enjoyed spending as much time with her as possible. But if he went to the soiree this evening, he wouldn't be able to travel to Bracknell until tomorrow morning.

As he wrestled with his thoughts, Lizette stepped forward and lowered her voice. "I know you do not enjoy social gatherings, but I was hoping you would come."

How could he turn her down now? He felt his lips curve into a smile. "I would be happy to attend," he said. "May I sit with you during the musical number?"

She winced slightly. "Lord Roswell already asked, and I accepted."

Tristan felt his smile slip, but he caught it. He couldn't let Lizette know that he was annoyed that his friend had done something so despicable. Lord Roswell knew he had feelings for Lizette, even though he tried to deny it. Or had he been so convincing that Lord Roswell had believed him? Either way, he would have choice words with his friend at his first opportunity.

"Perhaps I can convince Lord Roswell to sit with someone else this evening," he said.

Her smile reappeared. "That would be nice."

Tristan's eyes dropped to her lips, and he knew it wouldn't take much to lean in and kiss her. But to do so without an understanding would be terribly unfair of him. Lizette deserved more than a stolen kiss in the parlor.

He cleared his throat and took a step back. "I'm afraid I must depart, but I shall see you this evening at the soiree."

"I will be looking forward to it."

He stood there, watching her, not wanting to leave, but knew it was for the best. If he didn't go now, he might do something they both would regret.

Lord Ashington's commanding voice broke through the silence. "Tristan, a word." His voice was unusually stern.

When had Lord Ashington stepped into the parlor? He had been so distracted by Lizette that he had failed to notice that they were not alone.

"I will see you tonight," Lizette said before she departed the room.

Lord Ashington closed the door and crossed his arms over his chest. "What were you thinking when you spoke to Mrs. Everly about her sister, Mrs. Hendre?" he demanded.

"I was trying to understand why you have been paying Mrs. Hendre all these years."

"That is none of your business."

Tristan reared back. "How can I properly manage your accounts if you are hiding things from me?" he asked.

"There are some things that are more important than money."

"Such as?"

Lord Ashington uncrossed his arms. "I am asking you to leave this be. Just go on with your other tasks and let me have this one secret."

Not ready to concede yet, Tristan asked, "Did you know that Mrs. Hendre died three months ago, and her daughter collected the payment?"

"I did not, but that does not change anything for me."

As he opened his mouth to continue to argue his point, Lord Ashington put his hand up, stilling his words. "Leave it, Tristan."

Tristan knew he wasn't going to get anywhere with Lord Ashington and he had no intention of stopping. He needed to root out the truth, one way or another.

Lord Ashington must have taken his silence as acceptance, so he lowered his hand. "If you will excuse me, I need to return to the House of Lords. I only came home to retrieve some documents."

Tristan didn't stop the marquess as he left the parlor, leaving him to his own thoughts. Mrs. Everly had gone straight to Lord Ashington after she had left him, and now he couldn't help but wonder how they were acquainted with one another.

But he was going to find out.

Lizette watched as her grandfather's head started to droop and it was followed by a slight snore. She exchanged an amused glance with her aunt in the darkened coach.

Her aunt's voice was soft so as not to disturb the sleeping marquess. "I wish I could fall asleep as easily as my father can."

"As do I," Lizette said.

The coach hit a rut in the road and dipped to the side.

Her grandfather's head flew up and he gave them a sheepish smile.

"My apologies, I didn't mean to fall asleep," he said. "I'm afraid I haven't been feeling well as of late."

"No harm done," her aunt assured him. "We are in for a late night. Mrs. Bremerton is known for having her soirees go into the morning hours."

"I surely hope not," her grandfather declared. "I will stay until the musical number has concluded and then I will depart."

Her aunt shifted her gaze to meet Lizette's. "Speaking of the musical number, are you pleased by the prospect of sitting next to Lord Roswell?"

"I suppose so," Lizette said. She would rather sit next to Tristan, but she didn't dare admit that to her aunt.

"You suppose so?" her aunt repeated. "Lord Roswell comes from a fine family and would be an excellent catch for you."

"I have no intention of catching him, or anyone, for that matter," Lizette said.

Fortunately for her, the coach came to a stop in front of a whitewashed, three-level townhouse and it effectively ended their conversation.

The footman placed the step down before he assisted them out of the coach. Once her feet were on the pavement, she withdrew her hand and smoothed down her pale pink gown with a square neckline.

Her grandfather extended his arms to them, and he escorted them inside. The moment they stepped into the entry hall, she realized that this was a *crush*. The entire hall was filled with people, and everyone appeared to be indulging in conversation. No one seemed to give them any heed as they headed further into the room.

Once they found a place to stand, her grandfather dropped his arms and muttered, "I hadn't realized that this soiree would be so well attended." He tugged on his cravat. "It is sweltering in here."

"It is not that bad," her aunt argued.

Lizette's eyes surveyed the hall as she tried to discover if Tristan had arrived yet. Unfortunately, she saw no sign of him, and Lord Roswell had managed to catch her eye from across the room.

He tipped his head, and she responded in kind. She hoped that he wouldn't leave the group he was conversing with to come speak to her.

But she was not so lucky.

Lord Roswell broke off from the group and approached her. He came to a stop in front of her and bowed.

"Good evening, Lady Lizette," he greeted.

She dropped into a curtsy. "Good evening, Lord Roswell," she murmured.

Lord Roswell acknowledged her grandfather and her aunt before turning his attention back towards her. "I am looking forward to sitting next to you during the musical number."

"As am I," Lizette lied.

"I have heard that Lady Emmeline is playing the pianoforte and Mr. Petersen is accompanying her on the violin."

"How wonderful," Lizette said.

"Do you play the pianoforte?" Lord Roswell asked.

"I do."

"Perhaps you will be kind enough to play a piece for me the next time I come to call," Lord Roswell said.

"I would be happy to."

Lord Roswell turned his head towards the main door and revealed, "It would appear that Mr. Westcott is making an appearance this evening."

Lizette followed his gaze and saw Tristan walking towards them, causing her heart to skip a beat. It didn't matter where she was or who she was with, but just the mere sight of him caused everything around her to stop.

Tristan stopped a short distance away and bowed. "Lady Lizette," he greeted.

"Mr. Westcott," she murmured.

His gaze left hers as he acknowledged the other people in the group, and she felt the loss of contact.

Lord Roswell addressed Tristan. "I hadn't expected you to come this evening."

"Someone convinced me otherwise," Tristan said with a glance at her, "and I didn't dare refuse her."

Her grandfather spoke up. "It is entirely too warm in here. I am going to step onto the veranda for a moment," he announced. "Would you care to join me, Lizette?"

"I would be happy to," Lizette replied as she accepted his proffered arm.

As her grandfather led her towards the rear of the townhouse, the crowd started thinning until eventually they walked down an empty corridor that opened to the veranda. "It would appear that you caught the eye of two eligible gentlemen, amongst others," he said.

"Looks can be deceiving. I do believe Lord Roswell's interest lies elsewhere and Mr. Westcott and I are just friends."

"You two didn't appear like friends this afternoon in the library."

Lizette felt a blush form on her cheeks and attempted, "We were just having a lively conversation."

Her grandfather didn't appear convinced but, thankfully, he didn't press her. They stepped onto the veranda, and he dropped his arm.

"It is much better out here," her grandfather sighed.

Lizette felt the cool night air on her skin, but she wasn't cold. It had been rather stuffy inside with so many people. "I would agree."

Her grandfather sat down on the bench. "My apologies, I

am afraid that I am not feeling well this evening. I thought by stepping outside it would provide some relief, which it did, but I am still uncomfortable."

She noted his pale face before asking, "Do you want me to retrieve Aunt Anne?"

"I think that might be for the best," her grandfather replied. "She might have some of the powder the doctor prescribed for me in her reticule."

"Wait here," she ordered.

Her grandfather grimaced. "I don't intend to go anywhere."

Lizette turned and headed into the townhouse. As she walked down the corridor, she saw Mr. Slade approaching her from the opposite direction with a purposeful stride.

What now, she thought. She didn't have time for this.

Mr. Slade stopped in front of her, blocking her path. "Good evening, Lizette."

"Good evening," she acknowledged. "If you will excuse me, I need to see to my grandfather since he is…"

He spoke over her. "Have you had a chance to consider my offer?"

She gave him a disapproving look. "I believe I made it clear that I was not interested in marrying you."

Mr. Slade reached out and grabbed her arm. "It would be in your best interest to marry me," he said in a firm tone.

"Why is that?"

"If you don't, I will tell everyone that you were raised as a country bumpkin and everyone will stop fawning over you. You would be an outcast."

Lizette arched an eyebrow. "You are resorting to blackmail now?" she asked.

"You can pretend you belong in this world, but you don't," Mr. Slade said. "You belong with me, in Bridgwater."

She tried to yank back her arm, but Mr. Slade kept a tight hold of it. "Release me," she ordered.

"Or what?" Mr. Slade mocked. "You will scream? If you do so, you will be ruined and you will have no choice but to marry me."

"I would never marry you."

Mr. Slade's eyes narrowed and she feared that she had pushed him too far. "I was hoping you would come willingly, but I see that you are not being reasonable," he grumbled as he jerked her towards a room off the hall.

"I am not going anywhere with you," she said as she dragged her feet.

"You don't have much of a choice, at least not anymore," Mr. Slade stated. "We are going to elope to Gretna Green."

Lizette started fighting against him. "You will have to kill me first," she declared. Where were all the servants? Surely, someone could help her.

Tristan's voice came from behind her, and she had never heard a more welcoming sound. "Let her go, Slade," he ordered.

Mr. Slade kept a firm hold of her as he turned them to face Tristan. "She is mine. Leave us be," he spat out.

With a clenched jaw, Tristan said, "We both know that I am not going to do that."

"Lizette wants to be with me, but she is just confused," Mr. Slade stated.

"It is you that is confused," Tristan argued.

"Do you know what I can do with forty thousand pounds?" Mr. Slade asked. "I would be the richest man in Bridgwater."

Tristan took a commanding step towards them. "I tire of this. Lady Lizette doesn't belong to you."

"But she does to you?" Mr. Slade mocked.

"I never said that."

"You didn't have to. I have seen the way that she looks at you," Mr. Slade declared. "It is revolting."

Tristan put his hands up. "How do you think this will end

for you?" he asked. "Because I assure you that you are going nowhere with Lady Lizette?"

As Mr. Slade continued to argue with Tristan, Lizette saw movement behind them and she turned her head to see Lord Roswell creeping towards them. He put his finger up to his lips, indicating she should be quiet.

Lizette brought her eyes to meet Tristan's and she saw the worry behind them, despite his whole body being tense.

In the next moment, she felt Mr. Slade release her as he crumpled to the ground, unconscious. She turned back to see Lord Roswell shaking his fist but he stopped when he met her gaze.

"That man had a hard head," Lord Roswell joked.

Tristan appeared by her side, and he asked in a concerned voice, "Are you all right?"

"I am, thanks to you and Lord Roswell."

Lord Roswell interjected, "I believe I did most of the work."

Tristan ignored his friend's attempt at humor and kept his attention solely on her. "I had seen Slade from across the room and I saw that he followed you and your grandfather when you left the hall."

Lizette gasped. "My grandfather!" she exclaimed. "He isn't feeling well, and I told him that I would fetch my aunt."

"I shall see to that," Lord Roswell said as he walked swiftly down the corridor.

Tristan gently placed a hand on her arm and encouraged, "We should depart before anyone finds us here."

Lizette glanced down at Mr. Slade's body. "What about him?"

"Let the servants tend to him when he wakes up," Tristan replied as he started leading her away from Mr. Slade.

Lizette couldn't quite believe that Mr. Slade had attempted to abduct her, right here, during the middle of a soiree. Now that the threat had passed, she found herself growing irate at her old friend. He would force her into an unwanted marriage just to receive her dowry. Had he no shame?

Tristan kept glancing her way, but he didn't say anything. She could see the questions in his eyes but she was in no mood to talk. Frankly, she just wanted to be alone to sort out her emotions.

They stepped into the entry hall and she saw her aunt was walking towards her with Lord Roswell in tow.

Her aunt stopped and said, "Thank you, Mr. Westcott, but I will see to my niece now."

Tristan dropped his hand. "As you wish."

With an approving nod, her aunt gestured that she should follow her. "We will see to your grandfather and then we will journey home, together, as a family."

Lizette gave Tristan a weak smile. "Thank you for what you did for me." She hesitated before shifting her gaze to Lord Roswell. "For what you both did for me."

"It was our pleasure," Lord Roswell said.

"Come along, dear," her aunt ordered.

As Lizette went to catch up with her aunt, she snuck a glance over her shoulder to see that Tristan was rooted in his place, watching her. How she wished she could forgo propriety and run into his comforting embrace. But she knew that would no doubt ruin her reputation and his, which was something she was not willing to risk.

Chapter Seventeen

Tristan stifled the yawn on his lips as he approached Bracknell. He had been riding since first light and he was starting to get stiff in the saddle. He couldn't wait to get off his horse and stretch, but he didn't dare until he reached the Hendres' home.

He hoped this wasn't a fool's errand, and Mrs. Hendre's daughter wasn't as tight-lipped as Lord Ashington was. But what if she was? What would he do then? Could he just accept making payments to her and live without knowing the truth? No, especially since it had something to do with Lizette.

He had to discover the truth for himself.

Tristan rode into the village and saw a group of boys playing near the side of the road. He shouted down to them, "Hello, there."

The boys stopped and looked up at him.

"Do you know where I can find the Hendres' home?" he asked.

A brown-haired boy nodded. "Yes, Mister. Everyone knows the Hendres' manor. It is the biggest home in the village." He pointed down the road. "Just keep going and you can't miss it."

Tristan reached into his waistcoat pocket and pulled out a coin. He tossed it to the boy.

The boy caught it and gave him a toothless grin. "Thank you."

He urged his horse forward and continued down the road, ignoring the smell of freshly baked bread wafting out of the inn. Perhaps he would stop on the way out to get something to eat but, for now, he was on a mission.

As he neared the edge of the village, he saw a modest manor with trees lining the road to it. He assumed that this was the home the boy was speaking of because it did stick out amongst the small cottages. He headed towards the manor and noticed the neatly trimmed bushes that sat in the garden bed.

He pulled back on the reins and waited to see if a servant would come to tend to his horse. When none exited the manor, he dismounted and secured his horse. He cautiously approached the main door and reached for the knocker. He tapped it three times against the door and waited.

And waited.

He removed his pocket watch and studied the time. He refused to leave until he spoke to Miss Hendre, but where was she? What if he had arrived too early and she was still in bed?

A noise coming from within drew his attention. The door was opened, and he was greeted by a short, white-haired woman.

"I'm sorry about the wait. My hearing isn't quite what it used to be," the woman said, wiping her hands on her white apron. "What can I help you with, Mister?"

He returned his pocket watch to his waistcoat and replied, "I was hoping to speak to Miss Hendre."

The woman pursed her lips together. "For what purpose do you wish to speak to Miss Hendre?" she asked, clearly suspicious of his motives.

"If you don't mind, that is between me and Miss Hendre."

"I do mind—"

A sweet laugh came from within the manor. "It is all right, Mrs. Riddoch," she said. "I will speak to him."

The woman turned towards the person that was hidden behind the door. "But I don't trust him," she stated in a hushed voice.

"You don't know him."

"Precisely, he is a stranger," Mrs. Riddoch said.

The young woman appeared by Mrs. Riddoch's side. She had blonde hair, high cheekbones, and despite never meeting before, there was a familiarity about her that he couldn't quite explain.

Miss Hendre smiled, revealing two faint dimples. "I am Miss Hendre. How may I help you?" she asked politely.

He stared at her, not quite sure what he should say. Everything he had intended on saying had vanished the moment he laid eyes on her. She was not at all what he was expecting.

Mrs. Riddoch sighed. "Oh dear, he has turned mute."

"You can't turn mute. That is something you are born with," Miss Hendre said. "Isn't that right, sir?"

Tristan cleared his throat. "Have we met before?"

"I assure you that we have not," Miss Hendre replied. "Would you care to come in?"

Mrs. Riddoch placed a hand on the door and declared, "Absolutely not! He could be a murderer for all we know."

Miss Hendre gave him an expectant look. "Are you a murderer?"

"I am not," Tristan responded.

"There, now that is settled. Please come in," Miss Hendre encouraged, taking a step back.

Mrs. Riddoch removed her hand from the door and slid it into the pocket of her apron. She slowly lifted a small knife and held it up. "I will have you know that we are not some defenseless females," she said.

Putting his hands up, Tristan responded, "I assure you that

I mean you no harm. I just have a few questions for Miss Hendre."

Mrs. Riddoch slid the knife back into the pocket. "I won't have you harassing Miss Hendre either. You can ask your questions, but she doesn't have to answer."

Miss Hendre gave him an apologetic look. "I'm sorry, but Mrs. Riddoch can be very protective of me."

"I find that admirable," Tristan said.

Mrs. Riddoch stood to the side to allow him entry. "You should know that Miss Hendre is not taking any suitors at this time," she informed him.

"I am not here to press a suit." He stepped into the small entry hall and noted the faded yellow-papered walls.

After Mrs. Riddoch closed the door, she gestured towards a room off the entry hall. "Let us adjourn to the drawing room."

Tristan followed Miss Hendre into the drawing room and stopped near an upholstered armchair. Miss Hendre turned back around with a curious look.

"I'm afraid I did not catch your name," she said.

He bowed. "Forgive me. My name is Mr. Tristan Westcott, and I am the heir presumptive to Lord Ashington."

Miss Hendre's eyes grew wide. "You are Mr. Westcott?"

"I am," he replied. "Do you know of me?"

"I recognize the name because of the bank note your solicitor sent." Miss Hendre walked over to a writing table and pulled out a drawer. "I wish to return it to you."

"Pardon?" He had not been expecting that. He had just assumed that she would have kept the funds, despite being for her mother.

Miss Hendre held the bank note in her hand and approached him. "I do not feel it would be fair of me to keep this money."

"Do you know what this money is for?"

She nodded. "Which is why I am not entitled to it," she

replied, extending him the bank note. "I do believe the deal ended upon my mother's death."

Tristan did not move to take the bank note. "Can you tell me what it is for?" he asked, hoping he didn't sound too eager.

Miss Hendre lifted her brow. "You do not know?"

"I do not," he admitted. "I came all this way in the hopes of discovering the truth."

"Why did you not ask Lord Ashington?" she asked as she placed the bank note onto the writing table.

"He is not of the mindset that I should know," he admitted.

Mrs. Riddoch tsked. "Then you should not be here," she admonished. "It is evident that Lord Ashington does not want you to know."

"I can't go on not knowing, especially since it could affect someone that I greatly care about," Tristan said.

Miss Hendre considered him for a moment before saying, "I think I should tell him."

"Are you mad?" Mrs. Riddoch asked. "You promised your mother that you wouldn't be careless with this secret, knowing what is at stake."

"I know, but I'm scared of what George might do," Miss Hendre said.

Tristan glanced between them. "Who is George?"

"He is... was... my fiancé," Miss Hendre replied. "I mistakenly told him the secret and I fear that he has gone half-cocked on me."

"Why do you say that?" Tristan asked.

Miss Hendre winced. "He saw it as an opportunity to make an enormous amount of money by blackmailing Lord Ashington."

Tristan tensed. "Do you believe he will go through with it?"

"I don't rightly know since I haven't seen him in over a fortnight," Miss Hendre revealed. "I had no idea he was capable of such a thing or I would never have confided in him."

"What's done is done," Mrs. Riddoch said. "You mustn't blame yourself for George's actions. At least now you know his true character and were able to break off the engagement before you were too late. A husband is much harder to rid yourself of."

Miss Hendre looked at him with a sad expression. "You must believe that I never meant to hurt anyone."

"I do," Tristan said as he heard the sincerity in her voice.

Gesturing towards the worn upholstered settees, Miss Hendre asked, "Would you care to sit?"

"I would prefer to stand, if you don't mind," Tristan replied.

A line between Miss Hendre's brow appeared. "What do you wish to know?"

"I know that Lord Ashington has been paying your mother two thousand pounds for many years, but I am unsure of the…"

Miss Hendre spoke over him. "It has been eighteen years."

"Eighteen years?" he repeated.

She nodded.

Tristan continued. "I also know that Mrs. Everly is your aunt and she works for Lord Ashington's granddaughter as a lady's maid."

"No, that isn't right. She was a housekeeper for Mrs. Kent in Bridgwater," Miss Hendre said.

"She was, but I'm afraid Mrs. Kent passed away recently," he explained. "I sent for Mrs. Everly to act as a lady's maid to see to Lady Lizette during this difficult time for her."

At the mention of Lady Lizette, Miss Hendre exchanged a glance with Mrs. Riddoch and something passed between them. He just didn't know what that was.

Tristan put his hands out wide. "I'm afraid that is all I

know and that has brought me to your door. I'm hoping you can help me now."

Miss Hendre pressed her lips together. "If I do tell you the truth, what do you intend to do with it?"

"It depends on what the truth is," Tristan replied honestly.

"I'm not sure if I like that answer, Mr. Westcott," Miss Hendre said. "I want your assurance that you will do no harm with this information, especially when it comes to Lady Lizette."

Tristan grew solemn as he dared to admit, "I care deeply for Lady Lizette, and I would never do anything that would hurt her in any way."

Miss Hendre appeared pleased by his response, but she grew silent. Finally, after a long moment, she revealed, "Lizette is my twin."

Lizette sat rigid in the opened carriage as Lord Simon prattled on about his most recent hunt and she found herself growing increasingly bored with each passing word that came out of his mouth. When he did take a breath, would he even notice that she hadn't been able to get a word in since they had left her townhouse?

Most likely not. Lord Simon was vain and pretentious. So why had she agreed to a carriage ride through Hyde Park with him? She already knew that they would not suit, but Lord Simon had not come to the same conclusion that she had.

She nodded politely, knowing what was expected of her, but she would much rather be anywhere else but here, pretending to be enthralled with his conversation.

Lord Simon drew a breath before saying, "I find your company to be most tolerable."

Tolerable? Was that supposed to be a compliment? She

wasn't quite sure, but at least he wasn't talking about hunting anymore.

He continued. "Furthermore, you are beautiful, have an impressive dowry, and are the granddaughter of Lord Ashington."

Fearing where this was leading, Lizette attempted to change subjects. "I am those things, but I also enjoy reading. Have you read anything of note lately?"

Lord Simon gave her a blank look. "I have not."

The way he answered her question caused her to prod a little. "Do you read, my lord?"

"I can read," he replied, "but I do not read for fun. Books hold little appeal to me, but I do have an extensive library at our country estate that you might enjoy."

Lizette doubted that. She had no intention of ever visiting his country estate, if she had her way. It was time to prove to Lord Simon that they were vastly different people.

"I must admit I do enjoy reading, and I devour any books that I can get my hands on," she shared.

"But you are a woman," Lord Simon said.

"I am, and I thank you for noticing," she joked.

Lord Simon didn't even crack a smile at her attempt at humor. "How could I not notice?" he asked. "With you on my arm, I would be the envy of the *ton*."

"I care not what the *ton* thinks of me."

"That is because you are beloved right now, mostly due to your dowry, but if you started to turn mad like your father did..." He stopped. "My apologies. I should never have brought up your father. It is unsavory to speak ill of the dead, especially one as odd as your father."

"You think my father was odd?"

Lord Simon gave her a peculiar look. "Don't you?" he asked.

"I think my father was troubled, but he did the best that he could, knowing the fate that was going to befall upon him."

"You are being far too generous in your assessment," Lord Simon said. "He killed himself—"

She cut him off. "He did no such thing."

"Regardless, if you started to go mad then your husband would have no choice but to lock you up in an asylum."

Lizette's eyes grew wide. "I beg your pardon?"

"Your father was an earl, but you…"

"Are just a woman," she said, finishing his thought.

Lord Simon frowned. "I mean no disrespect, but a man cannot tend to his mad wife. It is better for everyone if she is tucked away, hidden from Society."

Lizette clenched her hands in her lap. "I think it would be best if I went home now."

"Are you angry with me?" Lord Simon asked, appearing bewildered.

"Is it so obvious?"

Lord Simon sighed. "This is not how I wanted this conversation to go," he said. "I was hoping to convince you to allow me to court you."

"Surely you cannot be in earnest."

"I am," Lord Simon said. "Even with the potential risk of you going mad, your dowry is more than enough to compensate for that."

"That is a relief," she remarked dryly.

"Does this mean you will consider my courtship?" Lord Simon asked eagerly.

Lizette looked heavenward. Her sardonic comment had been lost on him and he truly believed she would entertain the thought of him being her suitor. She wasn't sure if she should pity the man or send him on his way with a tongue lashing.

Definitely a tongue lashing.

As she opened her mouth, Lord Simon spoke first. "I know I am the second son, but my older brother is sickly. There is a good chance that he will pass before he weds and have children, passing his title to me. Which means you could be a marchioness."

"At least until you lock me away in an asylum."

"Yes, but I won't try to divorce you."

"No, you will just take up a mistress."

Lord Simon blinked. "What else would you have me do?" he asked. "I will still require companionship."

Lizette was trying to curb her anger, but she couldn't believe that someone would be this intolerably stupid. Lord Simon was trying to press his suit but, by doing so, he kept saying the most idiotic things. Not once had he mentioned that he cared for her, which she suspected he didn't. He was just after her dowry.

An image of Tristan came to her mind, and she wished that he was here with her. He had never once made her feel less of a person because of her father's struggles. He had always made her feel valued and, dare she believe, loved.

Loved.

How she wished that Tristan loved her.

She suspected he cared for her, but that might just be wishful thinking on her part. Although, what if he did love her? Could she entrap him in a marriage, not knowing if she would inherit a disease that could make her mad?

Lizette felt tears burn in the back of her eyes as she blinked them back. She couldn't- no, she wouldn't- do that to Tristan. She loved him too much to even consider the possibility of marrying him. He deserved so much more than what she could give him. And what if she did inherit the disease? He would be saddled with a wife that he would be forced to get rid of.

The carriage veered off the main road and onto a less traveled one. She brought her gaze up and asked, "Where are we going?"

Lord Simon gave her a sheepish smile. "I asked the driver

to take us to a more secluded location so I could press my suit."

"I'm sorry, but my mind has been made up," she said.

"I don't think I adequately explained myself."

Lizette gave him a pointed look. "I think you spoke plainly enough."

The carriage came to a stop near a large oak tree and the driver stepped down. As he walked away, Lord Simon reached for her hand and held it up.

"I would prefer not to beg, but you leave me no choice," Lord Simon said. "I must marry you or else I will be in dire straits. My father is cutting me off and told me to find myself an heiress to marry."

Was that supposed to impress her? "Lord Simon..."

He spoke over her. "Don't say no!" he pleaded. "What if I promised not to put you in an asylum? I could just lock you in your bedchamber with a nurse and..."

Lizette slipped her hand out of his. "As tempting as that is, I'm going to have to decline your offer."

Lord Simon slid back in his seat, looking defeated. "What am I going to do now?"

"You could go work for an income," she suggested.

He scoffed. "I think not. That is entirely beneath me."

The carriage door was wrenched open, and Lizette came face to face with her attacker from the coaching inn.

"Get out," he ordered.

Lizette shook her head. "I think not."

He reached in and grabbed her arm. "I said get out!" he exclaimed as he pulled her towards him.

Lord Simon stood up, causing the carriage to rock slightly. "I do not think the lady wants to go with you."

"I don't care what the lady wants," her attacker declared. "If you don't shut your mouth, I will kill you."

Slowly, Lord Simon returned to his seat and gave her a look of regret.

Coward!

Lizette fought against her attacker, but it did little good. He was much stronger than she was and it wasn't long before she was forced out of the carriage.

He yanked her towards the trees. "It will do you no good to resist," he said. "It will only tire you out."

"Let me go!" she exclaimed, hoping that she could attract someone's attention.

Once they stepped into a grove of trees, her attacker pulled her tight against him and covered her mouth with his large, callused hand.

"No one is going to come for you, and if they do, I will kill them," the man said, his warm, foul breath against her cheek. "Do you understand?"

She nodded.

"I am going to release my hand, but if you scream, I assure you that you will regret it." He lifted his hand. "Is that better?"

"It is," she murmured.

"On the other side of these trees is a hackney," the man shared. "The driver doesn't care if you live or die so do avoid making a scene. It will only end badly for you."

"Why are you doing this?"

The man sneered. "You, my dear, are worth a pretty penny and I have no doubt that your grandfather will pay me handsomely to return you to him."

"That is what this is about?" she asked. "Money?"

"What else would it be?" The man grabbed her chin and pulled it down. "But the condition in which you are returned is up for debate."

Lizette swallowed slowly as she felt fear well up inside of her. The way the man spoke his words, she knew he was in earnest. He cared little for her. She was only a means to an end.

He put his hand out. "After you, Princess."

"I am not a princess," she said.

"You could have fooled me." He shoved her forward. "Go on, then. I don't have all day."

Lizette started walking with her head held high. She didn't dare complain that her aunt had suggested she wear her least comfortable boots on her outing with Lord Simon and she doubted she could walk very far in them, especially since she felt every rock and unevenness of the path.

Her attacker must have noticed this because he picked her up and tossed her over his shoulder as if she were nothing more than a sack of flour. "I don't have time for this," he stated.

She started pounding on his back with her fists. "Let me down."

"Calm down, Princess," he mocked.

Lizette continued until she felt herself growing light-headed by the position she found herself in. She needed to conserve her energy if she wanted to escape, but would it even be possible? Her attacker seemed rather determined to ransom her off to her grandfather.

Chapter Eighteen

Armed with information that he could scarcely believe, Tristan rode towards Lord Ashington's townhouse. He had spent long enough with Miss Hendre that he was able to ascertain the truth, but even she didn't know everything.

He suspected there was only one person that did- Lord Ashington.

Tristan had no doubt that Lord Ashington would be upset that he had disobeyed a direct order from him, but he couldn't have gone on the way he had, not knowing the truth. He didn't regret his actions, but now he had to proceed cautiously. What would he even tell Lizette? Her whole life had been built on a lie, but did he dare reveal the truth to her?

Would she hate him if he did?

That constant fear had plagued him since he had left Miss Hendre's manor. The only thing he knew for certain was that he would not use this information to harm Lizette.

He reined in his horse in front of Lord Ashington's townhouse and a servant promptly exited to retrieve his horse.

Tristan hurried up the steps and addressed Brownell as he held the door open. "Is Lord Ashington in his study?"

"Aye, sir," the butler confirmed.

Without breaking his stride, he headed towards the rear of the townhouse. He stepped inside and saw Lord Ashington was hunched over his desk, reviewing the documents in his hand.

Tristan didn't want to startle the aging marquess so he stopped in front of the desk and cleared his throat.

Lord Ashington's head flew up. "Tristan, it is just you," he sighed in relief. "I thought I was going to receive a tongue lashing from my daughter."

"Why is that?"

"She summoned the doctor after we returned home last night, and he recommended I should rest for the next few days."

"Does he know what ails you?"

"It is old age, I'm afraid," Lord Ashington replied as he shuffled the papers in his hands. "What brings you by today?"

"I need to speak to you." Tristan walked over to the door and closed it. It would be best if their conversation remained private.

Lord Ashington looked amused. "I have been expecting this."

"You have?"

"It was evident by the way you looked at Lizette the other night that you held her in high regard."

"I do, but——"

Rising, Lord Ashington walked over to the drink cart. "And it was only a matter of time until you came to ask my permission to offer for her."

Tristan blinked. "I beg your pardon?" Is that what he thought he was doing?

"Come now, you didn't think I hadn't anticipated this outcome from the moment I sent you to retrieve her." Lord Ashington picked up the decanter and removed the lid. "I couldn't have planned this any better."

"You want me to marry Lady Lizette?"

"Heavens, yes," Lord Ashington replied. "Why else would I ask for you to watch over her? I was hoping that you two would come together on your own. Which you did."

"I... uh... don't know what to say." And he was being truthful. How had he not seen Lord Ashington's hand in all of this? Was Lady Anne in on it as well?

Lord Ashington poured two drinks and placed the decanter down. "I knew you were opposed to marriage, considering your past, but I had hoped you would reconsider once you met my granddaughter."

"I am not opposed to marrying Lizette..." He stopped speaking. Had he truly just said that out loud? He cared for Lizette, loved her, even, but that didn't mean he wanted to marry her. Did it?

But if he married Lizette then he could protect her from the truth.

A marriage to Lizette wouldn't be the worst thing. Perhaps she would prove less of a distraction once he could kiss her whenever he wanted to.

Lord Ashington walked over and handed him a glass. "You are smiling," he remarked. "I take it that you are thinking about Lizette."

"I am," he said as he accepted the glass.

"You two will make a fine couple," Lord Ashington asserted.

Tristan took a sip of his drink as he summoned up the courage to say his next words. He started off slowly. "I just returned from Bracknell."

Lord Ashington's smile faded. "Whatever were you doing there?"

"I was speaking to Miss Hendre, and we had the most informative conversation," he replied.

The marquess' face turned solemn. "You had no right to do so."

"You left me little choice in the matter," Tristan declared. "I couldn't go on, as I had been, being kept in the dark."

"I asked you to leave it alone. Do you not understand the consequences if the truth got out? Our entire family could fall into ruination."

"I understand."

Lord Ashington tossed back his drink and walked back over to the drink cart. "What now?" he asked. "What do you intend to do with the information?"

"I haven't decided."

"You can't tell Lizette," Lord Ashington exclaimed. "She has been through so much already that I worry this might break her."

Tristan placed his glass down. "I do worry about how Lizette might react, but I think she should know that she has a twin sister."

Lord Ashington shook his head vehemently. "If you did, she will no doubt start asking other questions; questions that I can't answer."

"You can, but you won't."

"Lizette is my granddaughter!" Lord Ashington shouted. "She maintains all the rights and privileges of her station in life. Do you want to take that from her?"

Tristan frowned. "That is not my intention."

"Pray tell, what is your intention?" Lord Ashington asked. "If you tell her the truth, there is no coming back from that. She will forever struggle with her place within Society."

"You don't know that."

Lord Ashington advanced towards him. "We must be sensible about all of this," he said. "You must marry Lizette and not utter a word of this to her."

Tristan crossed his arms over his chest. "You would want me to lie to Lizette?"

"It is for her own good," Lord Ashington replied.

"I won't do it."

Lord Ashington furrowed his brow. "You don't wish to marry Lizette or to lie to her?"

Uncrossing his arms, Tristan said, "I would marry Lizette, assuming she will agree to such a union, but I can't keep such a profound secret from her."

The marquess sighed. "I was afraid you would say that." He sat down on the settee. "I can't lose Lizette. I only just got her back."

"I daresay that you are underestimating Lizette," Tristan said as he moved to sit across from Lord Ashington.

"What if she hates me for the role that I played in all of this?" Lord Ashington asked dejectedly.

Tristan leaned forward in his seat. "What role did you play, exactly?" he asked. "Miss Hendre wasn't told she had a twin until her mother confessed it to her with her last dying breath, but she didn't know much more than that."

"Lizette was taken from her mother and swapped with my son's stillborn daughter," Lord Ashington revealed. "As far as the village was concerned, one of the twins had died and no one was the wiser."

"And Mrs. Hendre went along with this plan willingly?"

Lord Ashington nodded. "She was well compensated and..." His voice trailed off as the door was thrown open.

Lord Simon rushed into the room and announced, "Lady Lizette was abducted in the middle of Hyde Park."

Tristan jumped up from his seat. "How did this happen?"

"I tried to fight off the man, but he was too strong," Lord Simon replied. "I got a few jabs in before he knocked me unconscious."

Lord Ashington rose. "Are you all right?" he asked. "Should I send for a doctor?"

With a shake of his head, Lord Simon replied, "My only regret was that I wasn't strong enough to save Lady Lizette."

"You mustn't blame yourself," Lord Ashington said.

"But I do," Lord Simon responded, hanging his head.

Lord Simon's story did not sit well with Tristan, especially since the lord had no bruises or scrapes of any kind on him. Even his clothing was in pristine condition. This was not the appearance of a man that had fought valiantly over a woman.

Feeling rage building up inside of him, Tristan advanced towards Lord Simon and had the satisfaction of seeing him shrink back. "You are a coward!" he exclaimed, coming to a stop in front of him. "You don't even have a speck of dust on you. Do you truly expect us to believe you attempted to fight off Lizette's attacker?"

"I did try, but.. um… he overpowered me," Lord Simon stammered out.

"Liar!" He leaned closer to Lord Simon. "If anything happens to Lizette, I will hold you personally responsible for it."

Lord Simon swallowed slowly. "I know you are angry, but—"

Cutting him off, Tristan said, "I do not have time for this or for you and your pathetic excuses." He walked over to the door and shouted, "Brownell!"

It was only a moment before the butler appeared in the hall. "How may I help you, sir?"

"Send for Mr. Campden at Bow Street," Tristan ordered. "Inform him that Lady Lizette has been abducted and I need his assistance at once."

Brownell tipped his head. "It will be done."

Tristan turned back towards Lord Simon. He hoped the man wasn't truly as useless as he appeared, and he could garner some information from him. "Can you describe the man that abducted Lady Lizette?"

"It just all happened too fast—"

He spoke over him. "Think," he demanded. "What was his hair color?"

"It was dark, at least I think it was," Lord Simon replied.

Tristan scowled at the indecisive lord. "Was he tall?"

Lord Simon bobbed his head. "He was a giant. That is the only reason why he was able to overpower me."

Tristan took a step closer to him. "Can you tell me anything else about the man?" he asked. "Perhaps he had a scar?"

Lord Simon gave him an odd look. "He did have a scar. It was above his right eye. How would you know that?"

"Lucky guess," he muttered.

"Do you know the man that attacked us?" Lord Simon asked, his voice turning shrill.

Tristan didn't have time for this. He needed to speak to Mr. Campden and inform him that he had learned the identity of Lizette's attacker and possibly where he had taken her.

Lord Simon snapped his fingers in front of him. "Mr. Westcott?" he asked, impatiently. "Am I boring you with my questions?"

Tristan grabbed Lord Simon's hand and held it tightly. "I do not take kindly to people snapping at me," he growled.

"I was just trying to get your attention," Lord Simon whined as he shrunk back.

Tristan dropped his hand. "Go home," he ordered.

"But what of Lady Lizette?" Lord Simon asked.

"Lord Ashington and I will see to her," Tristan replied.

Lord Simon looked hesitant. "I could help, after all I have seen Lizette's attacker and—"

"No!" Tristan exclaimed in a firm tone. "We don't need, or want, your help."

"But—" Lord Simon attempted.

Tristan grabbed Lord Simon's arm and forcefully led him over to the door. "You are as useless as you look, my lord," he mocked. "Leave us now or I can't be responsible for my actions."

With fear in his eyes, Lord Simon departed from the study without another word.

Lord Ashington spoke up. "That was rather harsh."

"Trust me, Lord Simon is not the person we need right now," Tristan said. "He would just prove to be a hindrance."

"What now, then?"

Tristan walked over to the window and stared out. "We wait for Mr. Campden before we make our move and pray it is not too late to save Lizette."

Lord Ashington's soft voice reached his ears. "And if we are too late?"

Tristan closed his eyes at that thought. He couldn't lose Lizette now. She had taken a broken man and made him whole again. How could he go on without her by his side?

Lizette sat across from her attacker in a foul-smelling hackney. She wished she could open the windows and let the air circulate, but she doubted the man would let her. He had been glaring at her with his beady eyes since they had left Hyde Park.

She wondered how she was going to get out of this. She didn't dare attempt to flee from a moving coach. If she did, she most likely would end up dead on the street.

Perhaps her best recourse would be to speak to her attacker and try to convince him to let her go free. It was a long shot, but she didn't have much of a choice, especially since she knew she couldn't overpower him.

As she was gathering the courage to speak, the man spoke first. "We are almost there," he informed her. "If you try to scream or call for help, I will kill you and anyone that attempts to come to your aid." He pushed back his jacket to reveal a pistol that was tucked into the waistband of his trousers. "Do we understand one another?"

Lizette slowly nodded.

"Good."

Lizette wanted to keep the man talking so she could discover more about him so she said, "I'm afraid I am at a disadvantage since I don't know your name."

Annoyance flickered on the man's features. "You may call me George."

At least she had a name now.

"If this is all about the money, why don't you let me go speak to my grandfather and we can secure the funds for you?"

George scoffed. "I think not," he replied. "I am not letting you out of my sight until I have the money."

"How much are you attempting to ransom me for?"

"One hundred thousand pounds."

Lizette's eyes grew wide at the enormous sum that George spouted off so casually. "That is a lot of money."

"It is, but I have it on good authority that Lord Ashington has more than enough to cover that."

"I can't speak for my grandfather, but it seems as if it would take some time to secure those funds."

George shrugged. "The longer it takes, the more likely I will take it out on you." He removed a pocket watch from his waistcoat. "The ransom note should be arriving soon. I hired a street urchin to deliver it."

The hackney came to a stop and Lizette saw storefronts from out of the window. But none of the shops looked familiar. "Where are we?"

"You don't need to concern yourself with that," George replied as he went to open the door. "Do as I say or else you will regret what happens next."

Lizette shuddered at the harshness of his words. She had little doubt that he would make good on his promise.

George stepped out of the hackney and extended his hand back towards her.

She tentatively slipped her hand into his and allowed him to assist her onto the pavement. Once her feet were on solid ground, she tried to remove her hand from his, but he held firm.

Without saying a word, he placed it into the crook of his arm and started leading her towards one of the shops. They stepped inside and she saw there was a flight of stairs that was against the far wall.

George urged her towards the stairs and she felt dread in the pit of her stomach. What would he do to her once he got her alone in his apartment? What if he attempted to become too familiar with her? Fear gripped her and she came to an abrupt stop on the steps.

"What are you doing?" George seethed.

"I want your word that you won't become too familiar with me," she said with a stubborn tilt of her chin. She was mustering up all the courage she had, but her legs were shaking as she made her demand.

George chuckled. "You do not need to worry about that. I have no intention of taking your virtue. I only care about the money."

Lizette knew she didn't have much of a choice but to believe him. Frankly, she had little choice in the matter.

"Come along," George said as he continued up the stairs.

Once they arrived on the second level, he approached a door that had a number assigned to it- 231B. His hand went into his jacket pocket and he secured a key. He opened the door and shoved her forward.

"Get in," he ordered.

Lizette stumbled into the sparsely furnished room. An old, worn settee sat next to a fireplace and a lumpy mattress was shoved up against the window. The sun was partially blocked out from thick drapes, but there were enough holes in them to provide some light.

George closed the door and locked it. He slipped the key back into his jacket pocket. "Welcome to your new home for the time being."

Lizette wrapped her arms around her waist, unsure of what she should do next. She found herself in a precarious situation and she didn't see any way out of it.

Walking over to the window, George shoved back the drapes and pointed towards the windowsill. "I nailed the window shut myself so there is no chance for you to call for help." He walked over to a table that was tucked in a corner and picked up a loaf of bread. "Are you hungry?"

She shook her head.

He looked amused. "Starving yourself won't help you." He tore off a piece of bread and bit into it. "And I can assure you that it isn't poisonous."

Lizette watched as breadcrumbs flew from his mouth as he spoke. Even if she had been hungry, she wasn't now.

"Suit yourself, Princess," George said as he dropped the bread onto the table. "You will grow hungry soon enough."

He dusted off the crumbs from his hands and approached her. He stopped in front of her and she resisted the urge to step back. She didn't want to give him the satisfaction of knowing that she was afraid of him. Which she was. George terrified her.

His eyes roamed over her face. "It is remarkable how similar you are when you look closely."

What was he speaking of?

"You may have different hair color but your eyes are the same," George said. "Furthermore, my Rosamond has dimples when she smiles."

"Who is Rosamond?"

George smirked. "You don't know, do you?"

"Know what?"

Taking a step back, he replied, "Everything you know to be true is a lie. You are nothing more than a country bumpkin dressed up in fancy clothes."

Lizette furrowed her brow. "I don't understand."

"Your so-called parents stole you from your mother's arms

and raised you as their own," George said with satisfaction in his voice.

"That is preposterous, and not the least bit true."

"It doesn't matter if you believe it. It is the truth."

Lizette tilted her chin. "You are lying."

George reached into his pocket and pulled out a portrait miniature. "If I am lying, then how do you explain this?" he asked, extending her the small, gold, oval frame.

She accepted it and saw a young woman that did share many similar traits as she possessed. But that did not prove anything- at least to her.

George pointed at the young woman. "That is my Rosamond," he said. "We are engaged to be married." He paused, and his face grew crestfallen. "At least we were. She broke it off due to a misunderstanding."

"I'm sorry," she murmured, not entirely sure of what else she could say.

"We fought over you," George said.

"Me?" she asked. "Whatever for?"

George took the portrait miniature from her hand. "Rosamond is your twin and she only learned of your existence when her mother passed away."

Twin? Impossible. She had no twin. What nonsense was George sputtering?

"Your mother made her promise not to seek you out but to accept the fact that you two were on separate paths," George said. "When Rosamond confided in me, I knew that was a mistake and I saw an opportunity to become rich."

Lizette brought a hand to her head. "Are you truly saying that this Rosamond is my twin sister and I have another family that I know nothing about?"

"That is correct."

"That is unfathomable," Lizette said. "My parents wouldn't have done that to me."

George shoved the portrait miniature into his pocket.

"Have you never wondered why you didn't look like your parents?"

Lizette had never considered that before. "We look similar enough," she attempted. "My father and I both have dark hair."

George ran a hand through his hair. "If that is the case, then you and I could be related," he mocked.

"Regardless, I don't believe you," she said. "My parents wouldn't have kept such a secret from me."

As she said her words, Lizette knew that her parents had, in fact, kept secrets from her, but this was different. To imply she belonged to a whole other family was just laughable. Her mother had showered affection upon her and had never once hinted that Lizette wasn't her own.

The lines around George's lips grew hard. "You are a stubborn thing," he said. "I suppose I should have expected that, considering Rosamond has that vexing trait as well."

"I believe you are just confused."

George's eyes narrowed. "I am not the one that is confused, you are!" he shouted. "You are Mrs. Hendre's daughter, and you were born in Highworth."

Lizette tensed. How did he know where she had been born? "How did you know that?"

"Did Lord and Lady Crewe have a country estate in Highworth?" George asked.

"They did, but that is just a coincidence." Wasn't it, she wondered. It had to be. She had never heard of this Mrs. Hendre until now.

George tossed his hands up in the air. "This is pointless," he said. "You are just a dumb female in high Society. I don't know why I expected more from you."

"That is rather harsh of you to say. After all, you are expecting me to believe something that couldn't possibly be true."

"Why?" George asked. "Because you don't belong with the commoners, like Rosamond and me?"

"I never said that."

"Well, Princess," George drawled out. "You are one of us whether you want to be or not. This facade you have created is just that- a facade."

A knock came at the door and George reached for his pistol. "Wait here," he ordered.

He stopped by the door and asked, "Who is it?"

"Rosamond," came the reply.

George quickly unlocked the door and opened it wide. Rosamond stepped inside and her eyes grew wide when they saw her.

"George!" she exclaimed. "What have you done? You must let Lady Lizette go this instant."

"I think not."

"What you are doing is wrong," Rosamond proclaimed.

George tucked the pistol back into the waistband of his trousers and closed the door. "I am doing this for us."

"No, you are doing it for *you*," Rosamond asserted. "I want no part in this. I made a promise to my mother and—"

George cut her off. "You were foolish to do so. Kidnapping Lady Lizette is our chance to become rich."

"I don't care about being rich," Rosamond remarked.

"Your opinion will change when we have enough money to live comfortably for the remainder of our days," George said as he reached for her.

Rosamond stepped out of his reach. "Need I remind you that we are not engaged anymore."

"You will change your mind," George declared.

"I promise that we can have no future together unless you return Lady Lizette to her family, unharmed."

George reared back. "And forego the ransom that they will return for her release?" he huffed. "I think not."

"George, please," Rosamond said. "I came all this way to plead with you to do the right thing."

"That was foolish of you to do," George chided. "But now that you are here, I can't let you go until I have the money."

Rosamond stared at him, as if she were seeing him for the first time. "You would keep me here, unwillingly?"

George bobbed his head. "I would, because I can't have you going to the magistrate." He placed a hand on the butt of his pistol. "Why don't you use this time wisely and become acquainted with your sister?"

"George…" Rosamond attempted.

He put his hand up. "Save your breath, Rosamond," he said. "My mind is made up."

"If you go through with this, then I want nothing to do with you, ever again," Rosamond asserted.

A cocky smile came to his lips. "You will change your mind when I am a rich man."

"You are delusional."

"And you are wearing on my patience," George grumbled. "One more word out of you and I will tie you up and gag you."

Rosamond pursed her lips and narrowed her eyes at George, but she didn't utter a word.

George went over to the table and grabbed a chair. He repositioned it by the door and sat down. "If either of you tries to escape, I will kill you."

Lizette exchanged a worried glance with Rosamond. She did have an ally in the young woman, but she was no closer to escaping than she was before.

Chapter Nineteen

Tristan held the crumpled ransom note in his hand as he paced in Lord Ashington's study. The note had been delivered by a street urchin and they were unable to glean any information from him. He was just a messenger, nothing more.

It had felt like hours since he had sent for Mr. Campden and his patience was wearing thin. Where was the Bow Street Runner? Surely, he didn't have anything more pressing to handle at the moment.

Lord Ashington's voice broke through the silence. "You should sit, Tristan."

"I think not."

"You are making me tired just looking at you."

Tristan stopped and turned towards the marquess. How could he be so calm at a time like this? "How can you just sit there and do nothing?" he demanded.

Lord Ashington frowned. "What is there to do?" he asked. "After all, my solicitor is at the bank right now, attempting to secure the funds."

"That could take days."

"Let's hope that isn't the case."

"I could go and save her," Tristan replied. "Miss Hendre informed me that George has an apartment in Cheapside."

"You can't go by yourself."

"Whyever not?" Tristan asked. "I can handle my own against that ruffian."

Lord Ashington leaned back in his chair. "You aren't thinking clearly and that could get you killed."

"You underestimate me."

"Regardless, I would prefer if you stay out of harm's way since you are my heir."

Tristan ran a hand through his hair and he declared, "That means little to me right now. All I care about is getting Lizette back from that madman."

"Could it be that you found something that is more important than work?" Lord Ashington asked.

"I love her," Tristan admitted. "I don't know when I started falling in love with Lizette, but I suspect it was from the moment I first laid eyes on her."

Lord Ashington smiled. "I know. You have always been terrible at hiding your emotions."

His shoulders drooped. "Now you know why I can't lose her."

"I won't lose her either," Lord Ashington said. "We will pay the ransom and we will bring Lizette home to us."

"A hundred thousand pounds is not an inconsequential amount. It will take us many years to recoup that loss."

Lord Ashington gave him a pointed look. "Does that change anything for you?"

"Not for me."

"Good, because no sum is too great to ensure Lizette's release."

Before he could reply, Lord Roswell stepped into the room with a purposeful stride. "I understand that Lady Lizette has been abducted."

Tristan furrowed his brow. "How in the blazes do you know that?"

"I was at the club, and I overheard Lord Simon telling people of her dire circumstances," Lord Roswell said. "Was there a ransom note?"

"There was," Tristan confirmed.

"May I see it?" Lord Roswell asked.

"Suit yourself," Tristan said as he extended it to him.

His friend uncrumpled the note and read:

If you value Lady Lizette's life, you will place one hundred thousand pounds in a valise and place it outside of the servants' entrance. Do not tell anyone or I will kill Lady Lizette. Once I have the money, I will release her.

Lord Roswell looked up and asked, "What is being done to secure her release?"

"We are attempting to come up with the funds, but it could take some time," Tristan revealed. "Furthermore, a Bow Street Runner should be here at any moment."

Lord Roswell bobbed his head approvingly. "That is a good start. What can I do to help?"

"I don't think there is anything that you can do," Tristan said.

"Au contraire," Lord Roswell responded. "You might find that I can prove useful at a time like this."

Tristan wasn't convinced his friend could help, but he was appreciative that he was here, nonetheless.

The butler stepped into the room and announced, "Mr. Campden has arrived."

His words had just left his mouth when the Bow Street Runner appeared in the doorway. "I didn't feel like waiting in the entry hall since time is of the essence," Mr. Campden said.

"You were right to do so." Tristan gestured towards Lord Ashington and Lord Roswell. "Allow me to introduce you to Lord Ashington and Lord Roswell."

Mr. Campden bowed. "My lords," he murmured. "I regret to be meeting you under these difficult circumstances."

Lord Ashington tipped his head. "Mr. Westcott speaks highly of your abilities. I do hope you won't let us down."

"I will strive not to." Mr. Campden turned back to Tristan. "Tell me everything and no detail is too small."

Tristan heaved a sigh before saying, "I do hope you will be discreet with the information I am about to share."

"You need not worry about that. Discretion is a part of my job," Mr. Campden assured him.

"Very well," Tristan said with a side glance at his friend. He had no doubt that this conversation would remain private. "Lady Lizette was abducted from Hyde Park by a man named George Rabe. He was the fiancé to Lady Lizette's twin sister, Miss Hendre. He intends to ransom her for a hundred thousand pounds."

"You said he 'was'?" Mr. Campden asked.

"Correct. When Miss Hendre told him about Lady Lizette, he concocted a plan to abduct her and become rich in doing so," Tristan replied. "But she had hoped he had enough sense to not go through with his plan."

"Greed can corrupt anyone, if they aren't careful," Mr. Campden said. "What else can you tell me about this George?"

"Miss Hendre informed me that George has an apartment over a storefront in Cheapside," Tristan shared.

Mr. Campden eyed him curiously. "Do you believe that Miss Hendre played a role in Lady Lizette's abduction?"

"I do not," Tristan replied. "She seemed rather distraught by his intentions."

"Because if she did, I could be walking into a trap," Mr.

Campden said. "Did Miss Hendre provide you with an address?"

"She did, but I would like to go with you when you retrieve Lady Lizette," Tristan requested.

Mr. Campden shook his head. "Absolutely not!" he exclaimed. "I do not have time to watch over you."

"I assure you that won't be the case," Tristan asserted.

"You will only be a hindrance to me since I prefer to work alone," Mr. Campden pressed.

Lord Roswell spoke up. "I would like to go as well."

Mr. Campden huffed as he shifted his gaze to Lord Ashington. "Would you care to join us, too?" he mocked.

Lord Ashington put his hand up in front of him. "I am a smart enough man to stay back and let you handle this."

"Thank you. At least one of you have the sense to stay back." Mr. Campden brought back his skeptical gaze to meet Tristan's. "Can you at least shoot?"

"If I need to," Tristan replied.

"Oh, you will need to," Mr. Campden declared. "I can't promise that you won't get killed either. My focus will be on retrieving Lady Lizette, not trying to keep you alive."

"As well it should," Tristan said.

Mr. Campden looked hesitant, which was in stark contrast to how he usually was. "I would prefer if you stayed behind and let me handle this."

"I am going with you," Tristan responded. His tone brokered no argument.

Lord Roswell interjected, "As am I."

Mr. Campden looked heavenward. "What am I going to do with two pretentious lords that are determined to get themselves killed?"

"I am not a lord yet." Tristan walked over to the desk and removed the dueling pistols from their container. Then he went to hand one to Lord Roswell.

Lord Roswell pushed back his jacket, revealing a pistol. "You keep both of them since I brought my own."

"Why do you have a pistol on you?" Tristan asked.

"Don't you carry a pistol on your person?" Lord Roswell countered.

"I do not," Tristan replied. "I swore off pistols after my brother's duel, but it is time I pick them back up- for Lizette's sake."

Mr. Campden walked over to the door. "Come along, then. A hackney is out front to take us to Cheapside."

As they followed Mr. Campden to the hackney, Lord Roswell leaned close and whispered, "Lady Lizette has a twin?"

Tristan clenched his jaw. "She does, and I do hope you will keep that to yourself."

"You have my word," Lord Roswell responded. "When did you learn of this?"

"This morning."

"What does this mean to you?"

Tristan gave him a sideways glance. "It changes nothing for me."

"How can it not?" Lord Roswell asked.

"Because I love her."

Lord Roswell's steps faltered. "You love her?" he asked slowly.

"I do." There was something liberating about confessing how he felt for Lizette.

"Are you going to offer for her?"

"I intend to."

A bright smile came to Lord Roswell's lips. "I am agog. I can't believe you have finally fallen for a woman and are brave enough to admit it."

"You are an idiot," Tristan muttered.

"Ah, I see that love has not changed you one bit," Lord Roswell joked.

They departed the townhouse and stepped into the waiting hackney. Once they were situated, Mr. Campden said, "You will do exactly what I say, when I say it. Any deviation to my plan could get you killed."

"I can agree to that," Tristan said.

"What, exactly, is your plan?" Lord Roswell asked.

Mr. Campden smirked. "I don't have one yet, but it will come to me."

"Let's hope so," Lord Roswell said, "because I do not feel like dying today."

———————————

Lizette sat on the uncomfortable settee as she watched Rosamond stare out the window. There was no denying that they shared a very similar appearance but was that enough for her to dismiss everything that she thought she knew to be true?

How was this possible? Did her parents truly steal her away as George had said?

No! That was impossible. Her mother wouldn't have done such a thing; she was sure of that. So how could she explain Rosamond, or George, for that matter?

Rosamond walked over to her and sat down next to her on the settee. She lowered her voice and said, "I am sure that you have a lot of questions for me, but I think we should focus on trying to escape."

Lizette's eyes darted towards George. He was sitting on a chair by the door, his eyes closed, and he was slightly snoring.

"How do you propose we do that?" Lizette asked, matching Rosamond's hushed voice.

Rosamond let out a sigh. "I was hoping that you had an idea."

"I don't."

"Then we improvise," Rosamond said. "We just need to get that pistol away from George."

"I'm not sure if that is possible."

Rosamond turned her attention towards George. "I don't know what has gotten into him," she said sadly. "We were happy until I told him about you. Then he turned into a man that I scarcely recognized."

"Greed can do that to people."

"I don't understand why he wasn't just content with what we had," Rosamond murmured. "We were supposed to get married and start a family."

"I'm sorry," Lizette said, knowing her words were entirely inadequate for what Rosamond had shared.

Rosamond waved her hand in front of her. "It is not your fault. If anything, I should be apologizing to you."

"You have nothing to apologize for."

"But I do," Rosamond said. "I promised my mother that I wouldn't tell anyone about you, but I was so shaken from the revelation that I thought it would be all right to confide in George."

"As well you should since he was your betrothed."

Rosamond gave her a wry smile. "My mother was not keen on me marrying George," she admitted. "She felt I was settling with him, but I never saw it that way. I still love him, even though I know there can never be a future between us."

"That is to be expected."

"Is it?" Rosamond asked. "Because he is holding me hostage right now? It isn't very gentlemanly of him."

"No, it is not," she agreed.

"I did try the windows but they are nailed shut," Rosamond revealed. "The only way out of this room is by way of that door."

"And George is sitting in front of it."

"Precisely," Rosamond said, "but I am not ready to give up hope. Are you?"

"Perhaps we should just wait for my grandfather to pay the ransom," Lizette suggested.

"Then George wins."

"But we will both be alive."

"Will we?" Rosamond asked. "How do you know for certain that he will release you, unharmed?"

"He promised me."

A sad look came into Rosamond's eyes. "He made promises to me, too, but he broke them when they became inconvenient," she said. "Besides, I am not sure he will risk you going to the constable."

Lizette's eyes grew wide. "You think he would kill me?"

"Frankly, I don't know what George is capable of anymore."

"But he wouldn't hurt you, would he?"

Rosamond shrugged. "I want to say no, considering he has never hurt me before, but I fear that he isn't thinking clearly."

"Then we must try to escape." Lizette's eyes searched the room as she looked for anything that could be used as a weapon but saw nothing.

George let out a loud snore before his eyes flew open. His eyes settled on them and he asked, "What are you two conspiring about?"

"We were just becoming better acquainted, just as you had suggested earlier," Rosamond replied.

George turned his beady eyes towards Lizette. "Does this mean you have finally come to accept the truth?"

"I still have my doubts," Lizette replied.

"When are you going to realize that you are nothing more than a seaman's daughter?" he asked.

Rosamond interjected, "Leave her alone."

"Or what? You are going to make me?" George scoffed. "*Lady* Lizette should know the truth about her parents."

"Why should you be the one to tell her?" Rosamond challenged.

"Well, you aren't going to tell her," George responded. "You just wanted to let her go on pretending to live a lie."

"It isn't a lie," Rosamond said.

"What would you call it, then?" George asked. "She lives a life of grandeur and what do we have?"

"We have a good life."

"Do we?" George asked. "I have to scrape by to make ends meet and you are still living off Lord Ashington's graces."

"Not anymore," Rosamond said. "I am not entitled to that money, and I gave it back."

George gave her a blank look. "You are even more foolish than I imagined. That money rightfully belonged to you."

"No, the deal died with my mother."

"How do you intend to survive without those funds?" George asked.

Rosamond squared her shoulders. "I am not afraid of hard work," she said. "I could work at a shop or take in work as a seamstress."

"For how long?"

"My mother left me comfortable," Rosamond replied. "I could go on as I have been for years without an issue."

"What about the manor where you live?"

Rosamond pressed her lips together. "I do believe it is owned by Lord Ashington but he wouldn't make me leave."

"Why wouldn't he?" George asked. "He doesn't care about you or your mother. He only cares about himself and his precious reputation."

"You don't know him."

"But you do?" George asked. "You have always believed that everything will work out for you, but sometimes you have to fight to make it happen."

"I can fight, when the situation warrants it."

"You are naive, my dear," he said. "But once I get the

ransom from Lord Ashington, we can start over in a new village."

Rosamond shook her head. "I am not going anywhere with you."

George smirked. "We shall see."

Lizette spoke up with a question of her own. "How do you intend to collect the ransom if you are here with us?"

"My friend will retrieve the money and bring it to me," George explained.

Rosamond lifted her brow. "I assume your friend is Frank."

"It is," George confirmed.

"How do you know he won't take the money and run?" Rosamond asked.

George patted the pistol as he replied, "Because I threatened to kill his entire family if he betrays me."

"Frank has only ever cared about himself," Rosamond asserted.

"You have never liked Frank."

Rosamond nodded. "That is true because he is a jackanapes," she said. "Did you tell him about Lady Lizette?"

"I did not," George said.

"At least you can keep a secret," Rosamond muttered.

George's eyes narrowed. "I could use a little more gratitude from you," he said. "After all, I did all this for you."

"Not this again. I think we established that you did this for yourself."

"If it wasn't for me, you would have never sought out your sister," George said. "You should be thanking me."

"Thanking you?" Rosamond asked. "You are keeping me here at gunpoint."

George rose and stretched out his back. "That is so you won't run to the constable and tattle on me."

"You are unbelievable," Rosamond asserted.

"You may as well save your breath," George said. "I tire of your endless chatter."

Rising, Rosamond tilted her chin stubbornly. "I am not done speaking my mind."

George advanced towards her and Rosamond shrunk back. "Yes, you are!" he exclaimed. "Do not make the mistake that I won't hurt you."

"George, please," Rosamond murmured. "It is not too late to do the right thing and let us go."

"It is too late!" George said, tossing up his arms. "And why should I stop it? After today, I am going to be a rich man!"

"But at what cost?"

George pounded his chest with his fist as he replied, "It is *my* turn to be rich."

In a swift motion, Rosamond reached for the pistol that was tucked into his waistband but was stopped by George grabbing her wrist. He jerked her forward, so their faces were just inches apart.

"You thought you could relieve me of my pistol so easily?" he growled.

Rosamond attempted to squirm out of his hold. "You are hurting me," she admonished.

"If you do something stupid like that again, I won't be as forgiving," he said as he shoved her back onto the settee. "Do I make myself clear?"

Rosamond looked at him with wide, fearful eyes. "You do."

"Good, because I do not want to hurt you, but you leave me little choice," George said, taking a step back.

As she held her wrist in her other hand, Rosamond murmured, "You have changed, George." Her words were spoken with a profound sadness.

"I am a better man now," George declared.

"I don't believe that to be true."

George glowered at Rosamond for a moment before he

walked over to the table and picked up the loaf of bread. He took a bite out of it and chewed loudly as he approached the window.

"Where is he?" he muttered under his breath. "He should have already arrived with the ransom."

Shifting in her seat, Rosamond met Lizette's gaze and kept her voice low. "I'm sorry. I tried, but don't give up hope. This fight is far from over."

With a sigh, Lizette looked at the door and knew the chances of her surviving this ordeal were decreasing by the moment. She could feel herself slipping into the depths of despair, so she decided to dwell on something much more pleasant- Tristan. She truly hoped that she had the chance to tell him how she felt about him.

Chapter Twenty

Tristan felt himself growing more and more anxious as the coach traveled to Cheapside. He would do anything that it took to save Lizette, even if it meant that he must sacrifice his own life for her sake. For what was the purpose in his life if Lizette wasn't in it?

He glanced at Lord Roswell, half-expecting him to ask to be let out of the coach. After all, this wasn't his fight. Why should he put his life on the line? But to his pleasant surprise, Lord Roswell appeared calm as he met his gaze.

"It will be all right," Lord Roswell assured him. "We will get Lady Lizette back."

Mr. Campden huffed from his seat across from them. "I would prefer if you two remained in the coach and let me deal with this."

"I assure you that I can handle myself," Lord Roswell said.

"I doubt that," Mr. Campden remarked. "What would the son of a marquess know about fighting?"

"Plenty," Lord Roswell responded.

Mr. Campden didn't appear convinced. "Just try to avoid getting yourself killed. I can't even imagine the paperwork I would have to wade through if you died."

The coach glided to a stop and Tristan glanced out the window. "Where are we?" he asked.

"We are two blocks south of George's apartment," Mr. Campden replied. "You didn't think we would stop right in front so he could see us coming?"

Tristan shrugged. "I hadn't considered it."

"We need to have the element of surprise when we confront George," Mr. Campden explained before he went to exit the coach.

After they all stepped down onto the pavement, Mr. Campden gestured towards the alleyway. "Follow me," he encouraged.

Tristan followed Lord Roswell and Mr. Campden into the alleyway and attempted to ignore the pungent odor of excrement that seemed to seep off the walls.

Mr. Campden stopped in the center of the alley and spun back around. "I have an idea for how to save Lady Lizette, but it does come with some risks."

"What do you propose?" Lord Roswell asked.

Mr. Campden hesitated before saying, "We knock and hope that George will open the door for us."

Lord Roswell's brow shot up. "That is your brilliant idea?" he asked.

"I never said it was brilliant, but we just need to get into the apartment," Mr. Campden replied. "I will take the lead."

"Surely there is another way?" Tristan asked.

"I have considered every possibility and I feel that this is our best course of action. After all, from what you have told me, I do not believe George is a murderer," Mr. Campden said.

"But what if you are wrong?" Tristan pressed.

"I rarely am."

Tristan stared at the Bow Street Runner and he couldn't help but wonder if Mr. Campden was leading them straight into their own deaths.

Mr. Campden put his hand up. "If you are uncomfortable with my plan, you can stay behind," he said.

"No, I will go," Tristan asserted.

"Suit yourself," Mr. Campden said. "Stay close and, for heaven's sakes, do not jeopardize this assignment for me."

"My only concern is to retrieve Lady Lizette, unharmed."

"Mine, too," Mr. Campden responded. "Which is why you must trust me."

Lord Roswell interjected, "What would you have me do?"

Mr. Campden started out of the alleyway and spoke over his shoulder. "Keep your pistol close and do not hesitate to use it."

As they followed the Bow Street Runner out of the alleyway, Lord Roswell leaned close and asked, "How confident are you in Mr. Campden's abilities?"

"I'm not, but he did come highly recommended," Tristan replied.

No one spoke as they walked the two blocks towards the shop that housed George's apartment overhead.

Mr. Campden stopped at the door and said, "This is your last chance. There is no shame in waiting in the coach."

"Do not worry about us," Lord Roswell asserted. "We are all in."

"Very well, then." Mr. Campden opened the door and headed towards the stairs. Once he arrived at 231B, he knocked.

Silence.

Mr. Campden lifted his fist up and pounded on the door.

"Who's there?" a muffled voice from within asked.

"I have come to barter," Mr. Campden said.

"For what, exactly?"

"Your life."

It was a long moment before the door opened slightly and Miss Hendre peeked out. "You need to leave, or else George will kill Lady Lizette," she said, her words betraying her fear.

Mr. Campden shook his head. "I'm afraid I can't allow that."

Miss Hendre glanced over her shoulder before saying, "George is holding a pistol to Lady Lizette's head."

"Let me in," Mr. Campden ordered.

Hesitation showed on Miss Hendre's face. "I don't want Lizette to die."

Tristan came from behind Mr. Campden and said, "We are here to save her."

Miss Hendre stared at him for a long moment before she nodded and opened the door wide.

He followed Mr. Campden into the apartment and saw George holding Lizette in front of him, a pistol to her temple.

"Go away!" George ordered. "Or I will kill Lady Lizette."

Mr. Campden retrieved his pistol and brought it up. "If you do, then you will die."

George's eyes grew frantic. "How did you even find me?" he asked.

Miss Hendre spoke up. "I told Mr. Westcott about your apartment."

"You betrayed me?" George exclaimed.

"I did not see it as a betrayal since what you are doing is wrong," Miss Hendre said. "This is not who you are, George. Why can't you see that?"

George's eyes narrowed. "I will deal with you later."

"I don't think so," Miss Hendre said as she removed a muff pistol from the folds of her gown. "This ends now."

"You had a pistol on your person this whole time?" George asked in disbelief.

"Surely you did not think I could travel to London without one?" she asked. "I had hoped not to use it by convincing you to walk away before Mr. Westcott even arrived."

"You think you are so clever," George spat out.

"That has nothing to do with it," Miss Hendre responded. "I just didn't want to see you dead or transported."

George turned his pistol towards Miss Hendre. "Perhaps I should just kill you," he growled.

"Put the pistol down," Miss Hendre said with a plea in her voice. "You are vastly outnumbered, and this will not end well for you."

"We could have been rich," George whined, "and you threw it all away."

"You wanted to get rich at the expense of my sister and I can't allow that," Miss Hendre said. "She did nothing wrong."

"Why do you not hate her?" George asked. "She was given everything, and you were left behind."

"I do not see it that way," Miss Hendre responded.

"You should!" George shouted.

"I have no complaints about how I was raised," Miss Hendre said. "I consider myself most fortunate."

"But you could have had more."

Miss Hendre frowned. "That means little to me."

"You are a fool, then," George seethed.

Tristan took a step forward and said, "Please let Lady Lizette go. She is an innocent in all of this."

George turned his heated glare towards him. "Ah, yes, the high and mighty heir is here to save the day."

"I just want Lady Lizette back," Tristan said.

"Yet you are pointing a pistol at me," George remarked. "I have no doubt that you wouldn't hesitate to use that against me."

Mr. Campden interjected, "This place is surrounded by Bow Street Runners. There is no place that you can run to that we won't find you, assuming you even survive this ordeal."

George returned the pistol to Lizette's temple, causing a slight whimper out of her. "Put your pistols down and let me leave."

"We can't do that," Mr. Campden said.

"Then I will kill her," George exclaimed.

Miss Hendre lowered her pistol to her side. "I don't think you will, because you are not a murderer."

"You don't know what I am capable of," George stated.

"No, but I would like to believe you are still the same man I fell in love with," Miss Hendre said in a dejected voice.

George's face fell. "I am that man."

"Then prove it," Miss Hendre encouraged. "Put your pistol down."

For a brief moment, indecision crossed George's face, but then he blinked, and it was gone. "No," he said. "I'm afraid I can't do that."

As George's finger twitched on the trigger, a shot rang out and he fell to the ground, dead.

Tristan turned towards where the pistol was discharged and saw Lord Roswell was holding a smoking pistol.

Lord Roswell tipped his head towards Tristan before he brought the pistol down to his side. "By his own admission, George was not going to give up," he explained. "He left us with little choice."

"I agree, wholeheartedly," Mr. Campden said.

Lizette approached Tristan with a pale face, and he opened his arms wide, hoping she wouldn't chide him for his bold behavior. Instead, she rushed into them and laid her head onto his chest.

Tristan's arms came around her and held her close against him. "It will be all right," he murmured. "You are safe now."

"Thank you for coming," she said softly.

"Did you have any doubt?" he asked. "After all, it is not that easy to get rid of me."

"I don't want to get rid of you."

Tristan felt a smile come to his lips at Lizette's admission. As much as he wanted to press his suit with her, he knew this was not the time or place to do such a thing. But her words were encouraging.

Mr. Campden stepped closer to him. "It might be best if you depart before the constable shows up to investigate George's death," he said. "I will strive to keep Lady Lizette's name out of the investigation."

"That is most kind of you," Tristan acknowledged.

As he went to release Lizette, she looked up at him with red-lined eyes. "What about Rosamond?" she asked. "What will become of her now?"

"I don't know," Tristan replied as he only now noticed that Rosamond was crouched down next to George's lifeless body and tears were streaming down her face.

"We can't leave her here," Lizette said.

"No, we can't," Tristan agreed.

Lizette stepped out of his arms and slowly approached Rosamond. She placed a comforting hand on her sister's shoulder and said, "I want you to come home with me."

"I couldn't possibly…" Rosamond attempted.

"You shouldn't be alone right now," Lizette said, "and we still have much to discuss."

Rosamond rose. "I do suppose you make a good point." She wiped at the tears on her face. "I must look like a fright."

"I do not think I fare any better," Lizette responded.

Tristan stepped forward. "May I escort you ladies to the coach?" he asked. The sooner they departed from the apartment, the better.

Lizette readily took his arm, but Rosamond was much more hesitant. "I couldn't possibly impose…" she started.

"Nonsense," Tristan said. "It is my honor."

Rosamond placed her hand on his arm and murmured, "Thank you."

Tristan led the sisters out of the room, down the stairs and out onto the pavement. He knew there were a lot of questions that remained unanswered but, for now, he would relish in the fact that Lizette was alive and well.

To him, nothing else mattered.

———————◯———————

Now that Lizette was no longer George's prisoner, she was forced to confront the truth of Rosamond. There could be no denying that they were sisters, not after everything that had been said, but she had so many questions. And, quite frankly, she wasn't even sure where to begin.

As she sat next to her sister in the coach, she couldn't help but wonder what Tristan's connection to Rosamond was. Her sister had mentioned that they had spoken before. How was that possible? It would appear that Tristan had been keeping secrets from her, as well.

Tristan met her gaze and said, "I would imagine you have some questions for me," he hesitated, "for both of us."

"I do," Lizette responded.

Rosamond shifted on the bench towards her. "I am sorry that I put you in this awkward position. You were never supposed to know about me."

"Why is that?" Lizette asked.

"My mother... our mother... didn't want to disrupt your life," Rosamond explained. "She didn't want you to be burdened down with the truth."

"As you are?"

"It is different for me. If the truth ever got out, you would be ruined."

Lizette knew that Rosamond had a point but that still didn't explain Tristan's involvement. "You knew this whole time and never told me?" she asked him.

"I just discovered the truth this morning," Tristan said. "I traveled to Bracknell to discover why your grandfather was making yearly payments to a Mrs. Hendre."

"Is my," she hesitated, "mother alive?" Lizette asked.

Rosamond shook her head. "She passed away a few months ago, and that is when she confessed the truth to me."

Lizette turned her attention back towards Tristan. "Would you have told me about Rosamond?"

Tristan pressed his lips together. "I hadn't decided yet."

"Whyever not?"

"Because the truth can be damning, especially in this case."

"Didn't I deserve to know the truth?"

Tristan leaned forward. "You do, but I wanted to speak to your grandfather first," he said. "I was hoping he could provide more details about what led your parents to take you from Mrs. Hendre."

"My parents?" Lizette repeated. "They aren't truly my parents, are they? They deceived me, lied to me. For what purpose?"

"They loved you," Tristan said.

"If they had truly loved me, they would have told me the truth," Lizette asserted.

"I don't believe it was that simple."

"It should have been."

The coach came to a stop in front of her grandfather's townhouse and it dipped to the side as the footman exited his perch.

The door opened and Tristan exited first. Then he reached back to assist Lizette out of the coach. As she slipped her hand into his, he squeezed it and offered her an encouraging smile.

"We will figure this out… together," he said in a hushed voice.

Once her feet were on the ground, she withdrew her hand and waited for her sister to come stand next to her.

Tristan offered his arm but she didn't move to take it.

"Lizette?" he asked with worry in his eyes.

Her eyes stared up at the grand house. "Everything about

my life is a lie. How can I go inside, knowing that I don't truly belong here?"

"This is your home."

"No, it *was* my home," Lizette corrected.

Tristan moved to stand in front of her. "Nothing has changed, at least for me."

"But everything has changed for me."

With a glance at Rosamond, Tristan lowered his voice. "Besides a select few people, no one knows the truth. Your secret is safe."

She huffed. "I am so tired of all the secrets."

"Then let's go get the truth, once and for all," Tristan said, holding his hand up.

Lizette placed her hand in his, knowing she was relying on his support. "You will remain with me?"

"I am not going anywhere." His words sounding very much like a promise.

She allowed Tristan to lead her into the townhouse and they continued to the study. Once they stepped inside, she saw her grandfather sitting on the settee with a drink in his hand.

When he saw her, he jumped up, spilling the drink onto his hand. "Lizette!" he exclaimed. "I have been so worried…" His face paled when Rosamond came to stand next to her. "What is she doing here?"

Lizette gestured towards Rosamond. "Grandfather, allow me the privilege of introducing my sister, Miss Rosamond Hendre."

"She shouldn't be here," her grandfather said, his voice low. "It could ruin everything."

"Yes, well I do believe that the cat is out of the bag," Lizette stated.

Tristan moved to close the door before saying, "I think this conversation should remain private."

Her grandfather removed a handkerchief from his jacket

pocket and wiped his hand. "I should have assumed that this day would come," he said. "How did you two even meet?"

Rosamond spoke up. "My ex-fiancé was the one who abducted Lizette," she shared. "He became unhinged when I told him the truth about my sister."

"Rosamond helped save me from George," Lizette said. "Without her, I don't know if I would be standing in front of you."

Her grandfather's face softened as he addressed Rosamond. "If that is true, then I owe you a debt of gratitude."

Rosamond gave him a weak smile. "You owe me nothing, my lord. I couldn't stand by and do nothing as George tried to hurt Lizette."

Tristan walked over to the drink cart and poured a drink. "I think it might be best if you start from the beginning, my lord."

Her grandfather sighed. "Must we?"

"I do believe the ladies have earned the right to know the truth," Tristan responded.

Her grandfather gestured towards the settee across from him. "Would you care to sit?" he asked.

Lizette and Rosamond walked over and sat down.

Her grandfather returned to his seat and placed his glass down onto the table. "What I'm about to tell you has not been spoken of for years," he said. "It was a secret that I had hoped would die with me."

He continued as he met Lizette's gaze. "Your parents wanted nothing more than a child and they waited for many years until Elizabeth got pregnant. They were overjoyed and they planned for the future." He grew quiet. "But it was not meant to be. Their child was born dead."

Mrs. Everly's voice came from the doorway. "That is when I proposed a solution," she said as she slipped into the room. "I was Lady Crewe's lady's maid and I told her about my sister that just had twins a few nights prior."

She walked further into the room. "My sister's husband died in the war and she had no way to feed one mouth, let alone three. She was preparing to take them to the foundling's hospital when I approached her," she explained. "I found a way to let her keep one baby and receive a generous income for her discretion."

Rosamond spoke up. "How did she decide on which one of us to give up?"

"That was easy," Mrs. Everly said. "Their baby and Lizette were both born with a head full of black hair. It was as if it were meant to be."

Her grandfather reached for his drink. "For the first five years, everything was perfect, but then there were some pesky rumors about how similar Lizette and Rosamond looked," he shared. "Your father, who had only grown more and more paranoid with the passing of time due to his condition, convinced your mother to flee to Bridgwater and raise you in secret."

"But why didn't she ever tell me the truth?" Lizette asked.

"After your father died, she was so afraid of losing you that she continued the ruse, hoping you never discovered their deception," her grandfather replied. "She loved you more than anything else and cared little for her position in Society."

Mrs. Everly came to sit down next to Lizette. "You two girls were never supposed to know about one another," she said, "but I am so glad that you do."

Lizette clasped her hands in her lap. "What happens now?" she asked. "I can't possibly carry on pretending to be a lady."

"Whyever not?" her grandfather asked.

"Because I'm not one," Lizette replied. "I have no right to that title."

Her grandfather moved to the edge of his seat. "You are still my granddaughter, and always will be."

Mrs. Everly placed her hand over Lizette's. "I know this

must be hard for you, but your parents considered you the greatest blessing, especially since you wouldn't inherit your father's madness."

Lizette glanced down at their hands as she tried to process what they had told her. She knew she should be grateful for the sacrifices that her parents had made for her, but she just felt angry. Why had no one trusted her enough with the truth?

Tristan walked closer to the settee and asked, "Are you all right, Lizette?"

She looked up at him. "No, I'm not," she replied. "My own mother kept this secret from me; a secret that prevented me from meeting my real mother."

"Lizette, your mother..." Mrs. Everly started.

She cut her off. "Wasn't truly my mother," she stated.

Mrs. Everly's face fell. "She would be devastated to hear you say that."

Lizette felt a twinge of guilt at the words she had just uttered but she was so angry. What was worse was that she didn't know who she was the most angry at- her parents? Mrs. Everly? Her grandfather?

No. She was most angry at herself.

She had been given a life that most people would dream of, but she knew she couldn't go on pretending, not anymore. She couldn't be the person her parents wanted her to be. And by doing so, she knew that she was going to lose Tristan. She was below his notice now, and no matter how much she wanted to pretend there was a future between them, she couldn't entrap him.

Rising, Lizette murmured, "Excuse me. I just need to be alone."

As she fled from the study, she felt the tears building up in her eyes and they spilled over. She exited the rear door and hurried towards a bench that sat in the back of the gardens. She dropped down and let herself cry. What was she going to do now? She had never felt more alone, despite discovering that she now had a sister.

It was a short time later when she heard the sound of booted footsteps approaching her. "Go away. I wish to be alone," she commanded, not bothering to look up.

The footsteps stopped and it was followed by Tristan's rich, baritone voice. "I meant what I said earlier- nothing has changed for me."

"How could it not?" she asked. "I am not who you think I am."

"You are precisely the person I think you are."

She turned towards him. "How can you say that to me?" she demanded. "I am not a lady, and I am entirely beneath your notice."

He cocked his head. "Is that how you see yourself?"

"It is how you should see me," she replied.

"Then you would be wrong."

Tears filled her eyes as she said, "Just leave me be, I beg of you." As much as she wanted him to stay, she needed to let him go. It was for the best.

Tristan made no movement to leave. "I could leave you." He paused. "It would be much simpler to walk away."

Lizette winced at his words, knowing that he spoke the truth.

"But I have a problem," he said.

"What is that?"

He gestured towards the bench and asked, "May I sit?"

She nodded her permission.

Tristan sat down and held her gaze. "I'm afraid I have made the terrible mistake of falling desperately, irrefutably in love with you."

"You did?" she asked, her inconvenient heart taking flight.

"Yes and, you see, I can't just walk away from you," he said. "No matter what, you appear in my dreams. You are the first and last thing I think of every day."

"Tristan…" Her voice stopped. "You will be a marquess one day and I can't in good conscience entrap you."

"You would hardly be entrapping me." He held her gaze and asked, "I just have one question- do you love me?"

"That does not matter—"

"Do you love me?" he repeated, his words more forceful.

She pressed her lips together, knowing that he deserved the truth. "I love you with all my heart." Her words were soft.

Tristan reached for her hand and held it tightly. "Then marry me, Lizette, and we can figure everything out together."

"You make it sound so easy, but what if the truth about me ever comes out?" she asked. "We both would be ruined."

"Then we would sail far away."

"Do be serious."

"I am," Tristan said. "I refuse to let go of the greatest thing that has ever happened to me. You showed me that there is more to life than work."

"But what of your legacy?"

Tristan smiled. "All I care about is that you are by my side, helping me, and reminding me of how truly lucky I am."

Lizette glanced down at their entwined hands. "What of my sister?"

"She will always have a place in our home."

"Do you mean that?" Lizette asked.

"You and your sister are similar in appearance, but not identical. We might be able to convince the *ton* that you two are cousins. Some of them aren't very bright," Tristan said.

She giggled. "That is terrible of you to say."

"Do you have any more objections, or may I kiss you now?" he asked hoarsely.

Lizette's eyes darted towards his lips. "Do you not need my grandfather's permission?"

"He already gave it to me," he said as he leaned closer to her.

She placed a hand on his chest, holding him at arm's

length. "Are you sure, Tristan?" she asked. "I don't want you to wake up one day and realize marrying me was a mistake."

Tristan's eyes grew moist. "A mistake?" he asked with a shake of his head. "How could I ever think that about you? You came into my life for a reason. A beautiful reason. And I would be a fool if I did not spend the remainder of my days proving to you just how much I love you."

"But…"

He put his finger to her lips, silencing her. "I fell in love with you. Not your title. You. And nothing you will say- or do- will change my mind."

She felt her lips curve into a smile. "I feel the same way."

"Then say you will marry me and end my misery," he said as he lowered his finger.

"I will marry you, but you must promise to never leave me."

"Wherever you go, I will gladly go," Tristan breathed, closing the distance between them.

As he kissed her, the raw emotions that she felt from him were so powerful that they destroyed every barrier that she had carefully crafted around her heart, leaving her wanting more- needing more. He was her future; she was sure of that. Nothing else mattered.

Tristan leaned back far enough to rest his forehead against hers. "I love you," he said.

"I love you, too."

"Shall we go tell your family the good news?" he asked.

With a slight wince, she asked, "Do you think this is the right time, considering everything that has happened today?"

"I believe this is the perfect time to do so." Tristan rose and extended his hand towards her. "We will do it together."

Together. She quite liked the sound of that.

Lizette slipped her hand into his. "All right. I am amenable to that."

Tristan's lips quirked. "I do hope you will always be this agreeable in our marriage."

"I wouldn't count on it," Lizette joked.

While they walked hand-in-hand, Lizette knew that all of her problems wouldn't cease to exist now that she and Tristan were engaged, but with him by her side, she could handle anything.

Epilogue

Three weeks later...

Tristan grunted as Lord Roswell jabbed him in the side. He took a step back and said, "I think I have had enough abuse for today."

Lord Roswell put his cloth coated hands down. "I think that is wise since you appear to be terribly distracted."

"Why wouldn't I be?" Tristan asked. "I am to be married tomorrow."

"It is not too late to back out," Lord Roswell joked as he walked out of the chalked area.

Tristan followed his friend and went to sit down on a bench. "I have no desire of backing out. I have been counting down the moments until Lizette becomes my wife."

"You are past hope, I'm afraid," Lord Roswell teased.

As he removed the cloth strips off his hands, Tristan suggested, "You could take a wife."

Lord Roswell huffed. "Now you sound like my mother."

"Everything changed for me when Lizette walked into my

life," Tristan said. "I do believe I am a better man because of her."

"You are more tolerable than usual," Lord Roswell joked.

"I find that I have much to be grateful for."

Lord Roswell dropped the cloth strips to the ground as he said, "I will admit that you and Lady Lizette seem to complement each other nicely."

"That we do," Tristan agreed.

With a glance over his shoulder, Lord Roswell lowered his voice and asked, "How is Miss Hendre settling in?"

Tristan grinned. "Terribly, I'm afraid," he said. "She didn't have a chance once Lady Anne offered to prepare her for a Season."

"Do you think that is wise to introduce Miss Hendre into Society?"

"Lizette thought it was a good idea and I am a smart enough man to go along with it," Tristan replied.

"I just worry that the *ton* might start asking questions."

"We intend to introduce her as Lizette's cousin and Lord Ashington has generously agreed to take her on as his ward with a dowry of twenty thousand pounds."

Lord Roswell's brow shot up. "Twenty thousand pounds?" he repeated. "Miss Hendre will be an heiress."

"I will have my work cut out for me to ensure that no fortune hunters or rakes will come around Miss Hendre."

"I wish you luck with that." Lord Roswell rose. "Perhaps I will set my cap on Miss Hendre. She is handsome enough to tempt me."

Rising, Tristan reached for his blue jacket and said, "I wish you luck with that." He shrugged on his jacket. "Would you care to accompany me to call upon Lizette?"

"No, thank you," Lord Roswell rushed out. "I can think of nothing worse than sitting in a drawing room while you and Lady Lizette gaze into each other's eyes."

"Suit yourself."

They didn't speak as they exited the building and Tristan approached his coach. A footman stepped down and went to open the door.

Tristan turned towards his friend. "Will I see you at the chapel tomorrow?"

"I wouldn't miss it for the world," Lord Roswell replied.

"Would you care for a ride?"

Lord Roswell shook his head. "I think a walk will do me some good," he said before he started walking down the pavement.

Tristan moved to sit in the coach and closed the door behind him. He found he was eager to call upon Lizette. He knew that he would never tire of being around her. What made her so beautiful was that she was full of light, and it showed up in everything she did.

It wasn't long before he arrived at Lord Ashington's townhouse, and he promptly exited the coach. He hurried up the steps and was pleased when the door opened.

"Good afternoon, sir," Brownell greeted.

"Is Lady Lizette available for callers?" Tristan asked, stepping into the entry hall.

Brownell bobbed his head. "She is," he confirmed. "Allow me to announce you."

"That won't be necessary," Tristan said as he continued to the drawing room.

As he stepped into the drawing room, he saw that Miss Hendre was sitting on the settee, a book balancing on top of her head.

Miss Hendre caught his eye and explained, "Lady Anne thinks I slouch too much."

"Ah," Tristan said, not sure what to say about that.

Lizette rose from her seat and approached him. "Good afternoon, Fiancé," she greeted with a smile.

He reached for her gloved hand and brought it up to his lips. "Good afternoon, my love," he responded.

Lady Anne's amused voice reached his ears. "Are you going to stand there all day holding her hand or would you care to join us?"

Tristan released her hand and went to address Lady Anne. "I was hoping to take a tour of the gardens with my betrothed."

Lady Anne nodded her permission. "You may go, but do not dally for too long. Lizette needs to help with Rosamond's lessons."

He offered his arm to Lizette, and he led her towards the rear of the townhouse. A footman opened the door and then discreetly followed them outside, remaining on the veranda.

As they walked along the path, he said, "I daresay that tomorrow cannot come soon enough for me."

"I feel the same way," Lizette responded. "In hindsight, I wished we had eloped, considering how much time I have spent on the preparations."

"That would have been much simpler."

"But we don't do simple, do we?" Lizette asked with mirth in her eyes.

He chuckled. "We do not."

Lizette glanced over her shoulder before saying, "I do feel bad for Rosamond, though. Lady Anne has been relentless in her teachings."

"Has she taken issue with it?"

"She has never uttered a complaint to me," Lizette replied. "But I remember how daunting it was in my position to enter Society."

"I have no doubt that she will thrive."

"I hope so, because I have enjoyed having her here," she said. "I find it is much easier to keep pretending to be something I'm not to ensure Rosamond is given this opportunity. It makes me feel that my mother's sacrifice was worth it in the end to give me up. For now, I am in a position to help Rosamond."

"It is most fortunate that Lady Anne and Lord Ashington have taken a liking to her."

"After I told them what she did for me when George abducted me, they have been nothing but kind to her," Lizette shared.

"Have you worked out your differences with Mrs. Everly?" he asked.

Lizette bobbed her head. "I was furious at first that she had lied to me for all of these years, but I have since come to terms with the fact that she was trying to protect me and Rosamond in her own way," she said.

"What will Mrs. Everly do now?" he asked.

"She has asked to stay on as my lady's maid."

Tristan gave her a curious look. "Is that what you want?"

"Now that I know the truth, I am not ready for her to walk out of my life," Lizette replied. "Besides, I do not want to deny Rosamond the privilege of getting to know our aunt."

"You are as wise as you are beautiful," he said with a smile.

She returned his smile. "Flattery?" she asked. "You must want something."

Tristan brought his hand to his chest, feigning innocence. "Am I not able to compliment my betrothed without having an ulterior motive?"

Lizette shook her head. "Out with it."

Coming to a stop on the path, he turned to face her. "Mr. Slade's solicitor has sent word that he wishes to buy your estate in Bridgwater and was hoping you would consider selling it."

"What nerve," Lizette declared. "Does he truly think I would sell him my mother's estate after what he did to me?"

"The offer was more than generous."

"I care not," Lizette said. "After he slunk back to Bridgwater, I had been hoping to never hear from him again."

"Very well, then. I will tell him that you have no intention of selling the property." Tristan gestured towards a bench and asked, "Shall we sit for a spell?"

"I would like that very much," Lizette said.

After he assisted Lizette onto the bench, he claimed the seat next to her, leaving little room between them.

"I hope you aren't terribly disappointed that we aren't going on a wedding tour right after our ceremony," Lizette said. "I just didn't dare leave Rosamond right now."

"I understand, and you do not need to feel an ounce of remorse. As long as we are together, I care not where we are."

Slowly, beautifully, a smile spread across her mouth. "I don't know what I did to deserve you, but I am pleased that you are here."

"There is no place I would rather be." He leaned forward and lightly kissed her on the mouth. "You are an indescribable miracle of my life; the reason why I carry on," he said against her lips.

"I love you, Tristan," she murmured.

"And I love you, my dearest Lizette," he answered, kissing each corner of her mouth in turn.

Knowing they had their entire lives ahead of them for such pleasant endeavors, Tristan settled his back against the bench and Lizette rested her head softly against his shoulder.

"We should probably go back inside," Tristan suggested.

Lizette sighed. "Must we?"

"I suppose one more moment wouldn't hurt," he said as he kissed the top of her head.

The End

Author's Notes

I am not one to write author's notes, but I felt as if it were necessary in this case. The disease that I alluded Lord Crewe had was, in fact, Huntington's disease. It is a rare, inherited, and debilitating disease that causes the progressive breakdown of nerve cells in the brain. It causes involuntary movement, cognitive and psychiatric disorders, with symptoms widely varying between individuals. Before it was diagnosed by George Huntington in 1872, it was commonly lumped in with the differential diagnosis of dementia.

Huntington's disease can develop at any time, but it is most common to first appear when people are in their 30s or 40s. It is generally accepted that people may live for 10 to 15 years after the onset of symptoms. Many of the symptoms mentioned that Lord Crewe suffered from were typical of the disease. Sadly, there is no cure or treatment to slow down the disease due to a higher-than-normal rate of suicide for people who are diagnosed with Huntington's disease.

If you enjoyed Secrets of a Lady, check
out the next book in the series

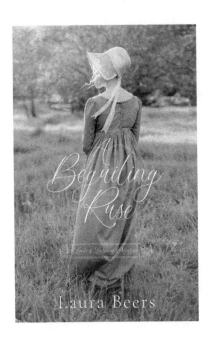

**He needed to marry her for her dowry but falling in
love with her foiled his plans.**

Miss Rosamond Hendre has had the most remarkable change of fortune for a daughter of a seaman. She went from living a simple life in the countryside to being introduced to high Society as the ward of a marquess. She is excited to embrace her newfound life, and she wants nothing more than to find a love match this Season.

Malcolm, the Viscount of Brentwood, needs to marry an heiress and Miss Hendre fits the bill. His family is on the brink of ruination and he doesn't have time for games. The problem is that Miss Hendre seems immune to his charms and constantly rebuffs his advances. But he isn't one to give up so easily, especially when so much is at stake.

Malcolm wants nothing to do with love, but he knows he must play the part of a devoted suitor or else he will lose Rosamond. But the more he plays the part, the more the line begins to blur between what is real and what is not. As his feelings deepen for Rosamond, Malcolm wonders if this battles of wills- and hearts- will end in happily ever after, or devastation?

Also by

_____

Gentlemen of London

A Treacherous Engagement
An Unlikely Match
A Perilous Circumstance
A Precarious Gamble
A Deadly Entanglement
A Devious Secret

Proper Regency Matchmakers

Saving Lord Berkshire
Reforming the Duke
Loving Lord Egleton
Redeeming the Marquess
Engaging Lord Charles
Refining Lord Preston

Regency Spies & Secrets

A Dangerous Pursuit

Also by

A Dangerous Game
A Dangerous Lord
A Dangerous Scheme

Regency Brides: A Promise of Love

A Clever Alliance
The Reluctant Guardian
A Noble Pursuit
The Earl's Daughter
A Foolish Game

The Beckett Files

Saving Shadow
A Peculiar Courtship
To Love a Spy
A Tangled Ruse
A Deceptive Bargain
The Baron's Daughter
The Unfortunate Debutante

About the Author

Laura Beers is an award-winning author. She attended Brigham Young University, earning a Bachelor of Science degree in Construction Management. She can't sing, doesn't dance and loves naps.

Laura lives in Utah with her husband, three kids, and her dysfunctional dog. When not writing regency romance, she loves waterskiing, hiking, and drinking Dr Pepper.

You can connect with Laura on Facebook, Instagram, or on her site at www.authorlaurabeers.com.

Printed in the USA
CPSIA information can be obtained
at www.ICGtesting.com
LVHW010606280124
769814LV00074B/2601